A SHOCK

Keith Ridgway

A SHOCK

PICADOR

First published in paperback 2021 by Picador

This edition published 2021 by Picador
an imprint of Pan Macmillan
The Smithson, 6 Briset Street, London EC1M 5NR
EU representative: Macmillan Publishers Ireland Limited,
Mallard Lodge, Lansdowne Village, Dublin 4
Associated companies throughout the world
www.panmacmillan.com

ISBN 978-1-5290-6479-7

1 3 5 7 9 8 6 4 2

A CIP catalogue record for this book is available from the British Library.

Typeset in Janson Text LT Std by Jouve (UK), Milton Keynes
Printed and bound by CPI Group (UK) Ltd, Croydon, CR0 4YY

Visit **www.picador.com** to read more about all our books
and to buy them. You will also find features, author interviews and
news of any author events, and you can sign up for e-newsletters
so that you're always first to hear about our new releases.

'There is a wall between you and me. I can see you, I can speak to you, but you're on the other side. What stops us from loving each other? It seems to me it was easier, once upon a time. In Hamburg.'

'Yes,' said Ève sadly. Always Hamburg. He never spoke of their real past. Neither Ève nor he had been to Hamburg.

The Bedroom
Jean-Paul Sartre
translated by Andrew Brown

The Party

She fries an egg but leaves it then, lying in the pan until it is completely cold. She bites at her nails and glances repeatedly at the window, seeing nothing but her tiny empty garden and the tiny empty sky, until eventually she sighs and lowers the blind. She feeds the cat, though not with the egg which she seems to have forgotten. While wiping the table she stops suddenly and listens. There is silence but for the usual sounds of the house in the evening and a light breeze outside – no hint of rain – and the tick of the kitchen clock. Perhaps it was that. She resumes wiping, and brushes absolutely nothing into her cupped hand, which she examines briefly then slaps against her hip.

Her neighbours had knocked on her door during the week, on Thursday, just as she was finishing her tea. Two boys. No, no. Men. They're men, and it annoys her, the way a part (what part?) of her brain insists on them as boys. They aren't boys. They are certainly men, and almost or perhaps even middle-aged men. Objectively. They are younger than her but they are not young. How could they be, buying a house? In fact they are probably the same age she was when she and . . . her husband had bought their house. Her house. So, thirty. About thirty. Probably they are older because it takes so long now to find the money. They are either older or richer. Probably both. To be able to buy, just the two of them, a house like this. It is exactly like her house, mirrored. When they walked through their front door they have everything on the right that she has on the left.

A couple, full of smiles, loud friendly voices, one of them northern, bits of tattoos poking out from under collars and cuffs, earrings, nice boys, men, and there they were at her door, one of them with a bag and both speaking more or less at once, all smiles though, and they have never done this before, it's always been chats over the wall in the summer, meeting out the front sometimes, the northern one calling over when they had a leak, worried that it would spread, but it didn't, but she had never, she thought, had the two of them together like this, certainly not at her door, and she looked from one to the other and was baffled as to what was going on, what on earth they were saying or what they wanted. She invited them in.

— It won't be insane.

— No, no, not at all, I mean it won't even be, it certainly won't be . . . oh this is lovely.

— We're keeping numbers down, oh it is lovely.

— Is this bigger than ours? It looks . . .

— It looks it doesn't it? It's lovely though. Much brighter, feels bigger doesn't it? You have the sink under the window, that's much better, ours is in that corner. Oh, well, that corner I suppose, ha, it's confusing . . .

— It's a mirror image isn't it?

— Yes I know, the same but opposite.

She nodded and smiled and motioned at chairs but they didn't seem to notice and all three of them were just standing there, the two boys looking at her sideboards as if a little annoyed.

— It was done, she said, ending a small silence that had risen like gas. Last year. The presses. I mean the cupboards. The floor, new taps, work, uh, work surfaces? All that.

— So bright. Cheerful.

— We should start saving.

— We'll add it to the list!

— The infinite list!

And they just stood there for a moment, smiling at her. The two young men, in her kitchen, with their faces and their hands and their necks.

— Do you want to sit down? I can make some more tea?

— No no no please don't, no need for that at all, thanks very much.

— We only wanted to let you know really.

— As I said, we're keeping the numbers down, and it's not going to be a wild affair, we promise. We're too old for that now.

They both laughed loudly at this, which she didn't really understand until she realised they weren't laughing because they thought it was funny, they were laughing because they thought she was old, and the one who had said it had said it without thinking and he had laughed to cover his very slight embarrassment, and the other one was laughing at his boyfriend's minute, barely felt discomfort, laughing at this small faux pas which he had stumbled into in this old woman's kitchen, and the fact that both of them were laughing a little too much at this was making them laugh a little more, laughing at the fact of their laughing, and it was only when all this was going on that she fully understood that they were telling her they were going to have a party.

She goes upstairs again, stepping into each room, looking around. It's warm. She stares out of windows but the sky is clear and in the back bedroom she scowls at it, gives a pantomime shake of the fist. There's never any rain. There hasn't been rain

3

in weeks. The cat follows for a while, complaining, then disappears. She can't hear anything, but the cat is skittish. But maybe she is making the cat skittish because she is skittish. *Skittish*, she says out loud. *Skitt. Ish.*

In her bedroom she closes the curtains almost completely, leaving a gap which she tests to make sure that it gives her a view of the front of their house. Impossible to see the door. Just their patch of gravel next to her patch of gravel. And the bins, theirs and hers, back to back with the wall between them, the colours matching, green, blue and brown. Had they done that on purpose? Maybe it's a coincidence. Maybe the bin men did it. She looks at her watch and the cat reappears, a living thing at her legs. A motorbike roars by. She sits on her bed and then lies on her bed, and then the cat joins her and she gets up.

— No, she says.

She goes to the wardrobe, deciding that she wants to change her clothes.

They had offered her things. For the noise. Not that there would be much noise. It would not be very loud, they said. They hoped, they said, that it would not be very loud. They had just wanted to tell her in person, rather than sticking a note through her letterbox. Notes through letterboxes wasn't very neighbourly, was it? *Bit passive aggressive somehow* said one of them, and *Yes I suppose so* said the other. So, they'd argued about that. One of them, that one, had said *let's just stick a note through the stupid old cow's letterbox*. Or something like that. *Anyway*, they said, *we thought we'd just call around. Really sorry to interrupt your tea. And bring some things*, said the other one.

— What things?

— Well, where are we, here we are, this is a

A Shock

He was pulling some sort of, what on earth, headphones? Big black things, with the big fat pads for the ears.

— Headphones here, for this, which is this old

A small . . . a phone?

— An iPod. My old iPod. And I don't know what you like obviously, or even if this is a stupid idea, you might not want to listen to anything at all, but there's playlists on there, some easy-listening things, some pop stuff, and some classical as well, you can, will I show you what, will I show you how this works?

— I know how an iPod works she said. I have an iPod.

— Oh! Oh well there you go.

He started to put it back into the bag, laughing again.

— Well you're all set for that already then, not that I think, you know, like we said, I really don't think it's going to be all that, well you never know, anyway, most likely just the music, the bass, and a bit of, ha, babble, and here are some earplugs as well

He laughed and showed them to her. A little box from Boots. He put them down on the table.

— It might get a bit loud at some point, said the other one. You know. And they, the earplugs I mean, might just let you get to sleep or whatever. Because you know the way these things go. They can go late sometimes, people won't leave. So the earplugs might just

— Well, ok. Thank you.

She had her own earplugs. She didn't have an iPod.

— And this is in case none of that works said the other one. He was holding a bottle of wine. He laughed, put it on the table. It's a nice red, well, we like it. In any case, that's yours.

— Thanks. There's no need for that.

— Well, it'll do no harm. And here's some chocolate mints, if you like that sort of thing. I love them. I could go through a whole box without even noticing.

— He could, and he does.

— Anyway, that's the lot.

She looked at what they'd brought for her. She pictured herself in the living room, in the armchair, her ears plugged with foam, drinking wine and eating the After Eights.

— What time is your party?

— Oh I don't know. I imagine it won't get going until after nine or something.

They looked at each other.

— Eight, nine. Whenever people show up I suppose. With the long evenings no one thinks it's evening until the sun goes down. Especially if it's a nice day, which is what's forecast.

— Saturday?

— Yes, Saturday. This Saturday. You'll be here?

— Yes. Yes I'll be here.

Where else would she be? They all looked at each other.

— That's everything. I think.

They moved towards the door, quieter now. She had not helped, she thought. She had been silent and they could see her face. She wanted to smile and laugh and joke with them. Tell them that it was fine, they weren't to worry, they should have a nice night, make as much noise as they liked, she wouldn't mind. But she did mind. She felt anger. She was angry. That, in any case, was what she told herself.

— Such a lovely house.

— So lovely.

— Thank you.

6

A Shock

— Bye!
— Bye!
— Bye.

She runs her hands over the wall as she goes downstairs. Over its peculiar bumps and mounds. She has put on a pair of pale cotton trousers which are too baggy but cool, and an ancient top that had been his. Hers. Hers then his now hers. It is difficult to explain. The cat is annoying her, following her, looking at her, making plaintive little noises.

— I don't know what you want.

In the kitchen she runs her hands over the wall between the fridge and the cooker. Stares at it. Turns her head and rests her ear against its cool lumpy surface. Everything is quiet. Everything. Nothing. Her hand in front of her is wrinkled, its skin doesn't look like her own. She lives less in her body now, she thinks. After all that. Her body is ceasing to be relevant, even to her. It has less and less to do with her. And it is healthy, it remains healthy, which is the strangest difference. It is like having an elderly friend who you rarely see.

The paint on the wall is a very pale green. She has no interest in repainting anything. *Ever*, she thinks, childishly. *Ancient*. Lives are like buttons.

She takes her head away from the wall and steps back and wonders if she's got the day wrong. She glances at the clock, and at her watch. It's far too early of course, but why aren't they in their kitchen, making preparations? Perhaps they are very organised.

She looks at the dent. It's up near the top of the wall, out of her reach. A dent. She doesn't know what happened. She thinks that it can't have been there before he died because he would have fixed it. But she also thinks that he might have dented it – banged

7

into it with a ladder or hit it with a stray hammer when he was doing something else, and that maybe he'd intended to fix it but died instead. His domestic life had been a cycle of breaking things then fixing them. Clocks, shelves, the boiler, himself. But maybe it had always been there. *Always.* An ancient indentation. Is that even the right word? A triangular bit of the plaster pushed in. A dark black upper edge to it – the start of a hole – that seemed wider now than it had been.

In winter she imagines that a draft comes through it and thinks briefly, for the duration of a slightly colder breath of air across her shoulders, that she should fix it. On the one or two times when she has been aware of noise from next door, she has looked at it suspiciously, as if it is responsible. Perhaps it would be a good place to put her ear. They'd had a fight once. Couldn't make it out. Except, perhaps, CUNT, very loudly, and a big, serious silence then. A door slammed. Maybe she was making that up, the door slam. She couldn't remember if there had been anything else.

The dent is a couple of inches long, like a corner peeled back on a yoghurt tub. No. Like a corner pushed in on something. The way you open a box of tissues. It was a year ago probably, the argument. It had embarrassed her more than anything. And there had been another time, not long after they moved in, when she had heard music and laughing and loud voices and had stood looking at the dent trying to make out what was going on. Maybe that had been a party as well. Maybe it had. And if so, perhaps this one would be the same. Not so bad in other words. Perhaps no one would turn up. Perhaps they were unpopular and no one would come. Perhaps it was too warm, perhaps it would rain, perhaps the world would end suddenly and without warning and the only remaining trace of humanity would be those robots, wandering through the cold empty universe like old women in empty houses.

She laughs.

She goes out to the hall again. Another motorbike roar. Then voices. Outside. She stops where she is. It's too early, surely. It is too early. They are just passers-by. Cars every few minutes. Sirens down on the main road. The rumbling planes. She thinks she might open the front door. She's allowed to do that. She lives here. Open the front door. Go out to her gate. Stand there looking up and down the street. People do that. It's a perfectly acceptable thing to do. Balmy evening. Neighbours, passers-by. *Hello. Yes, how are you?* She had wondered, quite often, if the CUNT was her. If they had been shouting so that she could hear. If they were drunk and they hated her and it hadn't been an argument at all but rather a bout of abuse, a bout of neighbourly elder abuse, and she was the CUNT and they had shouted it so that she would have no doubt. She had thought all of this several times and knew it was simply not true, that it was a manifestation of paranoia engendered by her depression, by the feeling of loneliness, worthlessness, with which she had struggled since his death.

So, whatever way you looked at it, it was her fault.

She goes upstairs again and lies on the bed and falls asleep.

When she wakes, the party has started and she cannot move. It takes her a little while to fully realise anything. The room is dim, as if forgotten. Her body has settled and failed. She is dead. Then she breathes and blinks her eyes and breathes again, and again. She has slept for far too long, a couple of hours maybe, and is confused and frightened, though she is also, as she begins to understand the situation, still alive, and still herself, and this is the room where she sleeps and has slept for most of her life. Various incorrect ideas about what is happening fall away from her and are immediately lost as she closes in on the truth, remembers who is dead, who lives next door now, who is having a party, that this is the party, that it has started, that what she is hearing is laughter and voices and they are not in her house they are next door, and that she cannot hear any music. She lies there, confused, still frightened, in a paralysed grip, the grip of everything which feels about to fall apart in her life, her diminishing life, and why is there no music? But she is not paralysed. She raises her head. The cat is curled up beside her but is also confused, and stares at her.

— Yes. Don't worry.

She strokes the cat and they make stupid noises at each other. Then the music starts up. She freezes.

— My god.

It has probably started up, not for the first time, but again. It is a throb and a pressure. The cat jumps off the bed and onto the wardrobe shelf and burrows into cardigans. She usually forbids that. But now she lets it happen. She might climb in there too. She might. This is awful. It occurs to her that perhaps the music stopping was what had woken her. Perhaps she could have slept all the way through it if the music hadn't stopped. Her dream had been something . . . something sharp, but it has fled now.

She could go out.

It is too late. There would be nowhere open. Nowhere for her.

She could just walk.

She eases herself off the bed and stands up. The cat watches her. She is stiff and her mouth is dry and she thinks she will brush her teeth and find her earplugs. When she turns to leave the cat makes a furious protest, and then leaps out to join her. She walks along the corridor in the gloom, not daring to turn on any lights, to the bathroom, wary of the wall, imagining that it is bulging with sound, like the skin of a drum, though of course it is doing nothing of the sort. But this is so loud. She is still half asleep, and she knows that she is, but this is so loud, this is not what she had expected, surely it can't be this loud? The cat is mewling behind her, following her all the way into the bathroom – *no rules tonight bauble* – and she splashes her face and brushes her teeth and rummages in the drawer for her earplugs, which are many years old, and all the while there is the throb of next door at her back, a boom and press of bass, like a heat against the wall, like a fire, and sometimes the haze, the flick of other things on top of it, singing and instruments and melody, things jumping and spitting on a pan. And the voices, all the voices boiling together, people having to shout to make themselves heard, shouting out, and you might think they're dying in there if it was not for the laughter, the huge bursts of laughter that come every few seconds, which punch through the wall as if directed at her personally. She stands in the bathroom staring astonished at her own face in the mirror and just listens. The cat at her legs.

Downstairs she considers what lights to turn on and settles for the lamp in the living room which throws light into the hall, and one of the kitchen lights, the one over the table. She isn't sure why she is thinking about lights so carefully, or at all. It is something to do with her presence in her own house. She is . . .

There is a fried egg sitting in the frying pan on top of the cooker.

What an astonishingly odd-looking thing.

She thinks then that she might have left the ring on, and is momentarily furious, but of course the egg is cold, as is the pan. She has no explanation.

The earplugs are still in her hand. She is trying not to attract attention. She is trying not to disturb the people who are making the noise. She is trying to be unobtrusive next to this.

What is wrong with her?

A little white island with a little yellow lake.

Obviously there is an explanation. She fried an egg and forgot about it. Has she eaten? She can't remember. Is she hungry?

She stands by the sink and pulls the side of the window blind towards her and peers through the gap. She can see a couple of people. Three or four people. Young people. One of them throws their head back and she thinks they're laughing but . . . he, maybe, he . . . is drinking from a can. Another has sunglasses pushed onto the top of their head. But the fence is quite high and all she can see are the top halves of faces, or just hair, or skin, butterflies amongst them. They might all be naked, she thinks. The sky is a deep dark blue, far from turning black, and a plane crawls across it, and it is still warm.

She takes the pan and scoops the egg into the bin and feels tearful and goes to sit down in the living room. She's put the earplugs down somewhere. She thinks she should eat something. The noise is ridiculous. She sits in the armchair in the corner and looks out at the hall. She stares at the wall, she thinks she can see it moving, the way you can see a pulse in a neck or a wrist. But she can't see that. It's not moving.

It occurs to her suddenly that the shared wall between two terraced houses is often called the party wall. She laughs.

— Party wall.

She's right isn't she? She thinks about it and decides that she is. This seems inordinately funny. It changes something. She laughs out loud, actually claps her hands together, has a little fit of the giggles. The party wall. What's wrong with her? Why is she sitting miserably in the gloom in her own house, just because next door is having a party? Yes it's loud, but parties are loud. She has made plenty of noise in her time. It will not last forever. It will, in a few hours, be over. This is not hell. Let them have their party. For god's sake.

She gets up and finds the earplugs beside the cooker and puts them in her ears and that improves things too. It muffles and distorts the noise. And it makes her own breathing and her own voice when she talks to the cat loud and warm in her head and she likes that and talks more because of it. The cat won't leave her side. *I would put earplugs in your ears too baby but you'd have my eye out wouldn't you? You'd have my eye out!*

She wanders around for a while. She looks out into the back again. No one there now. She goes to the front door, peers through the glass and can half see some shapes in front of their house. She pulls back when she realises that she is a face at the glass. She goes upstairs and goes through the complicated procedure of lying on the floor to peek through the curtain. They are smokers mostly out there, the rise and fall of their orange dots. They murmur and laugh a little. She worries that she can be seen and ducks her head and lies flat. The cat climbs on top of her and she laughs. She waits for a while, to catch her breath, and the cat settles, and then she tries to crawl backwards from the window and the cat is on her shoulder, confused, and she is laughing again, more giggles, and this is just ridiculous, look at her, lying on the floor with the cat practically sitting on her head, and it is no small thing for a woman of her age to get up from down here, with an animal attached, what on earth was she thinking, and she makes it eventually to the bed, still laughing, and manages to get awkwardly to her feet, calling herself a *ludraman.*

London, she thinks to herself. In England. Of the world's many ludicrous places she had to choose London.

She goes downstairs, opens the bottle of wine and pours a glass.

After a while, more people drift out to the garden at the back. Or they drift out there again. She can hear them. A clearer sort of laughter, more human, understandable, coming to her through the kitchen. She goes and looks but the fence makes it pointless really, just the tops of heads, just young hair and fringes and she wonders how long she has to live. Of course she might die tomorrow. He did. But if everything keeps declining at the same rate, and given the age of her mother when she'd died, and adding on a few years for better drugs and what have you, she might last another decade. That seemed absurd. What could she do with all that time? Although. It felt like no more than the click of a couple of seconds since he'd died, and a minute or two since they'd met, and maybe half an hour since she was a girl. The whole thing was absurd no matter which way you turned. And how banal, she thinks, how predictable and dull, to think of time at all.

There is only now, in all its perpetual detail, as deep as a well.

She goes upstairs and spies on them through the back bedroom. Youngsters. Light summer clothes. Chatting and laughing. Drinks, joints, cigarettes. Those machines with the big clouds. It is a big party. Well done them. She goes downstairs and has more wine. A novel thing these days, wine. She mustn't overdo it.

After a while she finds herself with her ear to the kitchen wall again. It is muffled. She takes out her earplugs and immediately puts them back in. She stares at the hole above her head, and looks around for a while. The hole looks terribly interesting. She wonders if it goes all the way through to the other side. Whether she can look through it.

Let's go to the party! Let's make some new friends! Find out what the young people are like now. See what they get up to. Come on. I'll look after you. This, his voice, still so easy to remember, and to hear saying these things, or things like them, though only glancingly. When she tries to slow it down, to actually imagine his face, and his voice, it falls apart. Not because she cannot remember, but because there is too much to remember and it all comes at once, and she is cowed by the scale of her loss. It seems too important and vast to be hers alone.

— Shoo shoo baby she says, bright as she can, ostensibly to the cat.

She goes to the cupboard under the stairs where there is a stepladder and she moves a couple of boxes to get at it. The boxes are light, just decorations, tinsel, and the step ladder is good, new – she bought it online after she fell from a chair while changing a light bulb in the living room. It was nearly the dying room she thinks and – because she is still battling something, or because of the wine – she laughs very loudly, a great explosion of mirth, good lord, and stops.

Would they hear that?

She hopes they did, but they wouldn't would they? Impossible to judge with the earplugs in. She probably hadn't been loud at all. No. Maybe one of them might have heard her. Young, good ears. A shy girl in their hall, leaning against the shared wall – the party wall! what is *wrong* with you? it's not funny – pretending to be interested in her boyfriend's conversation with his friend, but bored really, or that variation on boredom that comes chiefly from shyness, from wanting to be elsewhere. She would be listening to them have a conversation about politics, about sport . . . no, more likely politics, about the . . . what . . . the eccentric, in international terms, confusion of the British Left. She would be drifting off in her mind, thinking how nice it would be on her own, at home, reading a book, watching something, asleep, instead of here at this mostly male – but allowed, because also mostly gay – party, where the straight women are ostentatiously welcome, where the gay men think of themselves as the best sort of men, rather than what they might profit from, which was to not think of themselves at all, or certainly not as much, and to refuse that particular tail pinned on that particular donkey, but very few of them think like that, attached as they are to the business end of things, which they cannot, most of them – maybe she was being unfair – most of them cannot separate from the naming of the thing, and the naming rights, the bragging rights . . . now she has lost her train of thought.

The cat has vanished.

She stares at the step ladder. Yes. She had laughed. So maybe some shy girl on the other side of the wall who was not enjoying the party very much might have heard her. That was all. That was the thought. What if the girl, being curious, were to ask someone – *Who lives next door?* And on finding out that it is – what would they say – it's an old woman, some deaf old woman who lives on her own, what would happen if the girl, being curious, were to wander out of the house then, being just a little curious and quite a lot bored, having said to her boyfriend something like *I'll be back in a minute*, not that he cares anyway, talking now as he is loudly about the failure of social democratic parties in Europe, and off she wanders, away down the hallway, down their corridor hallway to the front door, which is open, excusing herself past people, squeezing past people, and out into the little patch of gravel, probably walking on the gravel because the path has people standing on it, and out the gate and to the right and then again to the right, and through this other little patch of gravel, two steps up the path which she has entirely to herself, and she lifts the knocker and lets it drop.

Moments are eternal.

She steps back a little. Sticks her head around the corner of the cupboard under the stairs and looks at the front door. Just shadows and glows. Nothing sharp or definite, nothing moving. What would she have done if a tipsy girl came calling? She laughs again, but much quieter now. No one would hear that. No one would ever hear that. She imagines the awkwardness. The girl at her door trying to make friends with her, trying to escape the boring party, wanting to come in, expecting tea because she is so tired of these lukewarm sweet drinks that fuzz up her head and all she wants is a good refreshing tea and the chance to sit down for a nice chat with an old lady, a chat about what, tell me about your life she'd ask, tell me about the war, what bloody war what are you talking about I've never been in a bloody war, no more than you have you idiot and there is no girl she does not exist.

She picks up the step ladder. She puts it down again.

If a girl like that existed she would not be so rude. So stupid. You are simply deflecting away any possibility of empathy, connection, offer of friendship. You are running away from your own story. You are bitter and lonely and terrified that you will be like this for the rest of your life. But if someone were to knock on your door and ask you your story you would turn them away. Because how can you tell your story? How, now? There was a person I loved. Who says person? A man I loved. A man. There was someone I loved. And there it is. And I love him still, more than I can possibly explain, in that way that she doesn't have to explain, in that way that everyone already understands, apparently, that same way that is not very different to anyone else who loves a person, a dead person, a gone person, as if all love is the same in the end, a click of the tongue, a single tear, and people nod and know, *isn't that terrible, she loved a man and he died, god love her, but better to have loved and died, loved and died, loved and . . .* Because he died, the end of all stories, and all stories are the same story, and here I am, the leftover part, the unresolved plot, the loose end, the woman in the house, the house in the woman, the cat, the unkempt garden, the clothes in the wardrobe that she cannot throw out and cannot wear, the furniture she moves so that she can forget, and moves back again so that she can remember, and remembering anyway whatever she does, lost in a little roundabout life, the shopping and the library and the visit once in a while from people who were friends but who now are strange old men, strange old women, who sit in her living room and talk about the television and their internal organs, so that they confuse one with the other, and she confuses them one for the other and they ask her how she's doing and she says *all right*. All right. I loved a person. She died. He died. That is all there is to it. A person. Love. Death. It is stupid. It is barely a story. It is not a story.

It is not a story.

She tuts at herself and takes the step ladder to the kitchen.

It is her life.

It feels foolish. To open the ladder and to set it sideways against the wall. So she does that and then stands back and looks at it, smoothing out her top with her hands. The cat has reappeared. The noise now is something she imagines. Perhaps it has stopped.

She goes and takes a sip from her wine glass in the living

room, fiddling as she walks back with one of the earplugs, reassuring herself that things are as bad as she imagines them to
be, and they are. But they are no worse.

She climbs the ladder and sees the kitchen from a new angle.
The top of the fridge is covered in dust. The table looks small,
the chairs childish, the sink below the window looks cheap and
useless. She hovers for a moment close to the ceiling, looking
down. It is like a doll's house. She turns and peers into the hole.
She can't see anything. She pokes her finger into it and immediately feels a drop in temperature. The rim of the hole feels
almost damp. She pinches an edge and it crumbles between her
fingers, plaster and paint dropping to the floor. She takes her
finger out and presses her eye to it. She can't really see anything.
A gap, then something dark and flat, presumably the wall on
their side. Why are there no bricks? She is surprised that there
seems to be nothing between two sheets of plaster. Is that how
they do it? It can't be. It seems absurd. It's nothing. There is a
definite smell of damp.

She gets a decent grip. Tugs, nervously, too gently. She tugs
harder and a small clump of plaster comes away in her hand and
the hole opens up to the size of her fist. She drops the clump and
pulls at another. It feels a little like damp clay, like soil she tore
as a child from the bank of a stream at the edge of a field, and
she hasn't remembered that in years. It would come off in big
pieces that held for a moment, then collapsed.

She drops another clump and the cat runs off.

— Sorry button.

She used to tell him about the place she grew up. He would
get her to describe it all in great detail, because he wanted he said
to draw a map of it in his head. She would ask him to do the same,
but he had grown up in a place he did not want to remember, and

he would make things up, castles and forests and elaborate and impossible fortresses cut into the sides of cliffs. That was their exchange. She took him back in time to a small farm and minute adventures. He took her to places that had never existed.

He'd have taken her to the party. He'd have negotiated an invitation with a breezy laugh and a bottle of something. He knew how to have people in a house.

Soon there is a hole the size of her head, and then slightly bigger than her head. She sticks her head in it. Definite damp. A leak, she hopes. Rather than rising. She taps on the other side of the cavity. Also damp. She can even see, a little to her left, but lower down, a bit of light, which seems to be a small hole, on their side, through which . . . The noise is slightly louder, especially the voices. A dozen conversations riddled with laughter. She thinks of taking out her ear plugs.

He'd have been laughing at her by now. He is dead and there is nothing of him left in the world at all. No one remembers him except her. He liked parties, liked people. He would talk to all of them, her hovering shyly at his shoulder. There are some who still remember him of course. She assumes. But they have stopped coming. And in any case, they had not known her.

She is surprised by the cavity. Surprised that it seems empty. There are wooden beams and there are wires and cables and there is something silver like a trestle to her right, and there are bricks beyond that. Old dark bricks and that's where the damp smell seems strongest – in that direction. There will be mice. The cat does a good job, but they have their paths and the tunnels and their halls, and the inside of the wall – she thinks, and thinks it's the way it should be – belongs to them. The cat does a good job. Where is the cat?

She leans too heavily and the plaster at her hands gives way suddenly and she sways slightly sideways, feeling the ladder tip away from her and for a moment she thinks she is going to fall completely, but she doesn't, she's fine, the ladder rights itself, and she is caught by the plaster on the left of what is now, suddenly, a very considerable hole.

They'll have heard that, surely.

She gingerly regains her balance, grabbing one of the wooden beams in the cavity as a support. The cat has reappeared and is lecturing her, the squeaks finding a way through the complicated hum of her earplugs, and they look at each other for a moment, one looking down, the other looking up. The pile of shattered plaster on the floor seems smaller than the gap it has left behind. She slowly descends the ladder.

Now what?

She goes and has another sip of wine. She doesn't care. He would hate this. He'd be angry. It will cost a fortune to fix. What have you done? His anger would be incredulous and would stretch and snap into laughter. He liked fixing things, improving them, making them over. She laughs at this thought. Everything is far too complicated to explain.

Back at the coalface. The cat is on the table, staring at the hole, astonished.

— I know baby. I know.

She washes her hands and peeks outside again. The dark is rising now, and the tops of the heads are silhouettes. She looks at the clock. She tries to forget how to read the time. She is . . . it is as if she is stuttering through time or time is stuttering by her, arrested as she is every few moments by some internal or external distraction which catches her, snags her, holds her somewhere away from herself for an instant and when she snaps back to now it is a different now to the now from which she was, she feels, some seconds ago, abducted. Again and again, in her own kitchen, kidnapped by some minute and ridiculous mechanism of violence. She thinks of it as violence. For every time she is propelled back into now, she has a definite though obscure sense of damage.

She snaps away from the sink, back to the hole. The cat is on the ladder, looking in, the brave thing, but jumps down as soon as she approaches. She looks at her work. It is the shape of a rough bell, a battered bell swinging right. The bottom of it is low enough for her to move the ladder out of the way and look in. Wooden beams. A narrow frame, plasterboard hung on each side of it. Cheap idea of a wall. Bricks to the right, the house proper. The kitchens of course were added on, and must have been added at the same time so why bother with bricks. She reaches in and feels around. Quite a wide cavity. The damp is just on her side. Theirs is more solid, drier. To her left, at about eye level, there is light. Definitely some sort of hole into their kitchen. She reaches for it, knocking a little more plaster off in the process. She thinks that if she tugs a line of plaster out on her side, as far as the hole on their side, she will be able to see through. As she is thinking about this she rests her hands on the plaster just below the level of her chest, as if she is looking over a fence, and she must think that's what she's doing, because she goes up on her toes, puts too much weight on it, and the whole thing suddenly crumbles and falls – plaster, paint, a great rubble of sheetrock, falling on her legs and her feet, and for a second she thinks that the whole lot is coming down, the whole wall, the whole house, and she stumbles backwards and loses her balance and falls with a clatter into the chairs around the table.

Clarity.

Not one then the other. Not day and then night. Not a

woman and then a man. There is only one moment, and it continues. The body had changed but there was only one face. In her memory, there was only one. In the parks sometimes, they would laugh and the rain would never fall.

She finds herself sitting on the floor. She feels fine. But also feels that she may very briefly have lost consciousness. She has been away, somewhere. Something took her and now she is back. She feels her head, and looks at her hand. Nothing. Her legs are covered in a chalky dust. The cat is standing in the door with a look of disbelief on his face. He appears to be talking to her but she cannot hear anything except the smothered confusion in her ears and she takes a moment to remember the party and to establish that it is still going on. She leans forward and peers over the cat towards the front door.

What an idiot.

She does not have words.

There is a dictionary on a shelf in the living room. But it works the wrong way around. There is no combination of words that can even begin.

Yes there is.

Why now?

Why not?

She is trapped in the place where she hides from the world and suddenly the world has wrapped itself around her, embraced her house with music and laughter. The world is here. And she feels she should say hello.

She takes her time. She dries her eyes. Fishes a tissue from her pocket and blows her nose. She climbs slowly to her feet, gripping the backs of the chairs, the table. She is lucky she wasn't knocked out but still feels that she might have been.

Perhaps she is dead?

She checks herself again for blood or bumps but there is nothing.

— Gather round, she says to the cat. Gather round and hear how sad I am. Boo hoo.

After washing her hands again, and shifting some of the rubble with her feet, and pulling away the last of the plaster above the skirting board, she tries to extend the big hole in her side of the wall so that it meets the tiny hole in theirs so that she can look at the party. But all the remaining plaster is solid now, she can't break it. She hurts her fingers trying. She presses herself into the hole and turns her head to the left and shuffles as far as she can in that direction, inside the cavity, towards the light. She laughs. She is this thin.

— Mother of god, she says, and laughs again. The cat is on her foot. She shuffles back and turns her head and tells him to get off.

— Go asleep now button. Go have a nice sleep. You'll be all right.

She thinks then about feeding him. There are hours until breakfast. Why would she feed him now? Nevertheless. She finds herself refilling his water at the sink and shaking some new chewables into his bowl. What is she at? She's not going any-where. He follows, peering at her, his eyes wide, chattering away as if she's not listening, which she isn't, but as if she should be, as if this is very important, this information.

— I don't know what you want baby. Shush now.

And she goes back into the wall.

She holds her breath and tries to squeeze further along, her left arm outstretched towards the light, such as it is, a glow from their kitchen.

She pulls in her stomach, her chest, moves another couple of inches. Behind her she can feel the plaster shift but it doesn't give. She turns her head. It is difficult. She cannot quite. He was very funny. Always very funny. The two of them in stitches on the bus. As a child she had always made her brothers laugh. Then a long time without laughter. Then she met her, and the laughter started up again, and didn't stop. Until he died. And since then it had been the memory only, and the stupid jokes she would fall into and he would be back for an instant then gone again, and the damage, the damage was considerable. Laughter, no laughter, laughter again, and then the ghosts. Two ghosts with the one face.

There is a rib of wood at her back stopping her. She pushes with all her might against it. She is not mighty. But something shifts. She moves another inch, another two, and she can see now, sideways, through the tiny hole. Light, shapes, the movement of figures. She pushes back and sideways again and she gets her head turned a little to the front and she can see.

She can see them.

It's as if they are not allowed near the wall. They stand instead to her left, near the garden, and in front of her, leaning on the counters, in little groups, moving past each other. She realises that there is a table against the wall. She can see the tops of bottles and cans down there. She can see the young people. She can see their full faces, their lips, their shoulders. She can see them happy.

This is great.

— Take off your life like trousers, she says.

She can't remember what that's from.

Then the music stops. What is this? The music has suddenly disappeared. Have they seen her? Oh god.

She tries to move back the way she came, but she can't. She is. She can't be. She is. They aren't looking at her. They are looking towards the door. She can still feel the wooden rib at her back. She is stuck. She thinks she's stuck. Possibly stuck. She cannot turn her head. Oh dear lord.

She goes through a complicated procedure of raising her hand in the crevice and holding it out to her side and then over, and bending it above her shoulder, out and over, and she pulls the earplug from her right ear, and immediately drops it, idiot, but the sound is crisper, clearer, of people, so close, and she can practically hear the words. But it's quieter now. The music has stopped. What is happening? There is laughter. They are all looking at the door out of the kitchen, the door into the rest of the house. Boys. Not boys. Young men. Young women. She sees them. In their T-shirts and tops, with their drinks. She sees a couple with linked arms. She sees a young man with a beautiful smile, leaning on another man's shoulder. She sees the bored girl. Well goodness. Her bored girl. There she is. That's absolutely her. But she doesn't look so bored. She looks anxious, poor love. She is standing with her arms folded, leaning against where the sink must be.

She thinks she can hear whistling.

Then a voice begins to sing. A man's voice. A single voice. Singing. He used to sing. She, too. The voice never really changed, one to the other. Nothing did. Not really. They had loved each other better, maybe. More carefully. This voice though. It's very good. Very full. It is commanding. It carries a melody, strongly. It's a good voice. Familiar, almost.

Then the whistling again.

Then the voice.

The bored girl has closed her eyes to listen. She no longer looks anxious. She is smiling. She is very pretty.

Her hand is still above her shoulder. She can't seem to lower it. As it's there, she puts a finger in the hole and pulls a little at the edges. It is smaller than her eye. The song is maybe French. She works at it with her finger, so that it becomes as large as her fingertip, then as large as the first of her knuckles. She pulls her finger out. It is as large as her eye now. The voice is beautiful. Full of emotion. She puts her eye against the hole and holds it there and looks at the girl.

The singing stops. There is a moment in which nothing happens.

Then there is applause, and there are raised voices and all the people in the kitchen seem to crowd around the door.

Except for the bored girl. She isn't bored though, she's curious. She has moved towards the table. She stands peering at the hole, an expression on her face. What is she doing? Oh. She is staring at the eye. Which is what she sees. An eye in the wall.

She lifts her hand.

She opens her mouth.

But wait. Wait until I tell you.

This story I have.

The Camera

HE WANTED A new camera, he said. He'd had a decent camera maybe four or five years ago, but he'd lost it, or – this was vague – he'd given it to a guy he'd been seeing, or this guy had stolen it, or there had been some sort of misunderstanding which led in any case to him losing this camera, as well as the guy, who'd disappeared to Germany soon afterwards, as if – and here Gary went off on a confusing contradictory rant, somewhat sentimental and embarrassed as well as everything else – as if the camera, or getting the camera, had been the sole purpose not only of this guy's involvement with Gary but also of his entire time in London. He was Italian. Or, Gary corrected himself, Sardinian in fact, which is completely different, and anyway he took off to Hamburg without warning, overnight, as if making a run for it. Which Gary admitted might have been only his own somewhat heartbroken perspective, having lost the guy, whom he quite liked, and the camera, which he'd liked at least as much. Though it hadn't been, he admitted, a particularly good camera – just an ugly clunky bridge thing, well out of date now. And he'd never fully mastered it, though frustratingly he hadn't needed to – it automated things so eagerly that it allowed him to be lazy. Now though, Gary said, with a certain comic haughtiness, now he felt that he was successfully putting laziness to one side. He was coming out of a shell he said. Not his shell, but one he'd borrowed somewhere, one that was not his and not him.

He was maybe a little high.

He was, he said, reading books again, not having read a single book for about a year. He said that he was much more, way more engaged with what was going on, politically – reading the news, listening to the political podcasts. He *knew* what was going on, for the first time in ages. And it wasn't, he said to Stan, as if Stan didn't know this, it wasn't good. Stan nodded. It wasn't good. Nothing was good. Stan smiled at his friend and went to get them another couple of pints.

It was the first time he'd seen Gary in more than a month. He'd put on a bit of weight, and he seemed generally much better. The last time he'd seen him he'd been a mess – precise and paranoid, hanging around the back room of The Arms refusing a drink, refusing company, nipping outside every five minutes and then nipping back in, in out, in out, doing nothing but drawing attention to himself and then freaking out over the looks he was getting. Stan had had a word. But Gary said he was waiting for someone. *Well wait outside.* And Gary had waited outside. He hadn't come back. There'd been a few text exchanges since, Stan trying subtly to enquire if he was ok, Gary taking forever to reply and then bombarding him with typos for an hour and going quiet again. But that was Gary. Always a bit high or a bit low. Always busy with himself. Good heart, bad head. Not exactly reliable. He'd asked Stan to meet tonight. They used to do this often – meet at The Arms midweek, just the two of them, chat over a few slow pints, veering between serious and stupid – books they were reading, a bit of politics, a little gossip. Stan had missed it, to tell the truth. Gary made him laugh. He'd worried that it would be weird or worse. But it was good.

The Arms was deserted. The older gentleman with the glasses who always said hello and goodbye to Stan but nothing else was sitting at the bar, spun on his stool to watch golf on the big screen. Harry was in the backroom, where there seemed to be maybe three or four people together, working the jukebox, a little boisterous. It took a couple of minutes for Harry to come through, apologetic.

— It's cos there's no one here. I drift off.

— Yeah, where is everyone?

— It's Tuesday mate. This is everyone.

Stan took the drinks back to the high table at the window where Gary fiddled with his phone.

— Here's some examples.

— Do you take pictures on that?

— Yeah loads.

— Examples of what?

— Cameras. Cameras I'm thinking of. Looking at.

He was looking at digital SLRs he said. Canon or Nikon. He showed Stan some pictures of chunky looking machines, all black and heavy and identical as far as Stan could see. Gary was reeling off model names – letters and numbers that could have been motorways or washing machines for all Stan knew about it. So he was looking into that, Gary was.

— They're expensive.

— They're fucking outrageous man you have no idea.

— Are you working?

— Yeah yeah I have shifts at B&Q again.

Gary was flicking through pictures of cameras. Stan thought

about the fact that to take a photograph of a camera requires two cameras.

— You back at your mother's?

— Stop worrying about me man it's embarrassing.

— I couldn't give a shit about you.

— You fucking love me.

— In your dreams.

— You're not my type much Stanley. I'm at my mother's. I'm working shifts at B&Q, and I got some jobs coming up with my uncle. I'm good.

— What uncle?

— My plumber uncle. Ronnie. Who you've *met*. Look at this thing.

Gary was doing his research, he said. Taking notes, working out what he wanted, reading reviews, watching all the features videos people made, listing the pros, the cons, how they compared, how they performed, all this, all that. But these cameras – the ones he wanted anyway – they started at about £750. And went up sharp. And that was before you got into lenses, which were the whole point of going for SLR. You were talking about a lot of money. A hell of a lot of money.

Gary, Stan knew, didn't have any money.

— Why don't you just use your phone?

Gary gave Stan a hard look. Held it. Held it a second more. Stan was smiling at him.

— Just go be basic white girl somewhere else Stanley.

— A bit racist.

— I could cut you.

— Also racist.

Gary was smiling as well now.

— Yeah, I grant you. Look at you. Cat got the cream, getting to joke about racism with your black mate.

— Ooof.

— Yeah.

— Fair.

— It's the project of a lifetime man, never give it up.

Stan nodded at that.

— Money, though, said Gary. I need money. Give me money. Not literally. I'm not asking you for money.

— You have your shifts at B&Q.

— Food money.

— Can you save a little? What's your mother charging?

He laughed.

— Uhhhh. No. No. I mean, I owe her. And I owe my brother. They're not coming looking for me, but you know. I'm not in a saving sort of place.

They moved their drinks around. Stan looked out the window, tapped his glass with his nail. What he could do with £750. This was his social life for the week. A couple of pints with Gary meant no cinema on Friday, unless he broke his own rules. Which he had done the week before when he'd gone to Brighton with Maria to walk on the beach and see their friend Meena who was pregnant and having some sort of crisis. And there would be, next week, probably, a visit from Maria's brother who would stay for a while because he had nowhere else to be, and that would cost more money, not because they'd be doing anything expensive, but they'd just be out of the flat more because good relations would require it, and stepping outside the door in London costs money.

He'd drifted off. Gary was deep in his phone.

— This place can't last.

— What?

— It's so empty.

— Tonight yeah. But weekends, the pub quiz. They're doing fine. I think Canon is the way to go.

Stan sighed.

— I'm being boring, said Gary. I know.

— Nah, it's not that. It's money. So much worry and energy about money, you know? It's just constant. It's control. Things which should be inalienable become contingent. All human endeavour is commodified. The obstacle to your access to the camera is the commodification of your desire for the camera.

Gary nodded.

— That's exactly right. I am being boring though. I mean, I know what this is, I'm fixated on this camera idea a little, and I know, I know. There are priorities. But this is not just Gary-wants-a-nice-thing. It's more than that. It's what I can do with it. I have this idea that it will . . . Ah fuck.

He pushed his pint to the side and put his phone down and put his arms on the table and leaned towards Stan.

— I want to do things. You know that. I am tired of just rolling through, you know? And it's exactly about what you just said. Look at us. Two intelligent good-looking men in our prime and not a bean between us. It's not the money. We don't need money, we need to be able to stop worrying about money, and scrabbling around for money, so that we can do the things we should be doing. The work you do, the hours you do Stan, that should . . . you should be comfortable. And I mean. Maria, she should be paid more than anyone, you know? Teaching is either as important as they say it is and she gets paid like it is, or it isn't and everything is bullshit. A teacher

— She's not a teacher.

— She's a librarian.

— She's a library assistant.

— All right. A library assistant. School though. Those kids with their library. She's an assistant? That's even more important, you know. Library doesn't function without an assistant. Those books, they don't . . . lend themselves out. Those little rich brats need help to reach the high shelves? What's that about?

— It's . . .

— I'm joking.

— Ok. Not obvious.

— Nice. Anyway, I am serious about this. I am serious. I don't mean to dis Maria. I know she hates that place.

— It's ok.

— Ok. But things like that. There's schools with fuck all, where they send the kids home on a Friday lunchtime because they can't afford to keep the fucking thing open, and there's schools with everything, with playing fields and labs and the best teachers, and with Maria and they pay her fuck all, right? Those kids are lucky to have her. But it's not luck is it? It's money. It's money that makes the difference. We didn't even have a fucking library did we?

— We did.

— Did we?

Stan laughed at him.

— Yeah. I mean it was shit. But it was there. I read *1984* there. Tony Benn's diaries. Solzhenitsyn I think? Mouldy old paperbacks. Mrs Dawson wouldn't let me take anything home.

— All right. Well I don't know what I was doing.

— I do.

— All right, all right. But it's not like what those kids have with Maria, right?

— No, it's not. Whole different world, that.

— Right. And on top of that Stan. The whole fucking set-up is racist. The Met, obviously. But housing, health, employment, all of it. Education. Run through with this . . .

— White supremacy.

Gary paused, looked at him, nodded.

— That's right. Right. It is. It completely is.

This was typical, thought Stan. Gary stayed wrapped up in his own life until he got bored with it, or a cop gave him a hard time, and then he'd come to Stan with a rediscovered sense of injustice. It had happened before.

— Come to another meeting.

— What? No no no.

He laughed.

— Come on, it wasn't that bad. I mean, it's just a different way of approaching stuff, you know. You'd get it after a while.

Gary took a sip, eyes on him.

— It was awful Stan. It was embarrassing. People laughed at me.

— No one laughed at you.

— They fucking did. That woman from the Pelican? I know her. When I was asking how things worked. When I asked who our MP is. She just laughed out loud. That's like . . .

— Janice? She's an idiot. No reason for you to feel embarrassed about that.

Gary looked at him, sharp.

— I don't Stan. I don't feel embarrassed in the least. It was embarrassing for her. For you. For everyone at that meeting. To laugh like that, to be so condescending, it was fucking outrageous man. I am never going back to that shit.

— Oh come on.

— Come on what? What are you going to tell me? There

were eighteen people in that room. Two black faces. In Camber-well? Are you kidding me? Spent most of the time talking about electing people from the meeting to go to another fucking meet-ing. And the rest of the time about fucking parking spaces.

— It was not a good meeting. But it's . . . it's work, you know. You have to be in it to change it, to make it do what it should be doing.

Stan sighed and looked out the window at the faces on a passing bus. Tired-looking people. He was tired of having this argument.

— I want to be doing things, Stan. But that's not me. Politics, yes, but that's not . . . I can't do meetings. You know? You're good at that, and you're right, you're in there and you're working at it, and I respect that, and I'm really glad that you're doing that, and I love it, it's great, but I can't do it. I don't belong in meetings and parties and formalities like you. What I want is to be on the streets when things happen. Protests. Arrests. Getting in the way. I want to be involved maybe with some groups that work about the police. You know. Brutality, deaths in custody. That stuff makes me so . . . and other stuff too, your stuff a little bit maybe, when you were on that march by the Aylesbury and all that shit. But I am, and you know this about me Stan. I am not good at talking.

Stan smiled at him.

— Are you joking?

The anti-gentrification march around the Aylesbury had been a mistake. They'd pulled down the hoardings. He'd had to duck out of it.

— Not to more than a person at a time. Not with strangers or rooms.

— You are good at talking.

37

— Yeah, but like when I'm with you, with friends, then yeah I'm ok. But I am not a talker Stan, generally. I am shy. Jesus, don't argue with me.

He laughed.

— Dyslexic. Faggot. Big weird head. Can't hold a tune. Can't dance. You like the beard?

— You can dance.

— I can dance, right, thanks. I have noooo natural confidence. And unnatural confidence is not good. Not a good way to live. Not in the long run. So. If I have a camera to cover my face, and can do something worthwhile with it. Do you think? Just be available you know? Turn up, take a few shots. Document. Witness. Let others do the organising and the talking and that. I just want to witness.

— Yeah.

— This isn't stupid?

— No.

— Ok.

— It's not stupid. It's the least stupid thing you've said all

— Yeah, yeah, yeah, serious now. I'm being serious.

— It's a good idea. It really is. And I'm . . . I'm glad you're thinking like this.

— Ok. Good.

He was. It was a good idea. It wouldn't happen. Or if it did it wouldn't last. But it was a good idea.

— Not a talker, though?

— One on one, people I know.

— I mean, I know you can lack confidence, I understand that. But you have plenty to say, and when you're . . . your voice is as important as anyone else's.

Gary gave him quite a look.

— Oh, said Stan. That's maybe not . . .

— Yeah.

— Sorry.

— Why do you ruin everything?

Stan laughed. Gary made a straight face, couldn't quite hold it, smiled.

— I'm kidding you. I'm kidding you. Seriously though, you think my voice might be as important as other people's? I mean, really, you really . . .

— Ok. Stop it.

— You really think that? Oh my days. I feel so . . . acknowledged.

— Yeah.

Stan was thinking now that maybe Gary wasn't high after all. Well, he wasn't sure how it worked, was he? He was doing the yabbering, but it made sense. He looked ok. His eyes were ok. Maybe he was just excited. That whatever had been going on for the last few months was now over, and he was trying to catch up on himself. Which was what he'd been saying, more or less. The half coded, half obvious way of speaking had become something that he didn't challenge Gary on. Not in a long time. Pointless. He didn't know what the problem was exactly, but there was some problem. Or there had been. He had seen him too often looking cold and clammy, twitching, scurrying away guiltily on the street, trying to breezily brush off Stan's enquiries, mostly by text. He'd admitted a couple of times to being *a bit too high for you right now Stanman, catch you later*, but Stan didn't know what that amounted to, not really. Gary had smoked a little weed for as long as he'd known him, but this was sharper than that. It was very different. He'd been living with a guy in north London for a while the previous year. And then there'd been some sort of house share in Bermondsey with some *friends* shortly after, but which Gary had referred to since as *the nightmare sitcom*. If he asked Gary a direct question, Gary wouldn't answer. But things slipped out, or were rationed out, and Stan noticed them, and didn't jump, and he thought that Gary probably appreciated that, appreciated that distance.

They had one more pint. Took a gossipy run through people they had in common. Stan caught him up on the meetings – factional gossip – and spent a while explaining how all that would probably play out in the local elections, and Gary sat glumly staring out the window at the Uber traffic and the fast-food bikes.

— Everything, he said, is wrong.

But they were ok. They walked together down to the Green. They hugged. Stan watched Gary cross at the lights towards his mother's down on Comber Grove. He didn't know what it was in the warm air, the cars creeping around the corner, the little breeze that disappeared as soon as you felt it, but it was something sentimental. Three pints of something sentimental probably. He remembered Gary as a kid. When they'd both been kids. And he missed that. And he wanted that back. But there was nothing much left of it now.

Maria's brother slept on the sofa and laughed with Maria about things that Stan assumed were family jokes because they made no sense to him at all. He was barely twenty. He seemed to always be eating, and playing with his phone, and Stan found it impossible to have a conversation with him. Maria would stay up late and Stan could hear them talking quietly, laughing. They argued once, but Maria wouldn't tell Stan what it was about.

He spent a lot of time sitting in Burgess Park, reading,

thankful for once for the weather. He lay on the grass. A couple of times he fell asleep, briefly, and woke up worried he'd been robbed. He was working too much, trying to do too many things, taking on more than he should. But it was all important. He was doing nothing that wasn't important.

There were texts from Gary, daytime, sensible, still banging on about cameras. He sent Stan some pictures he'd taken with his phone. A spilled bin on a footpath; a shopfront church shuttered in the dark; an empty road lined with globes of blurred white streetlights that looked like UFOs. All night-time, black and white, no people. Stan didn't know what to make of them. He thought about the cost of the cameras, thought about those big numbers, did some sums, shook his head. He recorded a couple of messages for Gary, telling him about the brother, about being out of the flat, telling Gary to come join him in the park some time. He didn't. Then the brother left, and he was looking forward to a few nights of nothing but restoring the flat, and Maria, to himself. But he only had one of those nights before Gary called, wanting to see Stan again. Maria didn't mind. Stan asked her to come along but she said she felt like a third wheel with the two of them, which Stan thought was cute camouflage for not really liking Gary. Or not recently anyway. She was, he thought, probably a little nervous about how he'd been behaving.

So about two weeks after they'd met in The Arms they met there again. Another Tuesday night. It was busier for no reason. A crowd of students in the back room. The older gentleman, watching the golf. The bus driver and his big friend, nursing their bottles of lager, doing a crossword. A table of four middle-aged women having a laugh. A few scattered others. And amongst them like a bit of grit in Stan's eye roamed Stoker.

Harry served Stan straight away, no chat.

They sat at the window again, Gary clearing empties back to the bar while Stan looked around, his gaze drawn quickly to the low table behind him where Stoker had settled, beside a woman Stan didn't recognise. Stan stared. Tried to catch her eye. Stoker leaning in, his shoulder against hers, whispering. The woman looked up. Maybe because Gary was back, pulling a chair out noisily. Or maybe she'd felt Stan's little community spirit, his small worry. She looked at him, worked it out from whatever he was doing with his face, and gave a barely perceptible, reassuring nod. Stoker turned and stared. A flash of something. And then the smile.

— Hello lovely boys. How are we doing?

Stan took it.

— Not bad thanks how are you?

— Oh I'm all right I am, more or less. Although I hate this state of things, don't you, this . . .

He gestured vaguely, towards nothing.

— It's the heat, it's inhuman, I can't stand it. I am against it completely. I was saying to Anna. I was saying to Anna that I'm lathered from morning to night, in my own juices, steeped. Marinated. Isn't that right Anna? I'm wet with it. Not made for this.

He looked dry as dead skin. He wore an old black suit rubbed to a shine and a yellow shirt, and maybe that made the jaundiced face, but Stan found him so generally disgusting that he wasn't sure. The man had looked for years like he was dying. Stan thought with some seriousness that Stoker was already dead. He'd never seen him anywhere other than The Arms. And never in daylight. And people worked so hard to ignore him that Stan sometimes felt that they couldn't see him. Gary for instance, now. No help.

Stoker stood up and came to their table. Stan stayed turned

in his chair to face him so that he could, after a minute or so, turn away. Gary, if anything, turned towards the window, something on his phone of great importance.

— Are you boys here for the duration?

— Of what?

— Anna, he stage-whispered, is drunk. Drunk and bitter. Terribly bitter. Thanks for the rescue. She gets this way. And are you?

— Am I what?

— Either of you, for the duration?

— Of what?

He looked briefly pained, but smiled again.

— Well that's fair. I was just saying hello.

— I don't know what you're asking me.

— That's an answer, that's fine. Lovely to see you both, and looking so nice. I can see you're set up for a heart to heart. I'll not intrude. I'm wanted at the Jamaican table in any case, I do believe. A round of lovely nonsense on the terrible cruelty of things. No doubt. Fuck the Tories, isn't that the cry? That's the cry. Fuck the Tories! God bless.

And his yellow smile flashed and he glanced at Anna, who was now on the phone, or pretending to be. He shuffled off towards the back room, his steps uneven and wrong, as he passed through furniture and parts of people's bodies. Stan felt an inordinate relief.

— What the fuck was that?

Gary shook his head, still looking at his phone.

— I'm not going to bore you with camera talk. I have just one thing to say about it. One thing and then we can move on to redistribution and your love of hip-hop. Whatever.

He thought maybe Stoker had left a smell behind him. A brief
unpleasant waft. He waved his hands in the air.

— Ok.

— I might nick it.

— What?

— The camera. I might steal it.

— Gary.

— Hear me out.

He hung his hand over the side of the table like it wasn't
working, but once in a while he'd flip it over, as if he wanted to
involve it but his arm was too heavy to lift, and his whole face
seemed to slump a little, as if he was tired but in a cosy, lazy sort
of way. He found a relaxed pitch somewhere under the buzz of
the room, making himself audible without raising his voice.

— I've been doing my research, yeah? Online, offline. I have
a head full of facts at this stage Stan, I'm driving myself mad.
ISO. Shutter speed. F-stops. You have no idea the things I know.
I've been on these little trips, little research trips into Oxford
Street. Annoying the assistants. John Lewis. Jessops. *Can you show
me this. Can I hold that.* Selfridges. *Let me see that other one. Thank
you and goodbye.*

Gary grinned and took a sip of his pint and then grinned
again.

— I'm annoying them, I'm annoying you, I'm *really* annoying
myself. So I was thinking. You know. If I've no money for a thing,
which as we have discussed is an injustice, as you said, in itself,
as you said so eloquently in fact, last time, so . . . why not correct
that injustice?

— I don't think you're going to be able to just walk out of
John Lewis with a Nikon under your arm.

— I know. But listen. Last time I was in there I walked home.

Bit of exercise. The Vulgar Square. White All. Downer Street.
Yesminister. That whole weird city from the TV news. You been
there lately?

Stan shook his head.

— The tourists Stan. The tourists. They are fucking legion. I
had no idea there would be so many. I mean, this time of year?
What are they doing? It's dreary. But there's thousands of them.
So many thousands. And every second one of them has a camera.
And maybe six out of ten of those have something on my
list. Nikons and Canons everywhere you look. Hanging around
the necks of people from all over the world. And you know me
Stanley, I'm not a snob. But these fuckers, these idiots . . .

Stan laughed.

— they're pointing them – and they're in fucking auto mode
I'm fucking sure of it – they're pointing them at bullshit soldiers
on horses and at bobbies, and statues of I don't know what, and
they for certain don't know what either, and at what they think
is Big fucking Ben, and at each other. You know, posing in the
only red telephone boxes left in London, have you seen these
things? Pristine. No hooker cards, no piss. They probably even
work. Photo ops for tourists with cameras that cost three month's
fucking rent. Shirley from Texas hanging out the door with her
little union-jack flag big cheesy grin for hubby to take a snap – a
snap Stanley, not a photograph, a *snap* – for the folks back home,
on a camera I could use to change the world.

They smiled at each other.

— And I am convinced Stan, I am convinced

He dropped his head low and Stan followed suit. Conspiratorial huddle.

— I am convinced that I can snag one of these things. If I'm
clever about it. And I can be clever Stanley, you know me. Grab

one of these beautiful machines. Grab it back from the industrial tourism complex. From the holiday fascists. From out of all that useless junk. Put it to *work* Stan. Restore some balance to the world of photography, and the world of travel, and to the fucking world itself.

He raised his eyebrows, nodded at Stan.

— I like it, Stan said.

— You do?

— Yes. I mean there are some potential downsides. A traumatised visitor who spent years saving for their trip, saving for a camera to document it. Losing precious photographs of their child, who is dying of cancer, maybe it was their dying wish to visit London. But I think, all in all

— Worth it.

— Worth it, yeah.

They were both slumped, heads resting in their hands, smiling.

— Could actually do it though. Probably. There are serious crowds down there. Bumping and jostling, waiting to cross the road, cameras slung over shoulders, not a care in the world. They rest on the hip, you know? All you need is a pair of secateurs and a bag of your own. Snip . . .

— A what?

— A pair of secateurs. Garden clippers. Or wire cutters. But my mum has secateurs for her balcony bushes, so. Snip, drop, go. Might take a little time to find the right sort of mark. The right place. The right time. But the whole area is swarming. It would work.

— Gary.

He smiled at Stan.

— I can do subtle.

— But you're not actually

Gary shrugged. Sat up.

— There's cameras obviously, all over. But you know, a base-ball cap. Sunglasses. Rain jacket. Find a blind spot after and dump them. Bag into another bag. Not a problem.

Stan laughed.

— Don't be daft.

He knew Gary wasn't being serious. He lifted his glass and put it down again. Outside, the buses and the syrupy night.

He was pretty sure that Gary wasn't being serious. But Gary's face had closed on him.

— You're not serious?

He shifted in his seat and ran his hand over his head and sighed.

— No man. I'm not serious. I don't have a death wish.

He looked around the bar. So did Stan. The older gentleman applauded a golf shot. Gary smiled.

— Not much of one anyway. First you'd hear about it would be a news alert.

— Don't think a camera thief gets that sort of thing.

— They'd shoot me Stan.

— Well I'm not sure about that, but

— Oh you're not sure about that?

— Who's going to shoot you?

— I'm in Whitehall, Gary said. I'm on that crossing, you know, literally across the road from the Houses of Parliament. I'm two minutes from Downing Street. There are cameras every-where. There are cops everywhere. And I'm going to prowl around looking for the right camera on the right person, I'm going to hang around, for hours maybe, with a pair of fucking

He laughed.

— a pair of fucking secateurs? A baseball cap, sunglasses, with my beard and my black skin? Stanley, bruv, I'm going to get shot.

He laughed loudly, shook his head.

— Of course I'm not fucking serious.

There was a shriek from across the room and Stan jumped, turned. A man stood up suddenly from one of the low tables. A woman ran in short steps towards the door, a snapped, sickly look on her face. The man stuck out a leg and stamped hard on the floor. Did it again, knocked against the table. Someone else stood up. Stan caught a glimpse of darting grey along the bottom of the bar to the corner, where it disappeared. He flinched. Mouse.

There was general laughter. The woman who'd run to the door stayed there, and the man went to join her, carrying their drinks.

— The fucking thing touched me! she said, furious. It was on my foot!

— Well it won't be back.

— And what were you trying to do? You want mouse guts all over your fucking shoe what's wrong with you?

He laughed. Gary was laughing too. They sat at another table, the couple. Some other people moved around as well. Stoker was chatting to two young guys Stan recognised from the Lettsom. Ran a youth group or something. He was clutching one of the guy's arms and they were laughing uneasily with him.

Harry had stayed in the back room during the commotion. Now he came through to the front clapping his hands, pretending nothing had happened.

— Who's next now please? Yes Lilly, same again?

— Bit busy for mice, said Gary. Usually only see them when the place is empty. Last week. Or when were we here? Last time. Saw a couple that night, nosing around in the corner.

Stan said nothing. He watched Stoker as the boys disengaged from him slowly and headed towards the door.

— God bless! Stoker called after them. God bless!

Stan eyed him, fixed him. He didn't know what he was. He liked to talk to everyone, liked to think he was everyone's friend, but Stan had never heard a good thing about him. Now he was looking around. Stan wanted to catch his eye, and his leg twitched, and he wanted to look at him, stare him down, unnerve him, let him know that Stan saw him, that Stan was fucking watching him. Anything, the slightest thing, and he would see it. Stoker didn't notice him. Didn't look at him. Instead he ran a finger over his thin lips and disappeared through the arch to the back bar.

— I absolutely fucking hate that guy, he said.

Gary followed his gaze.

— You hate Harry?

— No. Stoker.

— Who?

— Stoker?

— Who's that?

He looked at Gary.

— The creepy guy. Old suit. The skinny guy, looks like a fucking vampire. Came and said hello to us.

— Yano?

— What?

— Yano. His name is Yano. Where did you get Stoker from?

— Someone told me he was called Stoker.

Gary laughed.

— Bram Stoker? Someone was having you on Stan. Does have a touch of the Dracula about him. But he's all right. It's Yano. Or Yaniv. Or Yanko or something. Little strange yeah, but who isn't? Why do you hate him?

— I thought he was Irish.

— You hate the Irish?

— No, no. I thought his name was Stoker and that he was Irish and I hate him because he gives me the creeps. He says the weirdest things.

— Well I don't know. I don't think English is his first language. Was Bram Stoker Irish?

— No. I've seen him drinking leftovers close to closing time.

— Ok. I've done a bit of minesweeping in my time Stan. It's not, you know, it's not exactly the blood of the young.

He wanted to say to Gary that there should not be mice in a pub. That it should not be a matter of laughing and a bit of a commotion then forgetting about it. He wanted to tell Gary that he should have said that he'd seen mice the last time. Because he knew that they had been sitting at the same table, in the same position, and that meant that Gary had seen mice behind him, behind Stan, as he talked to him. Over his shoulder. At his back. Nosing. What did that mean? Nosing? They served food. They stored glasses on low shelves. It was disgusting. That was a different thing though. He wanted to say that Stoker, or whatever he was called, had something about him that Stan felt to be obscene. But he could not say that either because he had no idea what it meant.

Anxiety reversed through him and he turned cold and the night seemed glaringly bright and he bristled with discomfort. He hated every single stupid fucking thing.

They were quiet for a while. Gary watched him, looking where he was looking. Stan went for a piss and took his time and gave himself a bit of a talking to. But when he got back he was still shifty and shut down.

Gary asked him, nicely, about Maria, about work, about his

meetings. Stan couldn't shake his sulk. Stoker reappeared and stood near the door and looked at them for a moment but Stan only glanced and felt a tapping in his jaw of confusion and a milk-white dread, and Stoker went away.

Everything was wrong. They didn't have a second drink.

Stan didn't see Gary for a while after that. He put it out of his mind. He was busy with work, attending party meetings, union meetings, trying to spend all the spare time he had with Maria, who was depressed, and he wasn't worrying about Gary. Why should he worry about Gary?

Maria fell off her bike one day and Stan left work early to go and be with her and they told him that unless there was a doctor's note or a police reference number then he wasn't entitled to emergency time because there was no proof of an emergency and they were taking three hours off his pay and he owed them three hours. He got on to the union and they looked at the contract and told him he had no entitlement to the pay but he shouldn't have to make up the time. He told his boss and his boss said *fine, but I'll remember this*. Stan told him that he'd remember it too because his wife was injured, and traumatised, and here was Stan having to deal with a juvenile piece of intimidation from a new manager who was perhaps out of his depth and could maybe, *who knows*, do with some advice from central office about the handling of this issue and would he like Stan to put in a call? Then they had a brief staring contest that Stan won, and that seemed to be the end of it. Absurd.

Maria wasn't his wife, and she wasn't really injured, or traumatised, but she was depressed, Stan thought. She didn't want to do anything. She claimed she was fine. She'd had a scare, that was all, but she hadn't been hurt beyond a bruised arm and a cut on her leg. She was quiet though. She said she was working. And she did spend hours just writing in her notebooks. And that was good, because she hadn't done that in a while, and he knew that it was important. But he couldn't get much out of her. She was not fully there.

He next saw Gary at a demo against the plans to redevelop Elephant and Castle, down at the council offices on Tooley Street. He was right at the other side of what was a surprisingly big crowd, and Stan saw him and then lost him, saw and lost him again, and it took quite a while before he realised that he had a camera. Gary had a camera. Stan waved at him and Gary held the camera in the air and waved back and they both smiled at each other, but Stan was deep in conversation with a sympathetic councillor about strategy and he couldn't go over and when he looked for him later he couldn't see him. The camera had seemed something like the things he'd been looking at. He texted him but there was no reply. On his way home he called him but there was no answer.

Then a few days later there was an envelope on the doormat. Nothing on the outside. Inside, a photograph of Stan at the demo, chatting to the councillor. It was zoomed in. It was black and white. It was a good photo, Stan thought, atmospheric, like one you might see in an article about people to watch in South London politics. The Ones to Watch on the Left. Two men in conversation, caught side-on as they faced each other, with an out-of-focus background of figures and placards and movement. He could do with a haircut. He called Gary. Left a message.

— I really like it, thanks for dropping it in. Is this . . . oh, it's just paper. So it's printed? Like, just on a printer? See I haven't a clue. Camera looked great, from a distance. I look very cool don't

I? Be good to see you soon. You should come over. Or we can get a coffee or something. I'm around this weekend.

Then he sent him a text saying all of the same things, because there was a good chance that Gary wouldn't listen to a message for weeks. He put the photograph up on the wall in their main room. Maria liked it. She told him he looked conspiratorial and clever. And that he could do with a haircut. Stan wondered how Gary had been able to afford it. He didn't tell Maria about Gary joking that he'd steal it. He didn't want her to even have that in her head.

A couple of days later another photograph arrived. Again, an unmarked envelope, a black-and-white print, Stan on his own this time, walking towards the camera. He couldn't place it. Gary hadn't replied to his messages. Walking towards the camera but obviously unaware of it, looking to the side. Just head and shoulders. It might have been on the day of the demo, but the background was completely blurred and it was impossible to tell. Stan was wearing the same jacket. It was the only jacket he had.

— *Gary give me a call will you?*

Maria thought it was funny. Like he was a mafia boss, snapped surreptitiously leaving the funeral of someone he'd had bumped off. She started naming people he might want bumped off. He didn't think it was funny. He put it back in the envelope and left it on the table.

The next day there was another one. Stan, walking along Walworth Road. He'd been coming home from a meeting – he remembered this – he was eating a bag of crisps because he'd been starving and the meeting had run on, and his jacket was over his arm because it was warm, and his bag was hanging off his shoulder pulling his shirt sideways. He could see now that his jeans were a bit short on him. Maybe a bit tight too. He'd had a haircut. The photo was . . . two days old. And it was taken from above somehow. From the front, from somewhere across the road he thought, and from a height.

— What the fuck? he said aloud.

Maria wasn't there. It was early evening. It was warm out but the flat was cold. He stood with the photograph in his hand, examining it, wearing the same jacket, with the same bag on the table in front of him, looking at his own face from some impossible angle. He tried to think what buildings there were around there that Gary might have been in. What was he doing? He called him but it didn't ring this time.

He took down the first photograph from the wall, and put it with the other two into the envelope and put them in a drawer. He said nothing to Maria when she came in. But he also said almost nothing at all, so she asked him what was wrong and he told her. He took out the photographs and laid them on the table side by side. She shrugged. It was just Gary. She didn't find it weird. She didn't think it creepy. Just a bit . . . Gary. And, she said, he took good photos. She looked at Stan carefully. What, she asked him, was he worried about? He couldn't say. But he was anxious. The photographs, and Gary's silence, seemed to amount to something. He had a vague and, he told Maria, inarticulable idea that they constituted a challenge. He felt them as an affront, a *question*. He could not relax. Maria told him to go see Gary if he was so stressed about it. She seemed annoyed. It was just after seven. He put his jacket back on and went out.

It was still bright but the lights were lit. He walked beside lines of stationary cars and buses and trucks towards the Green and he could taste the fumes and his eyes were tired. He'd known Gary since they were teenagers. Fourteen, fifteen, Gary getting bullied and Stan deliberately putting himself beside him, just offering friendship by being there and Gary accepting, eventually. Like that. He remembered it like that. They used to go down the Elephant after school and sit in the shopping centre and talk about books and music. And there was Roy, and Ahmad and his sister Noor who was into football more than the boys. Gary didn't care about football at all, but Stan tried to care about it because it was the thing that people cared about when they didn't care about anything else. And he liked Noor. Then one day she had said something to Stan that made it clear she thought he and Gary were boyfriends. And he remembered how confounded he'd been by that, how embarrassed. He'd been so annoyed at Noor. *How could you think that?* And it made him back right off and leave Gary be. And he remembered that his mother had asked him where Gary was these days, *that nice boy Gary*. And his father looking at him suspiciously. And he remembered that he had gone for a long walk and had had a word with himself, told himself to be big, be brave – or don't be a fucking coward anyway – be friends with your friend, and he remembered going down there, where he was going now, going down and surprising Gary and he remembered how happy Gary had been to see him, and they'd gone out and got chips on Walworth Road, just the two of them, laughing, having a laugh. Like that.

So what was Gary doing, Stan thought, fucking with that?

The sky was blue but Comber Grove was dark. Old orange street lights and the hulking flats and it took Stan a while to remember which floor it was and how to get there. He went up the wrong stairwell and had to go back to the street and let his memory kick in. He was stressed and his stomach gurgled like a baby. His thoughts were shredded and he snatched at them. He thought about going home. Then he got it. Second floor. Right there. One from the end. The first stairwell. He could just forget about it. Go home.

Gary answered the door. Boxer shorts. T-shirt. He looked at Stan and broke into a great big smile.

— Stanley! Finally! Where you been bruv? You're like the busiest man in the world.

Bear hug. Stepping in to the hall. He'd lost his phone, Gary said. Then his mother appeared, looking out from the kitchen, suspicious first then smiling big when she saw him. Handshakes. Gary going off to get dressed. *Arms, yeah?* Stan was trying to be polite to his mother. He couldn't remember Gary's surname. *Mrs . . . Mrs . . .* He couldn't get it. So he talked over himself, *yeah it's Maria, yeah she's very well, and how are you? No, he died last year, well thank you, no he'd been ill a while. Yes she did. Eight years ago now. Yes ma'am.* He said *ma'am.* He said *ma'am.* She gave him a wide-eye mid-sentence but let it go and told him that he was Gary's only respectable friend, the others were all *gangsters* and then Gary was shouting at her from the bedroom, but they were both laughing, and Stan was laughing too, then Gary was there fully dressed and he had the camera in his hands and he was showing it to him. The camera, finally. *Look at it*, he was saying, *here*, and he turned it on and got Stan to hold it up to his eye and he got him to flip out the little screen and he showed him some of the pictures he'd taken, they were stored right there on the camera, and his mother was laughing, saying it was like he gave birth to this thing. Stan thought it was heavy. Thought it was heavy and that it looked expensive, and he found himself looking for scratches and knocks, and he even found himself examining the strap as if . . . and then Gary was taking it back and putting it away and while he was briefly gone his mother told Stan that it was like it was a baby, *this thing like his baby, he look after it like it a baby.* And she gave him a goodbye hug and told him to bring his girl to dinner, any time, there would be a welcome for them any time. Then they were outside, their bye-bye voices in the warm air, Gary still laughing, Stan feeling ambushed by this pretence, that this was pretence, made to feel that it was somehow he who was in the wrong, as if his worry should just be put away, forgotten, just like that.

— You don't mind do you? If we stay in it'll be three of us you know? She loves you too much.

— Yeah. Yeah. Gangsters?

— All of them. She's just bigging me up. No one ever calls at my door. She's just happy I still have a friend in the world.

— So did you steal it?

— Perfect crime, told you.

He laughed.

— My uncle gave me the money. Loaned me the money. He's a good guy.

— Which uncle?

— What do you mean which uncle? You know all my uncles? Ronnie. Guy I work with sometimes. Pretty sure you've met him.

— Ok. What happened with your phone?

Gary took a big breath. Sighed.

— Lost it at that demo I saw you at. First time out with the camera and I was so fucking nervous with it, and my hands were all muddled and I must have just put the phone down somewhere stupid or dropped it or something.

— I was calling. It was ringing. You can track them.

— Yeah. Didn't have all that set up did I?

— But it was ringing? I mean, the next day?

Gary looked at him.

— Yeah. Batteries, Stan. They work using batteries.

He was pretty sure that it had still been ringing a couple of days after as well, but he let it go.

— Anyway what did you think of the pics? Photogenic young man aren't you?

— How did you print them?

— Printer, Stan. Printer. Jesus. Do you like them?

— Yeah. Sure. Didn't actually know what was happening though.

Gary laughed. Like it had been a joke.

— I really like the first one, from the demo. Not quite sure how I did it. I took a lot of really shitty pics that day. That was one of about three turned out ok.

— Where did you take the last one from? You're looking down at me. You're in a building somewhere.

— I'm on a bus Stan. I was on a bus to central.

— That's from a bus?

— Yeah yeah. You can see all the grime of the window on it, which I sort of like, but it's framed all wrong. I think I cropped it for you. Everything is framing. But I'm learning, you know, I'm already learning. Went to this great exhibition at the weekend . . . the gallery down Peckham Road. These really . . . format, beautifully framed pictures of . . . bits of street and it's . . .

Stan strained to hear Gary's voice but was missing words as they came up to Denmark Hill and turned right. He just shook his head as Gary asked him a question crossing the road and a bus roared by. Stan hated the lights and the traffic and he didn't understand why Gary was fucking talking to him when he couldn't fucking hear anything he fucking said. When they got to the other footpath he slowed down.

— Jesus, Gary was saying. Anyway it's just these large prints, I mean really big prints, of street corners, doorways, bus stops.

There's a few bus stops. And park benches. Pretty sure one is Burgess Park down by the fake gates. No people in them. Just patches of space. And they are really . . .

He laughed.

— Are you listening?

— Yeah yeah. Patches of space.

— Well that's it. I really like them.

Stan nodded. But he didn't know what Gary was talking about.

— It's made me think about exhibiting. Which is yeah . . . dumb, I mean, I've literally started. But I fucking love it. And I am so full of ideas Stan. I am fat with ideas. Why are you walking so fucking fast?

Stan slowed, but then sped up again.

— I need to pee, he said.

— Go for it. I'll catch up.

He didn't need to pee. But he nodded sideways at Gary and ran. He ran furiously, as fast as he could. His jacket flailed and he slapped at it. He couldn't afford a new one. Maria couldn't afford to fix her bike. He had never lost a phone in his life. It took seconds for him to reach the door of The Arms. He thought about running on. About lengthening his stride and continuing, running up the hill and down the hill and all the way to Crystal Palace and on to Croydon, to Brighton, to the sea. He could run around the fucking world until he was running up Denmark Hill again and tap Gary on the shoulder. Clock it. Clock the planet. He stopped and went in.

Stoker was there, elbow on the bar, smiling at him. An awful, slow wink. A few others. Harry on the phone. Stan went straight through the empty back room to the gents and stood by the sink for a minute then dried his hands then washed them then dried them again and went out. Stoker was walking away. Walking away from the door of the toilets as if he'd been in there too. Or as if he'd been walking towards them and turned around. A pint in his hand. Walking quickly, not looking back, through the arch into the front bar. Stan followed him slowly. Gary was at the bar talking to Harry. Stan looked at his phone. He stood behind Gary and sent Maria a text telling her where they were. They went to their table at the window. Stoker hadn't said a word. He stood at the bar looking at small pieces of paper.

— You can still run.

— Still?

— I'm out of breath taking the stair. I don't even chase buses anymore.

— I never smoked. I missed the start of you describing this exhibition. What was it?

— Uh. Guy has these . . . oh ok, it's photos of places he's bought drugs. That's the hook. So he's gone back to these places and made these large format pictures of them. Really big. Bus stop. Park bench. Doorway. Corner. And there's . . . well, that's it. Simple, but beautiful.

— Who's the photographer?

— Michael someone.

— You know him?

— No.

— Is he black?

Gary half closed an eye and cocked his head at Stan.

— Is he black? I don't know Stan. I didn't ask. Why?

— It's . . . I don't know, it's the stereotype, you know . . . there's a stereotype of black guys selling drugs and white guys buying them. I thought he might be playing with that, you know, whether he's black or white.

Gary was looking at him like he was insane.

— Ok, I don't know where that came from my friend. But no. No people in this. Just places.

— Well, said Stan. I just thought it rang a bell. I saw this thing about a photographer somewhere was doing something like that.

— I don't think this is that.

— Ok.

— I think this is just what it is. Hey maybe he's Asian Stan. Or Latin. Really fucking with those stereotypes then.

— Ok, ok.

They were on their high stools at their high table. Gary was quiet for a moment, sighing, frowning, drinking his drink. Stan looked at him. A T-shirt and a jumper. A jacket on the back of his chair. He'd trimmed his beard. He looked good, he looked healthy, and Gary remembered when he had looked like shit. It wasn't that long ago.

— Why did you put photographs through our letterbox like that?

Gary closed his eyes for an irritated second, then opened them again. He waited and he looked at Stan and he took a breath.

— You weren't in.

— Not if you come by in the middle of the day, no.

— No. I was walking back from work.

He was speaking slowly. Holding's Stan's gaze.

— You can't just take photographs of people. On the street. Without their permission. I mean, it's a violation. It's . . .

— Stan.

— Well it is. It's creepy. It's weird. Taking photos of people and then putting them through their fucking letter box.

Gary stared at him. Then he dropped his head into his hands, and started to slide it out again, slowly, pulling his lower eyelids and the skin of his cheeks down with his palms and his fingers, so that he looked like a ghost face but black emerging out of his own hands, his big eyeballs focused on Stan who watched him with a feeling like disgust, as if this distorted, elongated face was something he should not be seeing, that it was none of his business, it was a private thing that no one should see, something personal and obscene. Gary pulled his fingers all the way down over his mouth, pulling his bottom lip and showing his teeth and his gums, and then his eyes flicked towards the street and he let go, and his face returned to something like a human face.

— It's not people Stan, it's you. My friend Stan. They went through your letter box because you're never fucking in. I lost my phone or I would have let you know. What the fuck is this?

— It felt like something.

— What thing?

Stan shook his head.

— What did it feel like?

Stan said nothing.

— Make you nervous did it?

— No.

— Yeah it did. It made you nervous. Like me joking about crime makes you nervous. Me taking your photograph makes you nervous. Me coming to your meeting makes you nervous. Even me getting sober makes you a little bit nervous. You think I don't see that Stan? Seen. Drug deals is bad-man stuff so it's black-man stuff. Must be. What are you really nervous about Stan? What is the thing about me, do you think, that makes you nervous, really? My height? My beard? My accent? No? My taste for cock? No? Let's see what else there could be. I wonder. What else is there Stan?

A Shock

Stan looked around. No one was paying attention. Stoker was standing at the bar, standing up straight, just his head bent forward at the neck, looking down at a small pile of paper, writing, writing on little pieces of paper.

— Christ Stan. You know how depressing it is to constantly have to deal with this shit? Again. And again. And again. It is so fucked up. You're a good bloke Stanley. You're an intelligent, decent man. But you have these big fucking zones of stupidity where you wander alone. I don't know where they come from or why they're there, but that's not my problem it's yours.

He took a sip of his drink. He looked weary. Different. He looked tired.

— It's a life's work Stan. For all of us. In this fucking country? It's generations of work. And I know exactly what you think because I think it too and I have to work every fucking day not to. Have to. What makes me shy? What makes me keep my mouth shut? What makes me not take an interest in things that I'm interested in? What do you think it is? Over-protective mother? I have it inside me and it's the work of a lifetime. For all of us. But you get to clock off and I don't. So. Maybe put in a little overtime Stan, just for a while, cos you need to catch up.

— I don't know . . .

— Don't Stan. Because you're only going to make it worse. You're either going to tell me that I'm imagining things. Or you're going to try and get some sympathy out of me for fucking up, or tell me that you're trying, or tell me anything at all. And I don't want to hear it. Just sort it out. Give me your number.

— What?

— Write down your number.

He was holding out a piece of paper and a pen. Stan glanced at Stoker. He was still there. Writing on a piece of paper, putting

63

it to one side, writing on another. Stan wrote down his number for Gary.

— I'm pissed off now. I'm going to go. When I have a new phone I'll text you. Give my love to Maria. Sort yourself out.

And he left. Stood up and took his jacket and shouldered open the door and was gone into the street.

Stan sipped his pint. Stared out the window.

He'd argued with Noor about it and she'd just ignored him from then on.

When he finished his drink he started on what was left of Gary's.

He remembered that the only time his father had hit him was when Stan had described some new neighbours by using a word that he had never used since. Never. Not once.

The place was quiet. Some people were watching the football but they didn't seem particularly interested. Stoker started walking around the room, handing out his pieces of paper. Stan watched a couple of people glance at what they'd been given, glance at Stoker, and go back to whatever it was they'd been doing. He didn't look at Stan, just held out what looked like the torn corner of a newspaper page. On it, in a very neat cursive script was *mouse*.

— Right everybody! Let's play a game. You've all been given an animal, and that's the animal that you are and it's up to everybody else to guess what animal you are by asking you questions about what animal you might be. Let's

— What are you doing? Harry asked him, loudly.

— Playing a game.

— Leave people alone, Harry said.

Stoker looked hurt. Then he went around the room and collected all the pieces of paper.

— Another time, he said. Another time.

Stan went to the toilet. There were was a guy at one of the urinals and they chatted about Stoker and discovered that they had both been *mouse*, and when they went back to the bar they asked other people and it turned out that everyone had been *mouse*, and there was laughter, and people called out *Are you a mouse? My first question is – are you a mouse?* which Stoker seemed to enjoy, and he joined in, and of course he was soon laughing louder than anyone else, and kept on laughing and calling out *Are you a mouse?* long after everyone else had stopped.

Stan stayed until they closed. He drank a lot. He couldn't afford it. But he couldn't help it. When he got home he slept on the sofa because he didn't want to disturb Maria.

The Sweat

HE DRUMBLED, STATS and notches. Wrong word. Insurmountable. He liked the long words, they felt manipulatable, like things in his mouth. Manipulatable. But they were too long, too big. They were cubes and blocks (oh! notches!) and he couldn't catch his breath. It was nice. It was fine. But what could he do with them. He had a mouthful of bricks and he was trying to build something in there. A house. An aircraft carrier. A maze of places he could go. He needed and wanted and required things that were smaller and more precise. Measurements is a long word for example. Seems inconsiderate. Something smaller. A tiny thing. So small. Notches for example, was a pretty good fix.

Notches

Not

Ches

Ot

Ches

Tch

Es

s

Fix

Ix

x

I

God no

x

Nothing was coming through him but innards, his inner-most. His skin was a leathery peel. A wet dry thing. He had been scraped and reapplied to himself and now he was dying in the street like an ant on a fire.

Notches.

He didn't know why he was repeating that word. So annoying. Such inconsideration.

Only small words from here on.

As a kid he'd sat by the fireplace and used the tongs (tongs?) to put tiny pieces of paper on lumps of coal (coal?) and pretended they were airplanes that had crashed onto the sides of volcanos and he waited for them to burn. Sometimes they just sat there curling and sometimes they burst suddenly into orange. Into flames.

He was going to get hit by a car. He wedged this thought against others and it held for a while. Little car units scurrying past him, running at his shoulder, barely missing him, coming the other way with their knife glint windows and their stares. There weren't many people around. Not here. He paused in the shadow of a corner and let the sweat out. Just let it come out.

He'd suck off pretty much anyone right now. Any passer-by. Any car driver. Any sort of astronaut, mountain climber, goat-herd, *sheep boy, idiot son of Donkey Kong.*

What was that?

His dad had been an immigrant but nobody could tell.

He couldn't remember if he'd imagined there being people on the airplanes. He supposed he had. But he didn't think that he'd been a strange boy, a weird boy. He thought that it was the burst that he'd liked, not some idea of people burning in a conflagration, melting in with the plastic and the toasted sandwiches and the crew. He laughed. Moved again. Toasted sandwiches. Wobbled a little, got it sensible. He was fine really. He was just sweating a lot.

He should eat something.

Oh. Fuck's sake. Car.

Facts stalked him, little fact units running at his shoulder as fast as he ran, which was not fast, given, so, so, so. So he was keeping pace, walking pace, a pole tied to his back and stretched across the road, hung with truthful items.

It is Saturday now.

It is past midday.

You are sweating very badly.

You are very high, still.

It is an excruciatingly hot day.

This last one he wasn't sure about. It fluttered on the end of the pole, scraping the wall opposite, ready to fall.

His pockets dug and scraped, coins and thugs and what he imagined for a stretch of narrow pavement toward the main road was a small rosary, small prayers and mutterings and with surely a calming value, worry beads, beads, don't think of beads, they are not beads. They were a clutch of pills in a freezer bag. Nothing to do with him. He had intended to keep them in his hand, ready to throw away if anyone looked at him sideways, but everyone had looked at him sideways since he'd left Sammy's, and he had them buried deep in his pocket now like a bullet in a wound – a terrible image which made him feel momentarily sick, where had that come from, and he took a sip of tepid water from the bottle which he found, bizarrely, in his left hand, which he had managed somehow, in a slightly disturbing sort of miracle, to not yet drop. The water felt good and holy, wet and main. But also so warm that he decided the hotness of the day was objective, was true, was real and brutal. Fucking hell.

Typical.

Maybe his hand had heated it, warmed it up. His elemental fingers.

They had, he decided now, in a bitter pop of clarity, sent him on the errand because he was an idiot. Not because it was dangerous or because he would be less suspicious, but simply because they were having a good time, and he had become a little restless, nothing he realised now that a shower and a cup of tea and a bit of that chocolate cake wouldn't have sorted out. He'd had a shower though hadn't he? While Duncan sat on the chair laughing at practically everything he said, including the prediction that they would die in an inferno because someone Sammy had turned away would lob a petrol bomb through the window and they would all be too fucked to escape. Duncan thought this was hilarious. But people are nasty, people are weird, people crack along unpredictable lines. Stop predicting then, he told himself. Where the hell was he? He pulled a hand across his forehead. It came back soaking. He ran it around the back of his head. That was worse. He sat down on a low wall. It was in a half shade. He stayed there about twenty seconds and then headed to a patch of grass by one of the big blocks. But as he got there he decided he couldn't sit down on the grass. It would look odd, and feel odd, and he needed to keep going. He was five minutes away.

From Honk's. Keep going.

A Shock

What?

Not *Honk*.

Frank.

He stopped and bent over and laughed for a minute or so, who knows, wheezing like a car that wouldn't start. He hoped some kind invisible stranger would stop and fuck him in the arse.

And so he marched, strode, strided, down the side streets between Cannibal and Feckem, in and out of estates with his jeans growing into his skin, his legs like the legs of someone else, parasitic, stapled on, something like that. His ways of thinking about things had been hacked and disrupted. Everything was immensely complicated. Stick to the facts. He was heading for Frank's. To pick up various things, deliver his freezer bag, hopefully have a cold drink, maybe even a shower, definitely a shower he thought now, he would refuse to leave without a shower, pick up various things, for himself, for Patrick and for Miguel, for Sammy? – he couldn't remember – and perhaps persuade Frank to come with him back to Sammy's. Then there would be a while there, time would pass or implode or whatever it did, before he probably slipped out for some food with Duncan, then home. Or back to Sammy's. In which case it'd be home in the morning. Or whatever. Monday was nothing. What was Monday it was nothing. He'd taken a bus from Sammy's to the Green. Hadn't he? He could probably have gone a couple more stops, but this was the way he knew.

The sun hunted him like a maniac.

That's it. Freezing, think of it, try to think of that, though hell . . . oh hell. He had been, he declared to himself – pausing for a moment on the kerb of a buckled dusty footpath that he was surprised to see he had been avoiding, walking in the road like a man

who was going to get hit by a car – scratching at the doors of hell,
and in a shimmer of fine detail he saw the surface of those doors
like a continent in turmoil, marching armies, fleeing citizenry, the
mountains filled with refugees and partisans, loaded guns in the
woodpiles, tied to the branches of trees, boulders propped by an
overpass, an indulgent father feeding milk and raisins to a small
girl in the shade of a gable, all that remained of a church of the
wrong column, his other children dead and unrecoverable in the
pit of the city where no humans any longer rummaged, though
there was rummaging, and over towards the sea, which was on
fire, there seemed to be a place of sordid and despairing coupling,
congress and varied carnal whatnot, and this distracted him a
moment. A moment. Which lasted deep into the seconds, not
passing over them but into them, deep down to their depths
where he briefly swam in almost tepid waters, his skin brushing
skin, chiefly the skin of the shirtless man he had seen step out of
a pedestaled doorway what felt like hours previously but which,
he confirmed with a glance over his shoulder, had been about
eight seconds ago. The man's beautiful back was getting smaller.
He thought for half a particularly deep second about following
him. That story took so much out of time that he stopped.
Christ. Hell. He adjusted his erection, appalled that he was cap-
able of one, and thought again that he would be hit by a car, if his
heart held out. The doors of hell, in any case, he clarified, had
been flung open as he stared at them, and he was pinned against
a wall. A wall of hell. Something like that. His back . . . to continue
where he had left off . . . ran faster than anything, his shirt a
bloody rag, and him a whipped fucking dog with no brains and no
one who loved him boo hoo – something kicking up a notch
there, bit of a second wind. Enough of this brains.

Notch.

A Shock

There was a moment which most weeks he walked past.

The route between work and home like a corridor.

Friday. Every Friday. Fridays.

The route between work and home like a corridor.

Most weeks he went on his way into rest, into meals, into seeing his brother and his nieces, drinks with the pals, old pals, a date, the football, maybe a dance, a lie-in in the mornings, the good healthy meals and the conversations and the calm body being a calm body.

There was a moment which most weeks he walked past.

But as a moment it was more of a small door.

Into relaxation, a good civilian, a citizen male, a man, a real man, a man at home in his life.

The route between work and home like a corridor.

But even perhaps in the toilet at work he might see it, glimpse it, set into the tiles under the hand dryer.

More likely in the corridor.

The route between work and home like a corridor.

Go for a drink with the work crowd, why not, why not do that, he might not see a thing if he does that, but he would see it then in the pub, it always happened that he would see it in the pub if he went to the pub, a good civilian, a good citizen after a week of work, in the pub.

The door beneath the bar, a tiny thing in the panelling.

As a moment it was more of a small door.

A real man.

Walking home he might see it in a wall or a bus shelter or the remains of a hedge, a knee-high hedge on a muddy patch between pavements.

A small plain door, with a handle.

A real door.

Sometimes, almost most times, he would see it and walk by, even give it a nod, a little nod, an acknowledgement, and continue home, continue as a real man, a citizen, and walk on by.

A small plain door, with a handle.

A real door.

But sometimes, many times, he would stop and stare at this small door, look at it, look at it.

74

A Shock

The door beneath the bar, a tiny thing in the panelling.

The route between work and home like a corridor.

But even perhaps in the toilet at work he might see it, glimpse it, set into the tiles under the hand dryer.

Look at it.

There is in his mind a flood, as if his mind is filling with blood, as if his mind is a body, which is a vessel, which is filling with blood, and it becomes impossible not to float away on his own blood.

But as a moment it was more of a small door.

Look at that small door, that tiny door.

It is beautiful.

Friday. Every Friday. Fridays.

But sometimes, many times, he would stop and stare at this small door, look at it, look at it.

A real man.

He thinks of his body as a vessel, and what is a man but a carried glass of water, a glass of water carried by a small child across a summer garden.

It is beautiful.

A child across a garden with a glass of cold water, that is a life, and the child concentrates so as not to spill a drop, but it does not matter, really, it does not matter, if it is only a life.

But sometimes, many times, he would stop and stare at this small door, look at it, look at it.

A real man.

Look at it, all the blood in his body filling his body.

A welling, soulful feeling.

This welling sense of himself, a body and a mind in blood, in the world, occupying exactly its own shape in the world.

He goes towards the door.

He would stoop then, stoop and go to the door and open it and he would climb inside into the space of his body and that would be it, that was where he was, that was where he was.

He opens the door and he climbs into the space of his body.

And closes the door behind him.

— Oh love, come in, come in, my god, what a day.
   Frank was wearing flip-flops, shorts, a blue singlet with something on it. He slumped. Sighed. He looked completely different.

Or perhaps he had been wrongly remembered. Did he have the right flat?

— You know, Frank said, I'd forgotten your face. I knew the name, but I wasn't entirely sure who it was that Sammy meant. Not ches.

— Tom, said Tommy.

— Tommy, of course. I know. Tommy.

Had they even met before? They eyed each other. Frank seemed happy enough about it. He was staring at Tommy's crotch.

— Haven't seen you in quite a while, have I? Was it here? Or have I seen you since? At Sammy's? I was there when? Couple of weeks now I think. Jesus look at you. Here, let me get you a drink.

He was mid-fifties, fit with a belly starting, bald, beard turning grey, a big scar across his lower leg, left, red. He was very sexy. Tommy swallowed hard, trying to seem level, at the same time wondering why. Always this need. As if anyone remembered anything.

He wanted a shower. He looked around the place. Ah. Ah yes. This place. There was a view of Buggers Park. Some weird paintings on the wall, lots of books and throws and drapes. A very gay middle-aged clutter. He had been here before. Once. It had been full of men. Now there was a cool air, Frank, and nothing else.

— Can I have a shower?

— Oh good idea. Yes. Here.

He led him to the bathroom. Helped him undress, rolling the wet T-shirt up over his shoulders. All the time talking, talking about the heat of the day, about the last time they'd met, taking the bag of pills with a pause and a close look, and then a thank you darling and a kiss, which was cooling and lingered, and then he was pulling a big white towel from a cupboard and turning the taps as Tommy wrestled off his boxers and stood there naked, feeling something like a child and something like a prisoner, but Frank just gave him another kiss, on the cheek this time, and picked up his clothes and left the room, saying that he'd make some cool drinks, that Tommy was to take his time, enjoy.

— Thank you Frank.

— Ooo ahhh, Frank said.

The shower was the most beautiful thing that had ever happened to him. He stood there with it in his hand, directing it first, still cold, at his thighs, using his hands to scoop it up into his groin, feeling glorious. Then over his head and his back. He washed with just the water, and then used a little of Frank's products. He thought about shampooing his hair but already he didn't know how long he'd been in there. Maybe he was taking the piss. He tried to pee but couldn't. He washed his armpits several times, and investigated his arse and squatted over the shower head and hummed a tune. He should stop. He'd been in there too long. When he stepped out and wrapped the towel around him he felt immensely happy. He had made it. He had travelled through himself and here he was, with another. He wondered why when he was high he always thought of his childhood, and he worried that they were the only two times in his life when he'd been happy.

— Glorious shower.

— Oh that was quick. I've put all your clothes on the fast wash, and they'll be out of the dryer before you know it.

— Oh.

— Well you couldn't have put them back on Tommy darling. Even your jeans were soaked. I don't know how you wear jeans on a day like this.

78

— Well I was out from last night.

— You've been at Sammy's overnight?

— I got there about 3 or 4 in the morning, he lied.

— Well anyway. You'll get them back clean and dry in about an hour. You won't get this sort of service anywhere else you know. Do you want some food? Look at you all lovely and sexy.

He sat on the couch beside Frank and ran his hand through his hair. His own hair. Frank didn't have any hair. He laughed. Frank squeezed his knee. He could hear the washing machine in the kitchen. And there was another sound, like a bigger, softer machine, Frank was on a laptop, on one of the sites, scrolling. On the coffee table there was a wet jug full of what looked like lemon soda with a lot of ice, several glasses, an ashtray, a pouch of tobacco, cigarette papers, a clump of weed in a large freezer bag, two small baggies of T, a pipe, several lighters, a little brown bottle, a needleless syringe, a wristwatch, three bottles of still mineral water, several more glasses in a different position, a note-book and pen, an orange peel, someone's phone – Frank's presumably, it wasn't his. There was music playing, that was the big soft sound – a sort of . . . jazz?

— Pour yourself a nice drink love.

— Thank you Frank. I really needed that. Feel a lot better now.

Where was his phone?

— And you look a lot better darling. Look at you. Gorgeous. You should eat. There's – what is there – there's fruit anyway, in the kitchen. Oranges, apples. There's a punnet of strawberries in the fridge which you're welcome to. There's smoked salmon . . .

— Where's my phone?

He was looking again at the things on the table. He had leaned forward and was lifting the weed, looking under the tobacco, at all the table's surface. He looked at himself. He was wearing a towel. He opened it and found only his genitals and a bruise on his thigh.

— I don't know.

— Oh fuck.

— Well

— I don't fucking believe it.

His phone was the tiny precise thing in which was to be found the way back to everything else. It was the way back to everything. The way out of the tiny imprecise slot of time in which he was currently hiding out. If it was lost, if his phone were lost, there was a chance that he would be trapped in here.

He stood up, leaving the towel behind him.

— Oh Christ. The washing machine.

He was both worried, frantically worried, and also relaxed because he was naked and he liked being high and naked, and he was more comfortably high now after the shower, and he knew he looked good, and he fancied Frank and knew they would have good sex, and he was really happy about that, but at the same time, interlaced, one sort of time with another, was the feeling that his phone was lost and that his phone being lost was a catastrophe the extent of which he could barely grasp, barely conceive of, which would leave him stranded like an actor who has to get off the stage but the wings are sealed and he's stuck out there.

— The washing machine, the fucking washing machine.

He was walking towards it, and Frank was following him, saying something, but he had no idea what. He got into the kitchen and stared at the suds turning a lazy circle and a flap of his T-shirt dragged across the glass like it was waving at him.

— Oh fuck.

A Shock

He crouched and tried the door and it was locked and he was about to burst into tears or throw up or maybe neither of those things but in any case none of this happened because Frank had said something that meant that he was now looking at the kitchen table where sat a pile of coins and his keys and a pack of chewing gum that he remembered buying at some point in his life.

— There was nothing else love, I promise. I mean obviously I checked, and I did think it was odd that you didn't have a phone or a wallet but there you are.

— Where are they?

— You must have left them at Sammy's.

— What? My wallet? Oh fuck where is my wallet?

Frank got on his phone and called Sammy's and eventually got Sammy on the line and Tommy could hear him laughing.

— How long did that take my Christ he's been gone hours is he ok?

— Oh he's fine, said Frank, staring at Tommy's cock. But did he leave his phone there? And his wallet?

More of Sammy laughing. Oh. Frank had put him on speaker phone.

— We talked about it! We had a twenty-minute fucking conversation about whether he should take them with him. He decided not to. They're here. They're in the safe. He's twatted. Stick him under the shower. Slap him around a bit.

— Oh well, that's fine then, they're in the safe love, you're fine.

— But I got the bus. How did I get the bus.

Sammy laughed some more.

— You said you didn't want to get the bus. You were afraid of people. You thought you were too sweaty.

— Oh you should have seen him when he arrived. Looked like a drowned rat.

— Is he ok?

— He's fine.

— I'm fine.

— Oh there you are you numpty. You all right?

— Yeah, yeah. I just didn't remember. Thought I'd lost . . .

— You're all right, you've just got the heebeegeebees. Have a shower, have . . .

— I had a shower.

— . . . something to eat. Have something to eat. Promise?

— Yeah I will.

— Do. Before you let Frank at you or else you'll forget. And call when you're coming back. And bring Frank with you. Gotta go, Miguel needs me.

He hung up.

Frank stroked his cock and they kissed for a while. Then Frank sucked him for some sort of length of time which was either very long or just an average length of time for cocksucking when cocksucking is amongst other things that you're doing, going to do, and then Frank bent him over, bent Tommy over the kitchen table and rimmed him, but then they moved position almost immediately because it wasn't working as well as it might, and Tommy leaned over a chair instead, bent right over it, a kitchen chair, gripping the edge of the seat first and then the actual legs of the chair.

He was sure he remembered getting the bus. Tommy was. But he couldn't have. Because he had no cards. They didn't take cash on the bus. They hadn't taken cash on the buses in years. Unless he'd taken a card out of his wallet. He lifted himself up a little, moaned, and reached out and nudged the coins and the keys on

the table but there was nothing there. Frank was very good at
this stuff. He forgot about everything for some period of time.
Tommy did. Just became the enjoyment, became the experience
of being rimmed by Frank in Frank's kitchen while the washing
machine spun.

Frank stopped then.

— This floor is hard, he said.

Tommy ate some salmon and a half a pot of spinach pine-nut
pasta and Frank made them teas and went out for a minute and
came back wearing only a jockstrap. They talked about Sammy
and who was down there at Sammy's place, or who had been
there when Tommy had left, and how Sammy was the sweetest
man they knew but that this couldn't last. And Frank said he had
a cough. That he, Frank, had a cough.

He coughed.

— He's got the cabinet, you know, I love that, and the safe,
and his . . . I said to him I said you should get a clipboard dear.

— He'd probably really like that Frank.

— He'd love it. He really would. We should get him one. I
should get on Amazon and get him one. He could write down all
the times, everyone's G timings and what have you, I mean he
does that anyway on his phone, he has some sort of system with
the cabinet, I can never quite work it out. Let's get him a clipboard, he'd love that.

And Frank went into the other room and got his laptop,
coughing a bit. He picked it up as if to come back into the
kitchen. But Tommy had followed him. They bumped into each
other.

— That's quite nasty Frank.

— I know. I should get some honey, some of that expensive

stuff, the cheap stuff is useless. Hakuna matata honey. Oh look at this. Messages. Look at this one.

They stood there, Frank holding the laptop, and scrolled through the messages that had come in on the website for Frank. Tommy thought he knew one of the men, face in shadow, a hard chest, nice cock.

— Is that Gary?

— Which Gary?

— From Sammy's.

— Black guy?

— No. Oh. No, yes, that Gary. No not that Gary. Is this guy black? There's another Gary.

— Which one love?

— Oh it's gone now, never mind. Are you high?

Frank laughed.

— I smoked a pipe while you were in the shower.

— Nice.

— First of the day. Have you been on it since last night? You look fresh though Tommy, look really good. A lot better than when you arrived, my god, what a mess.

— It's hot out isn't it?

— He's hot, look at that.

— Yeah.

— My god.

— But it is hot out isn't it?

— Yes, it is. I don't know what the temperature is but it got up to thirty something yesterday. It's not that hot yet, but it probably will be. Very hot. It's the climate warming.

— Will we sit down?

— I think we won't last the century that's my honest belief, I think a few more generations and that's our lot.

— Yeah?

They were sitting down now. Tommy stuck his hand between Frank's legs. Frank shifted a little, held Tommy's cock for a moment, then he put the laptop down on the floor and picked up the pipe. All the time talking, talking all the time. A day in an envelope. A day in a drawer. A put-aside day.

— I think so I really do. I mean people don't care do they? It'll take something horrible to make people care. You know, I don't know, New York melting, or Venice finally sliding into the sea. I don't like Venice. Have you been to Venice? No? I mean don't get me wrong it's full of the most amazing things, all those churches, that art, that beautiful culture, it's fantastic, but the tourists my god all these Japanese and Americans by the truck-load all stamping their way around after those little umbrellas, I hate them all I really do, and the locals are just furious now, they've been driven mad by it you can't blame them but they're so unfriendly and it stinks, it just stinks permanently of shit, of shit Tommy, it really does, I'm sorry but it does, literally of shit, actual shit, the whole thing is like a monument to human shit and I really think it would be better if they just took all that art off somewhere else, and maybe took some of the churches, they can do that sort of thing now, and then just let the rest of it slide into the stinking sea, with as many tourists as possible. Oh my god listen to me I think I become a bit of a fascist when I'm high I really do my god, I take it all back, what ridiculous nonsense.

— You just talk more than you would, you know, you take the things off.

— Yeah.

— The brakes. Not the brakes. You take off the things.

— Yes exactly.

— The wheels. Oh for fucks sake what's the word. You take the

— The blinkers.

— You take the blinkers off.

— There.

— No that's not it, that's something else. You take the things. Fucks sake. You take them off anyway.

— And talk too much. I know, it's awful.

— It's universal though Frank. We're all at it. Babble babble.

— Toil and rabble.

— What?

— Here hold that. Oh, that's nice. There's nothing I wouldn't say, that's what it is. The inhibitions are gone. So the slimiest things slide out. You see people as they really are you know, they can't hide. The aggression, the weird ideas, all that.

— Well that's paranoia.

— Well yes there's that as well. And the anger comes after it. Or with it. You know, like Arthur, you remember Arthur?

— No.

— Oh you'd know him if you saw him. Regular at Hamza's place in Lewisham. Or used to be. Sammy's a few times but I don't think Sammy, oh that's lovely whatever you're doing, I don't think Sammy ever liked him. Polish maybe, or Lithuanian, Estonian. One of those. And a beautiful body, and a lot of fun, and a lovely guy to talk to as well, but then at some point he'd just flip, get angry, start making accusations, everyone's got hidden cameras . . .

— Oh god.

— All that, you know. He was slamming of course and that just slipped him really, and he was stuck in it and Hamza put a stop to him coming over, but he was worried for a while. Hamza was. Wrapped it up for a month or so, went very quiet, Hamza did, couple of months, just in case.

— Do I know Hamza?

— I don't know love, do you? Look at me waving this around. Will you have a hit?

— Yeah why not. All my stuff is at Sammy's.

— I know that.

— I can't believe I left my phone and wallet there.

— Well it's in the safe. You trust him. I trust him too. He really looks . . .

Frank was holding the bowl up to the light.

— Is there anything in there? Oh god yes there is, my god, there's a whole chandelier in there. Ok.

— He really does, yeah.

Frank lit the lighter and held it to the bowl. Only brought it to his lips when the vapour burst. Little grey marble on a stick, Frank breathing, looking at Tommy, raising his eyebrows.

— Are you coming?

— Oh. Yes. I suppose.

— I mean, no rush obviously. I have to wait for my clothes obviously.

— Oh you know sometime we should go out to the Heath or something and just get naked and see what happens. Even over there sometime.

He looked around. Tommy did. The washing machine was starting into a spin. He stared at it for a moment or perhaps a little longer. He felt fine. Everything was good. But underneath everything was something else which was the annoyance, very predictable, and he could feel it in there like something he'd eaten. All the food had been disgusting but he felt much better.

He felt much better now. He was naked. He wasn't cold. It was warm, perfect. He went and stood in the doorway and looked at Frank who was putting some T into a pipe. Tommy played with his cock and watched him light up. Frank took a hit, offered the pipe to Tommy, who walked over and stayed standing and took it so that Frank could suck him while he took his own big hit, a big hit, a great big hit.

There was only the two of them.

He stood there, Tommy did, with his head back, his hands still holding the pipe (left hand) and the lighter (right hand), just holding them away a little from his face. He closed his eyes for a long time. Then opened them again almost immediately.

— Let me put these down.

They had sex in the living room until the spinning of the washing machine became too annoying.

— Have you had your PrEP today?

— Yes at Sammy's this morning.

— Good man.

— You?

— Oh me I'm undetectable.

— Oh yeah, I knew that.

He didn't. Well, he did now.

They sat on the couch and made out and Tommy played with Frank's arse gently, and they chatted some more about Sammy and about other people and about what they were doing.

Tommy could hear something weird.

— What's that?

— What?

— Is that jazz?

— Yes love. It's, what's that now. It's Mingus. I think.

He looked at his laptop, did something with it.

— Yes, Mingus.

— Mingus?

— Charles Mingus. You don't know jazz?

— I don't know anything.

— Bassist, composer, band leader, one of the real greats. One of the giants.

— Has that been playing all this time?

— Well not Mingus specifically.

— Jazz though? Music?

— Yes, I have Spotify on shuffle. Do you have Spotify? I'm addicted to it, I don't know myself with it, my god, it's every piece of music ever, at your fingertips, and all you have to do is look for it and it plays. You know. To have all this music. I would have to have been a millionaire before. You know. In the days of the LP and so forth. To have what I have now, for whatever it is I pay a month. It really improves my quality of life. It really does. I've said it to my doctor – it should be on the NHS. It should be nationalised and everyone should have it for free.

— But then what would Mingus live on?

— Mingus is dead love.

Tommy laughed, Frank laughed.

— All the great ones are dead. The young ones now I don't know what they're doing. Oh I'm an old fart I know but that's just how it works isn't it? What do you like?

— Oh you know, oral, lots of oral, I'm versatile, I love arse play and . . .

Frank was looking at him as if he hadn't noticed him there before. As if alarmed.

— I'm joking Frank, I'm joking.

— Oh my god.

They both laughed loudly, clutching onto each other.

— I thought, I thought, Frank was trying to say. I was thinking Oh my god just how high is this idiot?

They laughed and laughed and then Frank got some tissues and blew his nose and gave Tommy some water.

— Do you have some G?

— Yes but I don't share G love, as well you know.

— Mine is at Sammy's.

— Well there you are.

— It's been about . . . it's been hours since I had any.

— Tell it to the hand darling, you're not getting any. I shouldn't even have left it out. Temptation etc.

Frank stood up and took away the little bottle and the syringe and the notebook and pen and disappeared for a few minutes.

Tommy thought that was a bit much. He could hear odd little noises in the music. He liked it, the music. But inside it there were particular specific noises that seemed to him to be wrong. Wrong notes. He breathed in and looked out the window and all he could see was blue. He felt fine. A little annoyed at Frank. A little bored. Not bored. But he wondered what was going on at Sammy's. He looked for his phone to text but then remembered. He drank some water. Frank came back. He was naked. He was holding Tommy's wet clothes to his chest.

— What am I doing? he asked, and then turned around and disappeared again. Tommy laughed.

— You all right?

— I forgot they need to be dried didn't I?

— Thank you Frank.

— You're welcome.

He listened to the music again. In a moment of clarity he realised that the noises he had not liked had not been part of the music. They had been the beeps of the washing machine, indicating that it was finished its cycle and his clothes were clean, and he had heard them coming from the kitchen and had incorporated them into the Mingus.

— Into the Mingus, he said.

He peered into the bowl of the pipe. It was like a little patch of dirty snow, a winter pavement, a nice place for a crunchy, hesitant walk. They hadn't, he realised, smoked very much at all. He ran his finger over the trackpad of Frank's laptop and checked the time. 14:32. That seemed impossibly early. On the screen was a clutter of thumbnails of men. He opened a new tab to put some porn on, but then thought that Frank might be funny about him looking at his laptop and stopped and stood up and walked over to the door to the kitchen. His clothes were back in the washing machine, spinning around.

— Is it a dryer as well?

Frank was standing in the middle of the floor looking at his phone.

— It is. Not a very good one, but it's a light load.

— I thought the beeping was part of the music.

— The what?

— The beeping of the washing machine, when it finished.

— Oh it doesn't beep. There's just a click when the lock unlocks. But no beeps. Sammy wants us to go to his

— I can't believe I left my phone there.

— Do you want to smoke some more? I'd love you to fuck me.

— I'd love to Frank. You're very sexy.

They went into the front room again and smoked some more.

— I swore I could hear beeps. Usually it's voices.

— Voices?

— Oh don't worry. Not voices in my head. But I sometimes think that I can hear mumbles from another room or whatever. It's the T. I never think it's real. I mean. I do actually, I think there's someone outside the bathroom door in Sammy's all the time, talking, like having a conversation, and there never is. I come out and there's no one anywhere. And I've been convinced that there's been two or three people out there chatting while I'm trying to douche or whatever.

— Paranoia.

— Well, I suppose. But it doesn't bother me. I know what it is. I never think that there really were people out there. I come out and I immediately know that I've been hearing things, and I know it's the T, and everything is fine.

— You don't slam do you?

— Nah. You?

— Very very rarely. I mean. Not in about a year. I don't like it. It scares me.

— I know what you mean.

— What I get is that I see things.

— Really?

— Not like, I don't mean I hallucinate. Well I do actually don't I? Like you. But it's just peripheral, corner of the eye stuff, movements. Most of the time, like you, I know what it is. I know I'm off my tits and it doesn't bother me. But occasionally . . .

He laughed

— Occasionally I'll swear I've seen a mouse or a rat or some other nasty. Most of the time it's just a flinch and that's that. Sometimes though I've been convinced. Not in a while now. The weed keeps me sensible.

— Peripheral.

— Peripheral.

— Peripheral vermin.

— Peripheral vermin. Exactly. What a nonsense it all is. Such a lot of nonsense my god what on earth are we doing?

— We're having fun Frank.

— Is that what it is?

— I like to think of it as taking things to their logical conclusion.

He leaned over and kissed Frank for a while, and they touched each other's bodies, running their hands over their torsos.

— What do you mean?

— What do I mean what?

— You said something about logical. About logical. Conclusions.

— I have no idea.

— Oh Tommy.

— Oh no, I know. I know what I meant.

— Oh good.

— Taking T is like, it's a rational response to the world. To the stress of work and money and London and everything. People constantly. It's like, ok, you want me to have this ridiculously complicated life of managing a million things at once while you exploit and deride me and abuse me, well fine, I'll take something that makes me feel comfortable with that level of complexity, that amount of shit that I have to stress about, you know, like work, like paying the rent. You. People work in these jobs. They work in these ridiculous jobs. I know someone who works in advertising for fuck's sake I know someone who cleans the trains out in some fucking . . . out in Cricklewood. I mean what even is that? Cricklewood? What does that even mean? It sounds like a kids' cartoon show, you know, with cute animal characters. But. Anyway. What was? Oh yeah. I know a guy drives a bus. I know someone who is a junior doctor, and even they, especially they, you know, when you wouldn't think . . . just trying not to get absolutely fucked over every hour of every fucking day. Practically suicidal with it. You know? What am I talking about?

— Frank shook his head, smiling.

— I don't know love, you're far too high. I can't even see you. They laughed.

Much later they decided to go to Sammy's. Tommy felt that he would rather stay put, that outside was a level of unthinkable and that he didn't have it in him. But he also knew that he had to go there to get his phone and his wallet and that he should follow Frank's lead. Frank was messaging men on his laptop.

— Will we get someone over?

— It's up to you.

— What time is it? Oh it's nearly three o'clock. How are you feeling?

— I'm good. We need to go to Sammy's at some stage though.

— We don't really love, we could stay here. We've everything we need. Get someone else over if we fancy.

— My phone. And my

— Oh your wallet, yes, and your phone. Well, let's get an Uber. We'll get an Uber over there and maybe. There's this one, look, will I invite him?

— To Sammy's?

— Oh you're right. I can't invite him there it's against the rules.

— You could ask Sammy when we get there.

— Yes you're right. We'll get an Uber. Let me see.

A Shock

He was still looking at his laptop. They were both naked. Tommy put his arm on Frank's back. Kissed his shoulder. He wanted another body to occupy his own. Something to be in. Maybe he was cold. Frank coughed and his chest rattled like a piggy bank.

— Ah Frank.

— Will we ask this one?

— You're doing the thing.

Frank said nothing.

— Frank.

Nothing.

— Frank!

— What?

— You're doing the thing.

— What thing?

Tommy gestured at the laptop.

— You're in there.

He was still looking at the screen. He looked at Tommy.

— Where?

— There.

He licked his lips.

— Oh god I am amn't I? I'm sorry love.

He looked suddenly worried.

— Fuck. I always do this. Right. Right. What. Tell me something. Give me a purpose. I need some

— Let's go to Sammy's. Let's get dressed. Get our stuff together. Go to Sammy's.

— Right. You're right.

— What do you need?

— Well I need to get my stuff together.

— Let's get dressed. Let's get you dressed. Let's organise that one first.

— You're right. It's the thoroughness. I get very thorough. I need to be pointed at something. I'm an old fool. Good god. I could sit here for days and just not really notice. Have we had enough sex do you think? I'm not sure we have Tommy.

— We can have more at Sammy's.

— All right then.

— What do you want to wear?

— Come with me. Wardrobe. You can choose. It'll be fun. I can never decide what to wear. Are we . . . we're getting an Uber so it doesn't really matter does it?

It didn't take long to get dressed. By seven o'clock they were ready. Frank had wrapped his pipe in toilet paper and put it and his little bags of T and his bottle of G and his measure into a sort of pouch that he stuck into his jockstrap. Tommy worried that the pipe would break, but Frank told him that this was the way he always did it and that it would be fine. And he had a shoulder bag too, in which he had a change of clothes because of the sweat, and he had his weed and his headphones and a couple of toys he liked, and he also had a slice of carrot cake wrapped in cling film for Sammy, because Sammy liked this particular carrot cake which came from a cake shop in Battersea that Frank sometimes made a special journey to, because of his sweet tooth.

At the door, out in the air, Tommy felt suddenly anxious, afraid of several things that he could not quite identify. He was about to say to Frank not to close the door, that he'd left his phone inside, but then he remembered. What if Sammy had fallen asleep? Thrown everyone out and fallen asleep? What it someone had done something stupid and the cops had come? Why

had he left his phone there? Why had he even had his wallet with
him?

He looked over the balcony outside Frank's front door.

— What floor are we on?

— Fourth.

Frank seemed tense.

— Are we ok?

Frank was standing beside him.

— Let's just wait here a minute or two and be sure. We can
go back in and wait if this feels too much like

— We shouldn't have had that last hit.

Tommy laughed.

— What are we like?

After a minute of peering over the balcony and watching a
group of boys come from the direction of the park towards the
stairwell they went back inside, Frank fumbling with the keys
and laughing while Tommy stood at his shoulder telling him to
hurry up, that the boys were after them, that the boys would
throw them off the balcony, and Frank was laughing but also he
was fumbling with the key, and Tommy half believed that they
were about to die, or that he was about to die, to be killed, and
that the police would find no ID on him, and that because of that
he would be buried in an unmarked grave, and people that he
loved would never find him. But that's not how it works, and that
wasn't what happened.

When they were back inside Frank made them sandwiches
and a pot of tea. They drank the tea but the sandwiches just sat
there. They talked about dying, and about travelling to South
America, and about languages and how Frank spoke pretty good
Spanish, and then about how he was the only actual English
person, pretty much, that Tommy had spent any time with lately.

— Oh. Sammy of course, said Tommy, and they both laughed.

— My god how could we forget.

Duncan, said Tommy. I forgot Duncan as well.

— Oh yes, you like him.

— Do you not?

— Oh we've just never . . . maybe we're too alike. He annoys me to be honest. Always just a touch too loud, too pushy. Never stops talking my god.

— Yeah.

— But he has a lovely cock.

— Does he?

— Doesn't he?

— Well yes he does, but I thought you were a bit of a size queen to be honest.

— I am.

— Well then.

— Does he not? Duncan? Duncan with the grey hair and the laugh?

— Yes.

— Short, neat guy?

— Yes. You know him. I know you know him.

— Does he not have a big cock?

— Not especially. Average, you know. My size sort of thing.

— Would you credit it I've got someone else's cock and I've given it to Duncan. What cock am I thinking of?

And they thought that was very funny.

— Do you not mind heights?

Frank just looked at him.

— You're quite high up here.

— No I don't think so. Compared to some. Been here nearly twenty years now. Very lucky really. Good old Maggie.

98

— Gary, as well, said Tommy.

— What?

— Is English.

— Gary. Yes. No. Irish.

— What? No. He's from around here. Over there.

— We're thinking of different Garys.

— I think we're thinking of different Duncans as well. You sort of forget about the height after a while. I was going to say that you sort of forget about how high you are after a while but that's a different thing. Also true though. A different truth.

— You've lost me now.

— I have lost myself.

Tommy was looking out the window. He couldn't see any people in any of the windows in the block opposite. Then he saw a woman sitting in a living room eating something. A bag of crisps or a piece of fruit or something like that.

— Jesus, said Tommy.

— What is it love?

— I have things I need to be doing. I have . . . obligations. There's just the two of us. I mean, what are we doing? We're not doing anything, are we? We should. I should be. I have things that I need to do. I have things. I should never have left my phone. I'm not. This is not. This is not interesting. It's not on Frank. I'm against this.

— Against what darling?

Tommy looked around the room.

— Just, this. All of this.

It was panic that he felt. A familiar rising panic. He told Frank about it, and Frank rolled a joint and they smoked it together and Tommy calmed down and everything was all right.

*

In the Uber the driver was quite chatty. Frank seemed able to handle that, so Tommy didn't say anything. He just slouched down in his seat and looked out at the streets. They were inexplicable, the streets. He had walked to Frank's. The idea terrified him now.

— I have a family gathering later this evening. So I work for another hour or . . . yes, another hour, and then I will go to my brother's house.

— Is it a birthday?

— No. It is not for anything in particular. Well, my niece has graduated and so we will celebrate that of course.

— Oh good for her. What did she graduate as? In?

— She got a degree in psychology.

— Oh very good, that's very good.

— Yes it is. She is very talented I think. She will go now and perhaps do some more study so that she can practise.

— She wants to be a psychologist.

— Yes she does.

— Better watch out. Don't answer any questions!

The driver laughed.

— Is this bad traffic? asked Tommy. We haven't moved. Have we moved?

— We're in the same place.

— It's not so bad, said the driver. We're nearly there.

— My niece now is going for law. More brains in her than in the whole rest of the family she has, my god, I can't keep up with her at all.

He turned to Tommy and lowered his voice.

— We're in the same place.

— Will it be a happy gathering? Tommy asked the driver. I

mean, your family gathering. Because some aren't, necessarily, you know.

— Oh yes. We are a very happy family.

— Oh that's marvellous, said Frank.

— Happiness is lovely to come across, Tommy said. You burst into it, you know, like you're crawling in a tunnel and suddenly it opens out into this wonderful great space. Cavers talk about it, you know, people who, what are they called, they go down into the deep deep cave systems, tiny little tunnels barely the width of their bodies and they have to squeeze through, pressed down by all that rock, it terrifies me, even the thought of it, a mile of rock pressing down on your back, and under your belly there's nothing but the earth, ha, the whole earth, the whole planet, all the way down, all through the fire and you are pressed against it, and there is nothing, there is nothing at all between you and nothing, because you touch all the sides of this space, and sometimes it is actually literally like that, you know, not only are they crawling, or actually sort of dragging themselves, shuffling, through what is effectively a tube, because we think of these tunnels pressing on the back and the belly but they press on the sides of the body as well, so often they will have their arms straight out ahead of themselves and they will operate like climbers operate, finding handholds, grips, by which they can pull themselves forward, pull themselves through, inch by inch, and if they're lucky there is enough room for them to bend their legs and find a toehold and push themselves forward as well, because every part of them, every part of their body, from their shoulders to their hips, is pressed into the earth, pressed by the earth, they are buried in it, embedded, you know? and they usually have a rope tied to one foot, their left probably, in case they become stuck and they can be pulled back, and this must always be in their minds, this idea of just getting stuck, of pushing forwards and kicking forward, and feeling perhaps their shoulders or their hips simply sticking, jamming, like a piece of wood you stick in a wall or something, or maybe even their head, they misjudge the gap in front of them and they push maybe with their leg, maybe they have a good toe hold for once so they dig their foot in there and they give themselves a decent shove forwards, but they've misjudged the gap, and it's their head that gets stuck, gets jammed, think of the terror of that, for me anyway, that would be so completely terrifying, that you cannot, your neck cannot move your head, you cannot, you can't look any way other than the way you happen to be facing, you cannot move, your head is in a vice, and the vice is the planet, imagine that, imagine the terror of that my god, though of course these people who do this, these cave crawlers in the dark, they don't feel anything like that, it's a minor inconvenience for them, for one thing it's not their head it's their helmet that's stuck, they don't do this sort of thing without helmets and all the safety equipment that they need, they're not stupid, this isn't some sort of weird death drive that makes them do this, and if they get their helmet stuck they just ease themselves out of it briefly, maybe shuffle backwards a little, and they ease themselves out of their helmet so that it's stuck there, a piece of hard shaped plastic stuck in the planet like a piece of wood stuck in a wall, like the point of a nail driven into the wall is one way of thinking about it, and they push back so that they can get a better grip of their helmet and yank it out and maybe that means they have to go back, that that particular tunnel is just too small, too narrow, too constricted, so maybe they go back, or maybe if it's safe they chisel away at the little bit of rock that's blocking the way because sometimes it isn't that the tunnel is narrowing, it's just that there is an obstacle there, and they can remove it, or get past it somehow, or maybe their helmet doesn't get stuck, maybe the tunnel is incredibly narrow but they can get through it, and they probably have torn clothes, ripped clothes, and fingers that are ripped and legs that are cut and ripped as well, and they probably have bruises on their arms and their legs, blood may be running from wounds on their back, from wounds on their chest, they may be covered in sweat even if it's cold down there, even if it's in the dark cold depths, so deep that they are steaming, they give off a steam of heat and exertion, and they pull and push and bleed and then suddenly the tunnel bursts open into a huge and beautiful cavern like a train station, like a cathedral, like a city under the ground, a huge empty beautiful space, and they burst onto this suddenly, with a beautiful shock, and something which they had forgotten, something which maybe in their spirit they had forgotten, space and simple freedom, something which, no matter how professional and apparently fearless these people are, don't tell me they would not have begun, in those tunnels no bigger than themselves, don't tell me that they wouldn't have begun to suspect that there was nothing other than themselves, nothing else at all, and suddenly, with a gasp, with a loud gasp of pure amazement they would see, as if creation itself had happened again, as if the big bang had happened again, suddenly this expansion, this huge and sudden rushing apart of matter, and they would be in a new world, a new universe, in which they can see for millions of miles, millions of miles, not miles, for a long way, over rocks and cliffs and streams and lakes, a whole amazing openness, in which they can breathe, where they can look and keep looking, in which they can rest, and stop moving.

The taxi turned left between oncoming cars and there was a pleasant roll to the movement and Tommy rolled into Frank and Frank rolled with him. Just a little.

— Yes, it is, said Frank. But Tommy didn't know what was, didn't know what he meant. The driver looked in the mirror at Tommy. Tommy looked away.

— What I don't understand, Frank said, is how Sammy

— Are we nearly there?

— Yes we're nearly there.

— What time is it?

The driver looked at him again, but said nothing.

Frank looked at his wrist but there was no watch there. He had his phone in his hand.

— Nobody knows, he said. Nobody knows.

The Joke

SHE WAS FURIOUS, and the language she breathed out cleared her path.

She climbed the hill slowly, pushing the wrong gear, standing out of the saddle and injecting the pain in her legs back into the slope as if into the skin of an animal that had done her harm. She felt her back becoming damp. It was a blank-sky day, all of London suspended in a bowl of hot milk, her headache spooning through the sludge of her brain, her eyes almost closed, a taste in her mouth of the metal in the air and the shit in the metal and the blood in the shit. They didn't pay her enough, for one fucking thing. They didn't pay her enough and they treated her like some unwanted unnameable sap, something between a servant and a ghost. *What are you doing here?* was the permanent expression on their fucking faces. *Everything.* Ferrier. She hated Ferrier. My god she really did. Last few yards. Close to the summit. She shook her head to dislodge a bead of sweat that tickled her eyebrow but the shaking hurt and she stopped, and breathed out a long garbled curse that took in the school and all its staff and all its students, the air of London, the people of London, the stench of London, the heat of London, the hills of London, Denmark Hill in particular, and the stinking beast beneath it, whose hump she was now climbing like a fly, and she cursed the future and the past, and the eternal fucking present, and she damned the world to hell and hell to the world, and there was nothing, in, exist, tence, that, she, did, not, damn.

There.

There. Breathe. She sat back in the saddle and relaxed and her legs rippled, her muscles fluttered, a burst of butterfly pains that faded. She was too fit though. She was hitting the top too quickly, powered by rage and her rector femoris. Her quads, her glutes. She didn't have enough time any more to go through all the bad things. She had told Stan about this. How her anger and her hatred and her terrible thoughts climbed to the surface as she climbed the hills. How they boiled to the top like magma and belched out of her and how she liked to let it happen and how it had become a highlight of her day. He had smiled at her. And said it was probably healthy, she shouldn't worry about it. She didn't know if it was healthy or not, but she hadn't been worrying about it.

Up the hill in anger, down the hill in peace. More or less. Sometimes they got crossed over, when her mind was elsewhere. Sometimes there was no peace. The school, and Ferrier, had a lot to do with it of course. But she was, she thought, running out of uphill for the anger she had. She might change her route. Make it longer, with steeper inclines. Seek them out. Go home via Crystal Palace. Shooter's Hill. Vignemale.

She coasted past The Fox on the right and King's came into view, its chimneys and its helicopter pad and the city behind it, steaming. Her back cooled in the downhill and she breathed easier, though not very much. You could get a mask but they said that you suck harder through a mask so you end up getting the same amount of gunk anyway. She thought she should look that up. She wasn't sure who *they* were. Maybe they were Stan. She glanced to her right, at the station and the Sally Army HQ, and slipped out another curse – a precise unsubtle stricture.

The hill had home on one side of it and work on the other. It would be nice if each of them stayed put instead of following her up and down, down and up, like a pair of awful drunks.

Not Stan. She didn't mean Stan. She meant the flat.

She was stopped at the pedestrian crossing by the entrance to King's. She sat up straight and arched her back. Her head felt like it might burst and she glanced at the Maudsley with a sort of longing. There was a shuffling little crowd, always the shuffling little crowd, between the hospitals and the station and the bus stops – day patients, outpatients, sick people and their worry and their plastic bags, and the medical staff amongst them, out in their scrubs for a sandwich. She watched a doctor, or maybe a nurse, as he crossed from left to right. She wiped her nose and wondered what he wore beneath his papery sky-blue outfit. Didn't look like very much. He was eating an apple and carrying a book. She couldn't see the cover but his shape was such a pleasing thing that she decided it was a good book. Her eyes lingered on the back of him as the lights turned, and she wobbled off towards Camberwell feeling sad and slightly happy.

It was a humming day. The humidity. The white sky. She wanted a shower. But she did not want to go home. She cycled straight on, through the little valley of Camberwell to the plains of Burgess Park and found a place to take a couple of para-cetamol and read her book and dry out and think. Stan would be working for another couple of hours. And might have a meeting. She took her paracetamol, read, dried out, but thought mostly about the sky-blue doctor or the sky-blue nurse, and what his life was made of.

*

The cloud broke up into cities, immense structures that hung over her head, over London, and Maria spent long hushed minutes contemplating them, trying to grasp their scale, but their scale lay in not being able to grasp it. Sometimes giant airliners appeared against them or disappeared into them, and they were no more than specks, a speck, like a bus in Brixton or Hackney, against clouds that were taller, wider, thicker, deeper than Brixton and Hackney and Peckham and Croydon and all the places where she had lived her life, all put together, and her life was smaller than a bus. She stopped herself then. Stupid. But still. Clouds are very fucking big. That's the point.

The landlord had emailed to let them know that he hadn't broken the window so he wasn't going to fix it. This was a small shattered pane in the bedroom – they didn't know what had happened. A bird perhaps. But it was hard to see how a bird could have flown over the wall that backed onto the outdoor area of the pizza place next door, and dived to the ground floor and had enough speed to break a window, even if it had got through the bars, and there had been no corpse. That they could see. The space outside their bedroom was inaccessible. Two foot of nothing where litter accumulated in windy weather and stayed there rotting, or vanished in another wind. They had covered the pane with some cardboard at first. After a couple of days Stan found a piece of wood somewhere and used that instead, because rats can chew through cardboard.

Every day when Maria came in she opened all the windows and walked from room to room while the place cooled a little, and then she closed all the windows again before Stan came home.

One night Stan had been washing the dishes, listening to podcasts on his headphones, the kitchen window open. He'd been daydreaming, he'd told her, miles away, happy, enjoying the discussion, and the first couple of times he saw something moving just out of his field of vision he'd assumed – unconsciously, he said – he must have assumed that it was people walking by on the street. But it was a rat. It had come in through the window and was exploring the windowsill and nosing the plates waiting to be washed, licking them Stan thought, its long tail slapping glass. He had backed out of the kitchen and closed the door and she had never seen anyone so pale. It had taken him a couple of minutes to tell her. *Rat. There is a rat. A rat came through the window.*

Time had stopped and pooled at their feet and she did not know if it had been minutes or hours or whether it had ever ended. Neither of them could open the door, so they went out to the street and watched through the window as the rat ransacked their cupboards. It was a big rat. Stan wouldn't let her go to the pizza place to ask maybe one or two of the guys to come. She should have gone anyway. He wouldn't let her call anyone. They waited. She went back inside, stood at the kitchen door with her big boots on, her gloves, a broomstick in one hand while her other hand trembled on the handle but could not turn it. Just could not turn it. Eventually Stan ran back in and barged past her into the kitchen and pulled the window shut. He said it had climbed out dragging what looked like a bar of chocolate and had run off towards the main road. The kitchen looked and smelled like a place they had never been before.

Stan had been terrified. So had Maria. But with Stan it had seemed to stir something in him that he didn't understand. He had cried that night. He had cried and could not settle, and she had found him, when she woke from her thin sleep at dawn, sitting upright beside her, pale and twitching and watching the floor. He told her that the night was full of noises. She told him they could move. He didn't want to move.

On the way to work she didn't curse so much. The hill was longer and not as steep from the Camberwell side, and she was never as angry with Stan as she was with work. She liked that she was going against the flow, that she was not a part of the crowd of rich shits coming the other way on their stupid expensive bikes with their head cameras and their lycra and their attitudes. She could hear them sometimes shouting together at drivers. *Oi. Wanker. Fuck's sake. Watch it. Arsehole.* She took her time on the way up, sat back on the way down, wore leggings and a jumper, and didn't bother with a helmet. Drivers saw the helmet and recalculated the risk. She wasn't sure that was completely true. She hated a sweaty head.

Stan didn't want to move because he'd lived around there all his life and he was furious about it. They were on the list for a council flat. That was that. He wasn't going to be bullied from landlord to landlord. He was going to stay put. But if they could get a better place? One that didn't have a kitchen window beside the bins of the pizza restaurant next door? The council designated bin location? There would, Stan said, always be something. She had gone and spoken to the guys in the pizza place. They'd been defensive at first, but they said they'd make sure the bins were kept locked, and they wouldn't put stuff on the ground when they were full. And they'd stuck to that, more or less. And Stan had talked to people in the council, or to councillors or something like that, about moving the bins, and they'd said they'd look into it and that had calmed him down a bit, gradually. But he'd taken to wearing earplugs. It wasn't noisy, where they were. But in the silence he heard things. And he kept the windows shut and they no longer left food out anywhere, and he cleaned all the time, every surface, hunting for crumbs.

Flying down the hill with the cities overhead. The air was better on this side. There was more greenery. She could see some of the kids cycling, but not many. She could see more of them climbing out of expensive cars. Some of them getting off buses. All of them so neat and groomed, in their blazers or their jumpers or their shirt sleeves. Their neatly creased trousers, and their neatly pleated skirts. They flowed in her direction and every morning she argued and remonstrated with herself. It was not their fault. Do not hate them.

— What do you mean, assassinations?

— Murdering politishhhians, Misssss.

— In general?

— Yessss. We need to find out how Missssssssssss.

Laughter. The stage-whispering nonsense wasn't entirely to annoy her, they just seemed to enjoy croaking their voices through clenched throats, sounding like a huddle of ghosts around her desk, hissing their demands at her and giggling.

She eyed a dim-looking boy at the side, smaller than the others.

— Does it not hurt you to talk like that? she asked him. It looks like it hurts you. You look like you're in pain. Are you in pain?

He blushed and shuffled and the others laughed more quietly, coughed. Maria sighed. She pushed her hair back. This was Tuesday. No, Wednesday. These were Year 9 kids, spotty and sometimes entertainingly weird. But this was a little pack of them, and they were always annoying in packs.

— I'm not sure we have much on how to assassinate.

— Oh Misss, no. Not really.

— Not to do them really.

— We need to research what they change.

The voices were now more or less reasonable.

— What they change?

— Miss it's true.

— Their effects and effectiveness Miss.

— Mrssss Grant wants us to bick uh politician t'asssassinate.

Some of their accents were so thickly posh that it took her a moment to decipher what they'd said. There was a honking clip to the tallest boy, a sort of slur and bubble. He sounded like he was drowning, but he was an admiral.

— Mrs Grant wants you to . . . ?

— Pick uh politician to

— To assassinate Miss.

— To see what would happen.

The kids were always superficially polite. None of them had ever lost their temper with her. They had with teachers, though only rarely. She suspected it was a status thing. Teachers are on a par. Arguments can become heated with an equal, but you don't lose your temper with the staff.

— She wants us to choose a politician and work out what would happen, politically, if that politician were to be assassinated.

— It's good isn't it Miss?

— We're going to shoot the Prime Minister.

— Hat's too hobvious, said the tall drowning boy.

— Mrs Grant said that would be very complicated.

— She *said* it would be unpredictable, not complicated.

— She's a martist I think, said one of the girls with a quiet, hard voice.

— Is she Miss? Is she a Marxist?

— We should assassinate Corbyn.

— Hat's too hobvious too.

— Who then?

— The queen.

— Not a politician.

— He wants to shut down private schools. He'd put you out of a job Miss.

— Who? asked the dim boy, who reminded her of her brother.

— Corbyn.

— Is she a Marxist Miss?

She thought she probably was. She was an elegant woman who seemed perpetually amused. She had nodded at Maria a few times as they'd passed in the corridors. Grey-haired, about sixty, tall and thin and impressive, always wore a suit. But she taught history, and political science, in the sixth form. Maria hadn't known that she taught the middle-school kids as well. Perhaps she was covering. It did sound a little like a bored politics teacher covering a younger history class.

— But perhaps, Maria said to them, perhaps if you assassinated Mr Corbyn he would become a sort of martyr, and his policies would become more popular, and someone else with the same policies would become prime minister and shut down the school. And put me out of a job.

One of the boys, with glasses and spots, smiled at her breasts. Another boy beside him, also with glasses and spots, said

— That's the sort of thing we have to inculcate Miss. Who to kill to make sure we get what we want.

— Inculcate?

He blushed.

— What we have to work out.

— Calculate.

— Who to kill to keep you in a job Miss, said a girl in a head-scarf, not unkindly. A small handsome boy looked at Maria very seriously.

— Do you think assassination is a good thing Miss?

She had the vague sense of Ferrier, hovering behind her. A couple of the kids had dropped their heads.

— No. I don't think it is really, Maria replied. But it's an interesting puzzle Mrs Grant has set for you. Let's see what we have.

— Assassination?

Ferrier, leaning on the counter with her elbows as if she thought there might be smaller children out of sight on the other side.

— We won't have very much on assassinations I don't think. Some Kennedy biographies. Gandhi, I suppose. Mahatma and Indira. Complicated stuff. How on earth did Mrs Grant get onto assassinations?

— Spencer Perceval, said several of the kids at once.

— Oh I see. Well we'll certainly have an amount on the Per-ceval assassination. Maria?

She was already looking it up.

— Is this an essay or a project?

— Project.

— In groups?

— Yes Miss. Cells.

— What?

— Not groups. Cells. She's told us that we're cells. Like terrorists.

— We're going to be ISIS.

— Nah we're ISIS.

A Shock

— You and Josh? You're neo-Nazis bruv.

— Well that's a little. All right. Pipe down. No one is going to be ISIS in my library. And no *bruv*-ing either young lady. I wish Mrs Grant had let us know. We could have prepared some resources. First I've heard of it. Did you know about this Maria?

The tone was accusatory, of course. Maria shook her head, made a noise of some sort.

— Well sort them out with some Perceval and I'll have a word. See what she has in mind. Are you on a study break you children? No devices in that case please young man. Now, please. Thank you. Leave Maria to get on with it and go and do some study. Study space by the windows please.

She herded them away and Maria watched her go. She pitied her in the mornings and hated her by afternoon, and every day coming down the hill she persuaded herself that she had no reason to do either, and promised to try again. But Ferrier shut her down repeatedly, like a device.

Her brother came and stayed for a couple of nights. She didn't know what he was up to exactly, but he was up to something. She suspected after a while that he was seeing someone. Or meeting someone that he'd met online, and was using her place as a base. Which was fine, but why could he not simply say so? He couldn't. And she couldn't ask, because part of her thought that there was a small chance that he had genuinely come just to see her. To spend a little time with her. That he missed her.

They ran through their childhood sketches and talked obliquely of their parents and the things they had abandoned for now. He came and went and slept on the sofa. He tried to be friendly with Stan, but they were differently assembled, and she wondered about her love for each of them and how it differed. It troubled her that they didn't get on. Was her love too liberal?

They argued one night after Stan had gone to bed. A standard brother sister argument about not taking each other seriously. About not having respect. She thought that he was actually angry at Stan, not at her. Or he was perhaps angry at her for loving someone like Stan.

She thought about love a lot. Then he left.

She heard later in the week that Mrs Grant had been arrested and that all the kids doing her assassination project were now being investigated by the police as part of the Prevent strategy. She also heard that Mrs Grant worked for MI5 and had successfully flushed out a Year 9 plot to bomb Selhurst Park or the Den or possibly both. She also heard that Mrs Grant was a lesbian, or was married to Hugh Grant, or was the mother of Tom Holland, or was a widow who lived with three other widows in a castle somewhere up Sydenham Hill with a view of the whole city and their husbands buried in the grounds.

Stories floated through the school like bubbles, and fell or rose, were burst or lingered, according to a physics that was beyond Maria. But she knew that the staff were at least as bad as the kids. There had been some sort of fuss though. Ferrier informed her that the project had been cancelled. And that Mrs Grant was no longer covering in the middle school.

— Did she get in trouble?

— Trouble?

— Over the project?

— Decisions about what roles academic staff do or don't take on are none of my business Maria and if they're none of mine they're certainly none of yours.

She instructed her to take the *Assassinations as Political Strategy: Bibliography and Additional Resources* document off the shelf, and the Year 9 website, and archive it. What had begun as Maria's list of books about people she could remember having been assassinated had been turned by Ferrier into quite an interesting document. The counterfactuals of assassinations was apparently quite a popular field amongst historians and political scientists. And the uses of assassination. The achievements. The successes. The pride. Maria had been briefly lost in it. Operations Nemesis, Condor, Wrath of God. Later, she wondered whether her anger at Ferrier wasn't powered at least partially by envy. She took it accusingly up the hill and hated herself by the summit. Ferrier was good at her job.

She told Stan about it, and he sneered at the paranoia and stupidity of Prevent and at the reactionary attitude of the upper classes to any hint of non-state-sanctioned violence, and he laughed his assured, deprecating laugh.

— Some parent will have thrown a hissy. Precious Sebastian is being recruited to the Red Brigades.

And Maria thought that was probably exactly what had happened.

In the night when they could not sleep because it was too hot they would lie together side by side, naked in the dark, the duvet thrown off. She could hear Stan's sighs, and he would sometimes look at his phone, reading things at the lowest brightness setting, turned away from her. She would pretend to sleep in the hope that pretending would make it so. She would think about her father. She would think about Stan. And she would make herself stop. Then she would make a list of things to think about, and she would try to remember it, and try to go through it. Future things. A librarianship course. Becoming a research librarian. Taking a job in a specialist library, full of adults. Doing an archivist course. Working eventually in the British Library. Stan becoming a councillor, maybe even eventually an MP. Travelling, in France. Spending time in Lyons or Bordeaux or Marseilles learning French. Writing. Finding the time to write. No kids. Reading. Writing. Learning. Looking at the sky in France. And sometimes, though she would never tell Stan about it, sometimes she would lie there listening to the tiny scratching coming from the wood in the broken window pane.

— Would you like to go for a coffee?

Maria opened her mouth. This was a surprise, and she didn't know what to say.

She had seen Mrs Grant walking up the driveway as she was locking her bike. So she hadn't been fired then, or arrested. She was strolling, slowly, while an occasional late kid raced past. Maria glanced, and recognised her tall figure and the head of grey hair, but her gaze was drawn back and became a stare because Mrs Grant was smoking a cigarette. Astonishing. It was strictly forbidden, anywhere on the grounds. And Mrs Grant saw her looking. She took another few steps and dropped the cigarette and as she drew closer Maria felt she should say something. You can't stare at someone in silence – it's a judgement.

— Hello Mrs Grant.

— Hello, she said, a little curiously, but continued by.

— I just wanted to say . . .

Mrs Grant stopped, turned.

— I just wanted to say that I thought your project, for Year 9, I thought it was great. A great idea. The kids were excited by it, you know. It was a really clever way of getting them to think about political contingency, or whatever. So.

Mrs Grant smiled, did a little nod of appreciation.

— Who are you?

— Maria. Library assistant.

— The students need a sense of what's at stake. And anyway, these children are going to end up running things, aren't they? I think they should know early on that power is deciding who dies.

Maria nodded.

— They were excited?

— Yes, they all came to the library looking for resources.

— Well, good. That's good. Would you like to go for a coffee?

Maria opened her mouth. This was a surprise, and she didn't know what to say.

— Not now obviously. After you finish some day.

— Yes, sure. That would be good.

They exchanged numbers and in the midst of doing that Maria to her shame found herself wondering whether the other bit of gossip – about Mrs Grant being a lesbian – might be the truth.

— Well, not tomorrow, I have something. But the day after I'll message you. Perhaps we can go somewhere not too far.

— Perfect.

They walked together towards the same building.

— You smoke?

— No.

— Nor do I, said Mrs Grant. But I am annoyed at the school and I am sulking. I am sixty-four years old. And I am also fifteen.

— I won't tell.

— But I wish you would.

Maria laughed. Later in the library she sent Stan a text telling him that she had spoken to Mrs Grant and that they were going for a coffee later in the week and she told him what Mrs Grant had said about power. He replied *lol. fab. x.*

She needed to tell him so that it was not a secret, because a secret was what she wanted, and she was not allowed them.

Mrs Grant's first name was Anna. Anna Grant. Grant was her husband's name. She had been Anna Rollebon before they married. She was French but had lived in the UK, in London, for nearly forty years. She had been a university lecturer. She had lectured in French history, and European history, at the LSE and then at King's College. She had given up her job in 2005 when her husband, who was also a historian, had been seriously injured in an explosion. She told Maria all this within the first few minutes.

— What happened?

— An explosion.

— Yes, but I mean . . . what sort of explosion?

— A very bad one.

And she held Maria's gaze with her eyebrows raised, as if to ask her *what sort of questions are these? These are not interesting questions.* Maria nodded. Took a sip of her coffee.

— In any case, Anna Grant continued, he was severely wounded. Most of it they fixed up, eventually, but there had been a head injury which was of course the most important one, and they tried for a long time to do something about that but it was very difficult. They thought his brain damage would be great. But. It wasn't. He couldn't walk very well, and his voice changed, slowed, became a little deeper, and he was not as smart. No more sex. But apart from that.

A SHOCK

They were sitting in a small empty café at the bottom of
Denmark Hill. It smelled of detergent and Maria found the
noises of plates and cups being clattered and rattled behind the
counter annoying. She didn't know what the woman who'd
served them was doing. They had a table by the window and
Anna Grant looked mostly at the street while she talked. Her
grey hair was straight and perfectly cut, her face looked healthy,
surprisingly unlined, her mouth quite big, her blue eyes expres-
sive and quite beautiful. But she wasn't a lesbian, or in any case
she had been married. Maria shushed her thoughts about this
and blushed, mildly she hoped.

She hadn't noticed the French accent at the school. It was
slight.

— There were fragments remaining in his brain that it was
not safe for them to remove. It might have been all right. But
they didn't know. What they don't know about the brain is . . .
well they don't even know *what* it is, do they? They have no idea
how it works, really. They are like old people given a computer.
Worse than that. They are like old people manning the International Space Station.

She laughed a quiet but sort of snorting laugh, covered
immediately by her hand. The laugh was funny. Maria smiled.
You could see age in her hands – crumpled, dry-looking. There
were no rings. But she had a lovely silver bracelet on her left
wrist that twisted and flattened and twisted again.

— So they decided, because he was basically recovered,
enough to live a life, you know, they decided to leave things as
they were. He was ok, why risk killing him or making things so
very much worse. It seems sensible of course. But they told him,
Robert you must not make any sudden movements.

She made a face at Maria. Astonishment. There was a shrug.

— Can you believe this? Please, no sudden movement. No excitement. No running or jumping or falling over. Just calm, calm, calm.

She shook her head, incredulous.

— Robert was not a man who was ever calm. You have to know that it was, this was like a language he could not understand. No sudden movement! It was like telling him to stop thinking. He used to box, you know? He used to train at boxing, right up until the explosion. Which happened when he was fifty. He was fit, healthy. He would cycle, box, go for these huge walks – I would collapse and he would laugh at me and off he would go. Striding away. Always moving. Always sudden. So this news was terrible news for him. He thought, I thought, that he would be dead in a month.

She took a sip of her coffee, and made a face. And then a sip of her water. She glanced at Maria and then looked out the window again.

— But it didn't happen. He was very careful for a while. Anyway, he couldn't box anymore, no more long walks, no more sex – that was ok, we were together a long time – so his life was quieter, not so many things for him to do. And he would stand up slowly. Sit down slowly. Walk very slowly. But soon he started to go faster. He would forget. He would turn his head suddenly at a noise, and he would gasp, and I would gasp and we would stare at each other but no, it was ok, he did not drop dead. And he did not forget, no, he knew I think always that he could go at any second. But he stopped trying to avoid it. And then he was depressed anyway. He was not as smart as he had been. He was the same person. He was funny, and kind, and he was still Robert. But he couldn't follow complicated things. He couldn't read except for police novels, thrillers, some historical novels he liked.

But he would read his own books sometimes, and he would be, he would be very sad, he would become very depressed, because he could no longer really understand his own books. That was very hard for him. But we had friends, you know. Lots of friends. He didn't want to see them, but I invited people over anyway. And they would chat to him, and sometimes he liked that. You could see which ones were good for him, which ones weren't. Some of them asking him all the time how he felt, how he was, he hated that. But others were good. They would tell him things. About their lives and he liked that. The creative ones understood that. The writers, our comedian friend, a film director, we know several actors, maybe one or two academic people. But the bankers and the business people are just stupid. The capitalists. Just stupid. Anyway. Are you creative?

— I write.

Mrs Grant looked at her with interest.

— What do you write?

Maria blushed.

— I try to write. Fiction. I haven't really . . .

— What age are you?

— Twenty-four.

— Oh my god you are so young, it's fine. It's impossible to write anything until you are over thirty. I wrote a novel many years ago. It's somewhere. It was a terrible thing but it was in me like trapped

She did the laugh again.

— like trapped wind. I mean. It was a terrible thing but I had to expel it. Get it out of me. About a girl who falls in love, and then, oh it was so stupid, I cannot write. Are you good yet?

— Not yet. Not really.

— Read. Just read. That's all you can do. Just read everything.

Not the English. But the French. Some Americans. South Americans, not north Americans, they are terrible, but the South Americans, Central American, up as far as Mexico, including Mexico, so just that far north, they are very good, read them. Do you read Spanish?

— No.

— French?

— A little.

She looked directly at Maria. Her eyes narrowed, and she pulled the cup and saucer a little closer.

— You speak French?

— Un peu.

— No! No! Don't please. I have forgotten all of my French. It depresses me to hear it even. I cannot listen to the songs, I cannot talk to old friends. Speaking French now is like death. It is like death. I will speak French again when I die.

She both grimaced and smiled as she said this, one then the other then again. Maria smiled too.

— I won't, I promise. My French is really terrible anyway.

— It is a terrible language, so

The rattling behind the counter rose suddenly to a crescendo, and there was a loud crash, and silence. Maria didn't look over. Mrs Grant didn't either. She closed her eyes, as if this was yet another burden she would have to bear, and sighed.

— Sorry, the woman shouted.

Mrs Grant looked out of the window.

— I must tell you about the joke, she said. Would you like another coffee?

— No thanks, I'm fine.

— It is disgusting.

She said nothing for a long moment, and her hands stroked each other and her bracelet clinked on the table top.

— Our friend, the comedian, he was quite famous I think. Maybe not so much then exactly. But he was famous in the nineteen nineties certainly. He was a nice man. A good man. He was a friend of Robert's for many years. A little younger than us. He drank too much. Anyway. He was at the house one day, visiting Robert, and it was warm like this, and they were in the garden, at the table on the grass, down at the end under the tree. I was in the kitchen, I don't know, I think I was making some coffee for them. I was looking out at them anyway, watching them, because it was pleasant you know, to see them together, good friends, old friends, one of them not great, not well, not what he had been, and the other there to see him, to spend time with him, to talk, to laugh, to . . . it is kind of love. Company. Respect. Affection. That is love isn't it?

Maria nodded, but Mrs Grant was looking out the window – though probably not at anything. Her eyes were unfocused, clouded, and there was a smile that was not quite there but was nevertheless implied. A missing smile, and you could see where it should be.

— I watched them, talking. Robert in his nice blue shirt. Looking good. Listening to his friend. And his friend, our friend, talking, gesticulating a little, talking, telling Robert some story, hunched forward in his seat, you know, his head low, his hands moving. As if he was reaching out to tap Robert's arm, telling him some story, telling him something. And then there was this point, a point reached. The comedian straightened up, lifted his head, and stretched his arms wide, and stopped talking. And Robert, Robert looked at him for a moment. Saying nothing. Just looking at him. And then Robert started to smile, and then to laugh, and his laugh grew, it became louder, and he laughed and raised his hand as if to touch his friend's arm in return, and he laughed very loudly, and it was beautiful to hear, it had been so long, it was so rare. He threw back his head and he laughed. And of course his brain, whatever was in his brain, it moved then, it shifted. He fell silent, and he slumped forward very . . . definitively. He fell forward. Onto the table. His arms twitched for a moment and then he was still.

She looked at Maria. The missing smile was gone. Her face was entirely empty.

— He was dead of course. Instant death. He felt nothing. So. So it's good isn't it? He died laughing, happy. Suddenly like that. You laugh, you throw back your head, the universe ends. That is a good way to go.

— My god.

— Yes.

— For him, yes, I can see that. But for you. It must have been

— It was fine. He was dead. I would rather a shock than a terror, you know? A long decline. Already he could see that. I could see that. He would not have been a good patient, and I would not have been a good nurse. This was better. Maybe too soon, but everything is too soon. Today is too soon. Life is too soon.

She looked into her coffee cup, and then out of the window again. Maria needed to know. Just ask. She opened her mouth, closed it, sighed, looked where Mrs Grant was looking, and was aware that Mrs Grant turned to look at her.

— I don't know.

— What?

— I don't know what the joke was. That's what you want

to ask. Everyone wants to know. I wanted to know. He wouldn't
tell me.

— The comedian?

— Yes.

They were looking at each other now. For the first time Mrs
Grant held Maria's gaze with her own. There was a tiny piece of
discoloured skin at the left of her left eye, a sort of wart, or perhaps a scar.

— I asked of course. After some time. I can't remember how
long. He was devastated. He thought he'd killed Robert, that he
was responsible. And at first I thought that it was the trauma
that prevented him telling me. The way you might not want to
speak about the details of an accident. He wouldn't say, and in
the grief of that time, in his despair, I knew that perhaps it was
very difficult for him to say the words, those words which the last
time they had been uttered had caused a death. To say them again
to me. But I asked him again, later, after a few weeks. He couldn't
tell me. He told me he was afraid that I would laugh, and that if
I laughed my laugh would somehow echo or recreate Robert's
laugh, and that something terrible would happen. He was pale
when he said this. Pale, shaking. And then he said that he was
even more worried that I wouldn't laugh. That I would not think
it funny, that I would think it a stupid joke. That I would think
that he had killed my husband for nothing, for a stupidity, for a
joke that could barely be thought of as a joke. That Robert's
death would be worthless if it was in response to a worthless
joke. He told me this, his hands trembling, pale. Consumed by
despair.

She looked out of the window again and her face was almost
smiling.

— He was dead within a year. He went back to drinking. He travelled, strangely, haphazardly, with no apparent reason. I think he was simply spending his money. He would fly to Germany or to Mexico, stay away for weeks, living in expensive hotels. Drinking. He would write letters to friends. Not to me. I think he was trying, sometimes I think he was trying to find a joke. A joke good enough to die for. And if he found it he would come back and tell me, lie to me, that it was the joke he had told Robert. But he never came back. He died in a hotel in Istanbul.

She smiled fully. The little scar or wart by her eye seemed more visible now, as if the light had changed. Maria tried not to look at it. She was exhausted by the job of listening. She felt at once that this was fascinating, and interesting, that it was something of a privilege to be trusted with it, and also that there was something wrong about it all, something that wasn't entirely decent.

— So there you are, smiled Mrs Grant. But what about you? Tell me about you.

She cycled slowly though the traffic and her thinking was stalled. She could not gather up whatever it is that makes an idea. There seemed to be none of the material of memory available to her. As if she had met no one at all, or Mrs Grant had met no one at all.

Maria had looked at her, vacant, remembering suddenly that this was a conversation. And had said nothing much more than that she lived with her boyfriend in a terrible flat, she had no money and was very tired, and that she had to go home. Mrs Grant had seemed very mildly annoyed. She had sighed and looked at her phone and said something about going to a friend's place in Battersea. It was as if she was used to being disappointed by people who had nothing to say for themselves.

In the flat Maria opened all the windows and then lay on the bed for a while. When she got up and walked into the kitchen the rat was on the sideboard, looking at her. She was almost certain that it was the same rat. A long-bodied rat, an old crafty rat, a mother and a biter and a teller of jokes. She looked at Maria and chewed, looked and chewed, looked and chewed.

— Get the fuck out of my kitchen you absolute fucking cunt, Maria said, calmly, evenly, her eyes on her eyes. Then she took a step forward. When she spoke again it was louder.

— Get. Out. Of. My. Kitchen.

She stared into the tiny reddened eyes, two punctures in the world, behind which there seemed to be nothing but a mechanical darkness, a machine, snickering on death. The rat stopped chewing. Maria shouted as loudly as she could and her voice came from somewhere she had not realised existed.

— GET OUT YOU FUCKING CUNT GET OUT GET OUT GET OUT

The rat froze, drew back, moved to the side, moved again, and then with a speed that shocked Maria, ran or jumped or flew through the open window and was gone.

She slammed the window shut. She ran around the flat slamming all the windows shut. She sprayed every kitchen surface with disinfectant and wiped it down, and then did it again, and she washed every piece of cutlery that had been in the jar by the sink, and she washed the jar, and she washed the windowsill and the window and the floor and the wall in the corner where she found that the toaster had paw prints on its side, as if the rat had lifted it to get at the crumbs underneath. She threw it out. And she threw out the cloths she had been using, and the rubber gloves, and she told Stan when he came home that the toaster was broken and they needed a new one and that she had cleaned the kitchen because she was bored, and that Mrs Grant had been self-obsessed and weird, and that she was in a terrible fucking mood and she was going out for a cycle.

— Ok, he said. Ok.

She went to Burgess Park and sat staring into the lake, which is not a lake, it is a pond, no more than three feet deep, and on its surface floated the reflection of a single structure so vast that it obscured the falling sun and glowed like a city on fire.

Mrs Ferrier was picking books off the floor.

— What happened?

— Oh a boy was upset, it's all right. He pushed them off the table.

— Here, let me.

— Thank you Maria. I don't know what got into him. He was sitting there working for a while and then he just became furious, swept the books off the table and stormed out.

— Brat.

— Oh it's stress. He shouted sorry from the door. An angry sorry, but a sorry nonetheless. They have so much pressure put on them. I know you think they're all spoiled and you're right of course, but they don't know that. Not yet. They think it really will be the end of the world if they don't get to go skiing at Christmas.

— Skiing?

— Don't put them on the returns trolley. Some of them might be checked out. I heard another couple of boys talking about a holiday in Italy. And one of them said it depended on his term report. Whether he could go.

Maria laughed. She had never been to Italy. She collected the books and put them on the counter and began looking them up.

— How was your coffee with Anna Grant?

She felt a flash of annoyance and turned and looked at Ferrier, who was smiling.

— She told me she was meeting you. Yesterday in the common room. First time she's spoken to me in years. Wanted to know what you were interested in. I suspect she was worried you'd have nothing in common.

— Well. It was . . . she talks a lot.

— Yes?

— It was nice. She told me about her husband though, the death of her husband. Such a terrible thing.

Mrs Ferrier looked at Maria for a moment. Nodded. She picked up her pen again, and continued whatever she was doing. Nothing was said. Maria looked through the window to the playing fields where two girls seemed to be dancing. Or just messing about. Running. Jumping.

— I hadn't realised she was French.

Mrs Ferrier put the pen down again.

— She isn't French, Maria.

Ah. There.

— She isn't?

— No. She's from the south coast somewhere. Poole I think. And as far as I know she has never been married.

The girls on the playing field were lying on the grass. Maria breathed. Coughed.

— Well, perhaps I misunderstood.

— She is a terrible liar. I mean. She really is. There's something wrong with her.

Yes, Maria thought. Probably.

Later on Ferrier used a soft voice that Maria had never heard before.

— There is virtually no one on the staff who hasn't been taken in at some point. She spins yarns, and it's wrong. She's embarrassed people. But really she is the one who should be embarrassed. She should be ashamed actually Maria. Really.

And she touched Maria on the arm with what she must have thought was kindness.

She cycled up the hill and her legs didn't hurt, but she could not fire up any anger. It did not seem to be there. Her body was too fit. She wanted to sleep but she knew it wouldn't let her. She took a detour down to Deptford and looked at the Thames. She went to Rotherhithe and cut back to the Old Kent Road through streets she didn't know, trying half-heartedly to get lost. Perhaps Ferrier was the one who was lying. Perhaps that. One or the other of them, entertaining themselves, and how was she to know? And what was wrong with it anyway? Making things up and saying them and making a world out of that. What was wrong with it?

The sky paraded overhead and the planes roared through it, tiny little interlopers. All that human achievement.

Something was wrong with it.

She dreamed one night of strawberries. They were huge and she could not bite them or fit them whole into her mouth so she left them where they were and was puzzled at what was denied her. When she woke she wrote a paragraph about a woman who finds some strawberries that are too big to eat. Her dream was softly odd and liquid and it flooded her, and her paragraph was a blotted box of basic cogs that made her furious and tired.

She texted Anna Grant.

Why did you lie to me?

There was no reply. But their eyes met in a corridor at the end of the day, and Maria tried to kill her with a look, and nearly broke the bike getting home. She felt the vibration of the text as she turned off Camberwell Green. She tried to ignore it, but there was nothing in the flat to distract her.

I just like to entertain.

Stan had some sort of problem with Gary that she couldn't really understand. Photographs, which Gary had put through the letter box. Stan seemed to think this was an affront. She didn't know why. They were like an old married couple, Stan and Gary. They had a childhood loyalty that had outlived their friendship and Maria had long thought they should call it a day, even if she liked Gary a great deal. But Stan increasingly seemed to annoy him, and she could feel Stan's discomfort whenever Gary's name came up.

She told him to go and talk to Gary if it was bothering him so much, and he did, and she had fallen asleep still waiting to hear him come in. In the morning, after a brief panic, she found him on the sofa. Only her brother and Stan when he was drunk slept on the sofa. Her brother looked like an angel, but Stan looked like a heap of clammy sorrow. She left without breakfast and got an apple on the way.

*

That evening when she asked, he said that Gary was using again.

— Using what?

— I don't know. But he was obviously high. I'm not going to see him for a while.

— Is he ok?

— Yes he's fine. Staying at his mother's. But, you know, he was just . . . the way he's behaving just isn't acceptable really. Some of the things he was saying. He's an angry guy. And taking it out on his friends is not . . . it's not funny, it's not right, it's not what you do. He should know that it's not what you do.

He wouldn't tell her the details. Some dumb omerta of their schooldays. He wouldn't even look at her. Why had he stayed out getting drunk? No answer. Because he was sad about his friend? Why not say so? He couldn't.

In bed she pretended to sleep and the glow of his phone and the heat of his body pushed her towards the broken window. Something was wrong with her life. It was misdirected.

She thought she should text Gary. Make sure he was ok. Her brother the same. All these men with their unsubtle ghosts. Maybe it was them. She thought also, specks against her great confusion, about love, and secrets, and loyalty. She thought that it was probably, all of it, made up. And she thought that from the edge of her bed to the wood in the window was as much as she could manage. That everything else is the world. And the world has no paths. And nothing can make them. And that we are no more than interlopers here.

Am I forgiven? Anna Grant had asked. And Maria had not known how to reply.

*

A Shock

In the morning she was up first again, while Stan slept on. She showered. When she went back into their room it smelled bad, and she dressed quickly. She left the bedroom door open. She left the kitchen door open. She stood for a moment and looked at the window. The kitchen window. Then she opened it. And she left for work.

Five minutes later she came back. He was still asleep. She closed the kitchen window and left again.

The Story

— There's a story that my grandfather used to tell me. He had been a sailor – on trawlers first, off . . . Brittany, battling the . . . Atlantic. Though he didn't like fish. Then on cargo vessels all over the world; then finally, unhappily, on a ferry between . . . a ferry on the Channel.

— La sleeve.

— The sleeve, yes. He liked being on the sea, but he loved to be on the ocean. He thought the ocean was the stuff of the planet itself, and he was in awe of it, and it nourished him. Land was small and dreary and cut up. And he seemed genuinely to not understand how anybody could accept that a border was a real thing. It was an absurdity. He railed against borders. Stupid doodles on the world. Anyway, the story he told me was about a border. He was helping some people cross it. The details were always vague. A small boat, a foggy becalmed sea, a group of frightened refugees or fugitives approaching the coast in complete silence, waiting for the sound of a bell to guide them to safety. My grandfather was tense, standing up in the prow, not able to see the hand at the end of his outstretched arm. There was no bell. Someone whimpered and was quietened. A cough was smothered in gloved hands. The distant shush of a rippled beach. And then a single low tone, far off but clear. A bell. My grandfather turned his head and held his breath and just as his lungs began to fail it rang again. They made for it, navigating by ear, slightly to port, straight ahead. The encouraging bell. And then. Then there was a second bell. Another bell, a different one. A single low tone, far off but clear, slightly different to the first. A different direction. A different bell. Oars were lifted and the sailors huddled and conferred. My grandfather was new to this, but the others weren't, and they were in no doubt. They turned around. They headed back the way they'd come, carefully, slowly, grimly, shrugging off the increasingly desperate pleadings of their passengers. Not tonight. Another night.

She takes a sip of her wine.

— We are, my grandfather told me, surrounded by traps.

— Which grandfather was this?

— I haven't yet decided.

— A different one.

— A different one.

— Can they navigate by sound? In the darkness? Ships? Boats? Does sound not turn around on them? Would they not use lights?

She puts her fingers on the base of her glass and looks up over the rows of bottles to the patch of empty wall beneath the ceiling. Then she turns and looks at him.

— Foghorns, Yves.

He considers that.

— Fair enough. Foghorns. Yes. I still think. It wouldn't suffer by the replacement of the bell. Beacons maybe. Lights in the darkness, just as thrilling.

— No. I like the bell. I like the sound of the bell.

— Fair enough.

— We are surrounded by traps. Appealing little noises in the darkness. They sound like signals. They draw us in.

— Very good.

They are at the bar in The Arms. They sit at the end, at the wall that divides the front bar from the back, they being in the front, next to the archway, perched on stools, Yves leaning against the panelling, looking at the side of Anna's head, and past it to the rest of the front bar, which is almost empty, except for people. Yves is the same man that Stan calls Stoker and Gary calls Yan, or Yanko. Anna is the woman Maria thinks of as Mrs Grant. She is Anna Grant.

— Who did you meet? asks Yves.

— No one.

— I met a man from Colombia.

— Was he an interesting man?

— He was. He was interesting. Melancholy. I told him the story of the wretched woman and he told me a story of a mountain.

— Which wretched woman?

— The woman in the wall.

— I don't know that.

— Which first?

She takes a sip of her wine. Her bracelet slips along her wrist.

— The mountain.

— There is a mountain in Colombia. There is a sparrow there, a small bird, some sort of small bird, which is called the Heart of Jesus. But in Spanish. What is that in Spanish?

— Le coeur de

— Anna that's French.

— Oh Spanish. I'll have to look.

She takes out her phone.

— Go on anyway, she says.

— This bird is peculiar to the region, or this variety of this bird in any case, is peculiar to the region. Certainly in its behaviour it is peculiar to the region. When the Spanish arrived and one or some of them got it in their heads to climb the mountain, they would find the little corpses of this bird scattered near the summit, and the locals, the indigenous people, told them that

— El corazon de Jesus.

— That's it. But the local people, the indigenous people had another name for it of course in their own language, but anyway. They told the Spanish that this bird died because it kept trying to fly to the sun, and it would fly too high, and its heart would burst, and down it would fall, dead. And that is why there were so many little bird corpses on the summit, and near the summit, and the Spanish named the bird El cortisone

— El corazon de Jesus.

— That's it. And the scientific amongst them wondered if a bird could get high enough into thin air in order to kill itself, and apparently there were papers written and philosophical Spanish gentlemen who pondered this a long time, this question, and wondered what it could mean, and wondered too if the echoes of the story of the Greek boy

— Icarus.

— That one. They wondered how these local, to their minds, savages, could have heard that story, and wondered if the Greeks had been there, and wondered if perhaps all the world's people came from the same original story, but of course that would have been a dangerous thought to have, given that they were killing these beautiful people left right and centre for their gold and with the declared justification that they were not worth a damn one way or another, and do you know this isn't even the start of the story, this is all just preamble Anna, I haven't even got to the start of it yet.

— Go on then.

— But of course the locals were well ahead of them anyway because to their way of thinking there wasn't a multitude of these Hearts of Jesus – what would that be?

She touched her phone a little.

— Los corazones. De Jesus.

— That's lovely. Well to their way of thinking there was only one. Only one corazone. And the many dead birds were just the same dead bird, stuck. Stuck in a loop. Doing the same thing again and again. Never learning its lesson. Up it flies for the sun, and it falls down dead and off it goes again. Like that other Greek boy

— Sisyphus. Are we still preambling?

— And there was something about the way these people, very specifically indigenous, very specific to that area – he told me the name but I can't remember, but these are not your Mayans, who were just up the way a little, or your Incas, Anna, or any of the more famous, the Aztecs, the more famous civilisations of those parts, these are a different band of people, gathered around this mountain with the dead birds at the top.

He takes a sip of his beer.

— And this now is the story.

— Well thank god Yves, mon dieu.

He laughs at her.

— Very good. Now this mountain that they were living around and at the foot of, and a little bit up the sides of et cetera, the Spanish asked them the name of it, according to them. And every time they asked they got a different answer. Or probably what it was was that each time a different one of them asked they got a different answer, and it was only when they compared notes as it were, when they met at the end of the day and one would say to the other, *well now, the locals showed me up The Ear today*, and another would ask what The Ear was, and he would realise that it was the mountain that he had been told, by the very same locals, was known as The Storm, and a third would pipe up saying that the locals had told him that it was called The Bulldog, and another The Impossible and another The Burp of the Sheep, and another God's Thumb, and so on and so on.

— The Burp of the Sheep.

— And of course these Spanish, these terrible colonialists, these awful men, were furious, thinking that they'd been lied to left right and centre, and they went into the villages and raised a terror demanding to know what the locals called this mountain.

— Did they kill?

— Over this? No I don't think so. The man just said they were furious. You know the way violent men are constantly furious. Out of shame. That sort of thing. Assuming deceit. They probably knocked people about a bit. The Met on Rye Lane on a Sunday morning. Bloody, boisterous. You know. Seeing lies left right and centre. They kicked up an awful fuss anyway.

— You need to work on this bit.

— I do. In any case, it emerged of course that no one was lying to them. That they had been told the truth each time they'd asked.

He pauses, and regards Anna. She purses her lips. She sits on the barstool with her legs crossed, her hands lying loosely in her lap. She wears a soft black leather jacket over a thinly striped top, dark red trousers, sandals. A full-looking bag lies crumpled at her feet as if fallen from a great height. Her hair is tied back in a loose ponytail, strands of it falling over her face, which is very lightly made up.

— I think it's obvious, she says.

— Is it?

— The mountain has many names. She eyed him almost nervously, and smiled then.

— You are disappointed.

— No, no, it's obvious of course. If they're not lying . . . well then.

He looks around the bar. Has a sip of his drink.

— Go on then.

— No it's all right.

— Oh for god's sake Yves, tell me how it ends.

— The mountain had all those names. All of them. And more. Hundreds of different names. It had a different name depending on where you were when you saw it. A matter of perspective Anna. In one village it looked a little like a bulldog. In another it looked like an ear. If you were climbing it from this angle it might be Boulder Mountain. From that angle it might be Goat Mountain. If you're coming down it on this path it's Rushing Mountain. On that path it's Pigtail Mountain. Et cetera.

— That's good.

— He told it much better.

— Your Colombian?

Yves drinks the last of his beer, his eyes on Anna over the rim of the glass. She looks into the silence he has left and finds his eyes and laughs. And he finishes his drink and laughs too.

— One bird, many mountains, says Anna.

*

Harry comes with a new pint for Yves and stands by them for a while and they talk in low voices about the socialists.

— Are they Labour?

— I asked. Labour adjacent, one said.

— What's that?

— At the scene of the crime.

— Anti-Corbyn?

— No, no, pro-Corbyn.

— Are you a socialist Anna?

— I am, very much so. You are too Yves.

— I'm a fascist, says Harry.

— You are a gentleman Harry.

— I hate everyone.

— No you don't. You know everyone. It's not the same thing.

— Should we join their group? Yves asks.

— I'm not a joiner, says Anna.

— You won't join me for another drink then?

And they all laugh, though Yves is so delighted with his joke that he goes for a walk around the bar telling people about it.

— What are you working on Anna?

— The murder of Camus.

— KGB?

— Probably not.

— Novel?

— Probably not.

Harry fills her glass from a bottle he brings up from under the counter and puts back there.

— I have one for you.

— Go on.

— Writer

— What sort of writer?

— French writer. Goes to Mexico. For some reason. No, he goes to do a profile of a drug baron. You know, a commission.

— A journalist then?

— And novelist.

— All right.

— And he goes to do this profile for a big magazine. And he gets, much to his surprise, to meet this drug baron. And the two of them hit it off. They like each other. The drug baron is a charmer. Not at all intimidating, not to the writer anyway. But he has this immense power. Which the writer envies. And the writer has no power. But he has no responsibilities either, and he writes. And the drug baron envies that.

— Oh Harry.

— What?

— This is a movie.

— No.

— They will make the journalist a woman. They will make it a comedy.

— No. Well, it could be a movie. But it's not. It's about the violence, and about the sort of violence they end up doing to each other, and about ideas of masculinity and so forth. Sexuality. Gender.

She looks at him. He stares at the counter top. Aligns a couple of beer mats.

— They become lovers?

— Sure.

He won't look at her.

— That could be interesting.

— Yeah.

He scratches his head.

— Think about it some more, said Anna.

— Ok, says Harry, and moves away.

Anna watches him.

Yves comes back.

— I have hurt his feelings.

— Harry's? Why?

— What is the wretched woman?

He looks at her.

— A woman in a wall.

He stares.

— Yves . . .

— Oh! Yes! Yes! This actually happened near here Anna. On that big estate that nearly fell down. The big towers. Near the Old Kent Road. A woman. Let me get this right now. I'll get it wrong.

— You told the story of the mountain very beautifully Yves.

— I know. But this has facts in it.

Yves stares at the floor for a moment, getting the facts straight. Anna looks at Harry. He is laughing with John about the golf. John loves golf. Harry catches her eye, comes over.

— I have been reading a great book Anna. Do you know it? By that woman.

— Spark?

— What? No. Not Spark.

— I keep on telling you Harry. Rename the pub. Put her picture up. Create a cocktail called The Abbess of Crewe.

— I know. I know.

— She lived five minutes from here.

— There are probably legal issues.

— You could relabel the toilets. The Bachelors, and The Girls of Slender Means. There's nothing about her around here. She's been forgotten, and it's a great injustice that you could remedy Harry.

He stands leaning on the bar scowling at the little pile of beer mats.

— She'd hate it of course. I'm sorry Harry. What's the book?

— Oh I don't know. Spanish writer, or South American maybe, I can't recall the name. But she was on the radio. And it's this peculiar thing about a woman who moves into a small house in a great big forest. And it's just her in the forest. In this house. And she has this mad idea that she can make, she can open up a bar in the sort of barn that is attached to the house. There's no one around for miles. It's the middle of nowhere. But she gets it into her head that if she puts up a nice neon sign over the barn, people will come. That they'll see it or something, or feel it, and they'll come, and she'll make them drinks and play her favourite music. And it's like a fantasy she has. But at the same time, she goes to the city and makes enquiries about having a neon sign made, and she designs it, and orders it and everything. And then has it installed. Mad. This is mad. She doesn't even have any stock. No beer, no spirits. No license or anything. Just this big neon sign. And then Anna, listen, then the book starts talking. The book you're reading. It starts speaking. It's hard to describe. It's like the book speaks up.

— What does it say?

— No, it's not that. It's more that. You become aware that you're reading a book. I don't know how to explain it. It's terrifying.

— What does the sign say I meant.

— Oh. Something stupid, what is it, something communist. She's a communist. Used to be a guerilla fighter. I can't remember.

— Sounds great. Show it to me.

— It's upstairs. I'll go and get it later. Yes sir what can I do for you?

Yves looks up and gently touches Anna's elbow.

— So the council have been making a mess of this estate over there and I can't remember the name of it. So let's say it's the Salter Estate. The Salter Estate off the Old Kent Road. And the problems are legion Anna. There are problems with the heating. With the windows. With the walls. So it's the middle of summer and it's sweltering hot and in this one tower in the middle of the estate they can't turn the heat off. One of those systems that does the whole building. There are so many problems with those. Whoever designed them should be shot.

— Shot?

— If we demand shooting they might get a slap on the wrist Anna. That's how it works. Demand the stars, you might get the moon.

— Clever.

— The heating is on full blast. And it's nearly 30 degrees outside. And they can't turn it off. And the hot water is practically boiling. And a lot of the windows are rusted up and can't be opened. And not all of these flats have balconies. These conditions are preposterous Anna. They are inhuman. And the council has people on site, and contractors on site, and they're all down there with their vans and their hard hats and their yellow things that

— Gilets.

— Well they're all there in their jillys with their clipboards arguing about who is responsible for what, and people are going berserk. And there is one woman, near the top, and she is so desperate that she poked a hole in her flimsy wall, these ridiculous

148

flimsy walls they have, and these big empty gaps between them, the places built as if by children, these walls that were supposed to be filled but never were, with insulation or something like that Anna, I'll work on that.

— You'll fill it in.

— Yes. I will. And she is after coolness that's all it is. Just looking for some cool air. And the plaster comes away and there's a cooler space there, and it looks like she might fit. And she squeezes herself into the wall cavity and gets stuck. And the poor woman is there for hours. Hours. Sweating now with the anxiety of it as well as the heat, and she isn't discovered until her husband, who is a porter in King's, he comes home and his wife isn't there, she's not there Anna, his wife is nothing now but a screaming in the wall and he can't even find her, whatever way she's managed to do it, he can't even find her for a while, and then he had to get the fire brigade out because he can't pull her out, the poor woman, stuck in the wall like that. God.

He trails off, troubled, unhappy.

— What happened Yves?

— Ah they got her out eventually. Bloody council.

— It's all right. She got out. Don't worry.

— Still though Anna.

— Facts.

— I know. I know. I should know better.

— They used to put women in walls all the time.

— Who did?

— Men. Usually priests bricking up nuns.

— Why?

— I don't know. Pregnancies. Talking. Embarrassing someone. Brick her up!

Anna jabs her finger at the air.

149

— Disgrace! Brick her up!

— That's terrible.

— Many ghost stories of course. About bricked-up nuns. Think of the anger, Yves. A death like that, well you're just asking for trouble.

— It's murder.

— It's worse than murder.

— It must have been awful. Screaming. Trying to get out.

— Bloody fingers, yes, those ghosts, a lot of bloody fingers in those stories, nails torn off, broken fingers. Days of waiting.

— Days?

— At least. Weeks maybe. They'd have to starve to death.

— Oh my god.

— And there were monks, kings, oh I don't know.

— There was that boy from Camberwell in the roof.

— What boy?

— In the attic. You know Roy. Not Roy. Ron. You know Ron the plumber?

— No.

Harry walks by.

— I know Ronnie, he says.

— He's a plumber isn't he?

— Depends what you need doing, says Harry, and disappears into the back bar.

— Ron is a handyman then, and his son. Or his cousin or nephew or something like that Anna, was trapped in a roof, in an attic, for days.

— How did that happen?

— They were working on a house somewhere in Hampstead or somewhere. Some old mansion in the rich places, in the rich west Anna. Out west. Notting Hill or some such. Putting in a new kitchen or something like that. And it was a Friday I think. And Ron finished a bit early and completely forgot about the boy. And the boy had left his phone somewhere, and couldn't get out of the house and he hid in the attic. And the family came home and he stayed there out of embarrassment for the whole weekend.

— Embarrassment?

— I'll ask Harry.

Anna smiles into her wine. She uncrosses her legs and then crosses them the other way.

— Men brick themselves up out of embarrassment, she says.

— I'd kill myself, said Yves. If I was bricked up.

— But how Yves?

— I'd stop breathing.

— I wouldn't wish it on anyone. I really wouldn't.

— What would you wish on them instead?

— My grandfather used to wish

— The sailor?

— The sailor. He used to wish people a quick death. A sudden death. *May your death come as a shock to you*, he'd say.

— Not very friendly.

She laughs.

— Yes. People often thought that, and he'd have to explain. But some people know immediately what you mean. No lingering. No pain. No suffering. A shot to the back of the head on a sunny day. Something snapping in your brain. A happy death.

— Would you not want to say goodbye?

— To who?

— Loved ones. Friends. To have a last drink with me here.

— I will have a last drink with you here Yves. And this might be it. So live it

She raises her hands and smiles widely.

— Live it and enjoy it and savour it and fill it with magic. Because who knows?

People are looking.

— Who knows? she asks loudly, when death will come to claim us.

Yves seems embarrassed. His eyes dart around the room and he slouches. Anna brings her arms down and grins at him.

— What would we say, Yves? To each other? If we knew that I was to be hit by a bus in the morning? We would be maudlin, dense. We would suffocate each other. Much better that we have a lovely evening and go our separate ways in full expectation of the same time same place, and then I get hit by my bus.

— I will be very sad.

— You are very kind.

— I will organise some sort of commemoration.

— Please don't.

— We will have free drinks and we will talk about your life.

— Harry won't allow it.

— Won't allow what?

This is Harry, pausing with two pints in his hands.

— A free round in the unlikely event of Anna being hit by a bus.

— I won't allow it, he says, and goes through to the back.

— There was a writer.

— You don't like writers.

— I didn't say I liked this one.

— Go on.

— There was a writer.

Anna has a full glass of wine in front of her. She sits in the same position, if slightly turned now towards the man she is calling Yves.

— There was a writer, she says, for the third time. He lived in Chelsea because he thought it was important for him to live there. That a sort of cachet attached to a Chelsea address, and it would help him, somehow, in his career. This was in the 1970s. And his flat is basically a room. A tiny room at the top of a decrepit mansion house, landlord from hell, all the rest of it. He's an idiot of course. Those days he could cross the river and be in a squat in Kennington or even up here, around Wilson, Dagmar, all squatted in those days. Civilised days those, you remember?

— I do. You knew your neighbour.

— But he's an idiot. And he can't stand his tiny room on top of all these boiled vegetable flats, and he looks around for something else. And he finds a flat, not a room, but a proper flat, first floor on one of those squares with the locked parks in the middle. And he goes to see it and it's beautiful. Wood panelling, parquet floors, window overlooking a big back garden. There's a kitchen, a living room, bathroom, bedroom, something else, and he can't quite believe that it's available to him at this rent that he can afford. And he says he'll take it. But the landlady, this quiet sweet mysterious woman, doesn't immediately agree to let him have it. She asks him first if he knows about the . . .

She opens her hands, closes them again.

— The Maigrets.

She looks at Yves. He raises an eyebrow.

— No, what am I saying. The Maynards. Colin and Florence Maynard. The couple from the newspapers. And of course, unworldly aesthete he, he's never heard of them.

— Doesn't read the newspapers.

— He doesn't, Yves.

— Hasn't a clue.

— Not the first.

— About the famous Maynard murder.

— No!

— No?

— No! No murder!

— Oh.

— After living in the flat for just over a year, the Maynards disappeared. Vanished. Not a trace. And I mean, not a trace. The flat completely undisturbed. As if they've popped out to the shops. No missing clothes. Their car where they'd left it. No sign. Police all over because of some connection she had to the Home Secretary. A cousin or a niece or some such. But nothing. Nothing, ever. And the landlady, she just wanted to make sure that this writer knows about all that, and that it isn't a problem for him. And he's an idiot and in he moves. And he loves his new home. And he is happy there. And nothing bad happens. Nothing at all. But he does become increasingly fascinated by the idea of their disappearance. He doesn't really think that anything bad happened. He thinks that they just decided to leave, to step out of their lives. He thinks they're fine, living on a beach somewhere. And he thinks that's very powerful. It fills him with optimism. This notion that such steps are available. That we have such power. The power to vanish. He thinks of it a lot. And when he goes on his holidays, he decides to try and travel without leaving a trace. To see if it can be done. And these are the days before CCTV everywhere. Before mobile phones. When cash is still king, Yves. He buys a new bag, packs it with new clothes. In the middle of the night he dyes his hair, shaves off his beard. He puts on clear glasses. Before dawn he quietly leaves the flat and walks to Victoria, and he gets on a coach to . . . Chester, and then another into Wales, and he gets local buses to Pembrokeshire. Lovely down there Yves. Lovely coast. And he's disappeared. No one saw him leave. No one knows he's gone. It takes four days in fact, for people to realise he's not around. Another three days before the landlady finds out. She gets onto the police immediately. They search the flat. The last time anyone saw him was a neighbour, the day before he went, coming back to the flat with some shopping, all smiles. And he was never seen again.

— But I thought he was . . .

— Yes.

— I thought he was only seeing if it could be done.

— Yes.

Yves shakes his head.

— So what happened?

— He was going to book into a little hotel. But he knew as soon as he did that his adventure was over. And he was quite enjoying this notion of having disappeared. It was dusk now, and he hadn't slept the night before, and he went for a walk along the cliffs.

— Ah no.

— Yes. He fell into a sort of gully. He was knocked out. But he was alive. Upside down, unable to move, and the tide coming in. He didn't stand a chance.

— But his body?

— It was stuck down there for a couple of days. The next big sea shifted it. Took it out, carried it off. Never seen again.

Yves sighs and stares. He puts his glass to his lips but puts it down again.

— I don't know who can tell that story, he says.

— No one can.

— No.

— It untells itself.

— It does.

— It self-destructs.

— It reveals itself, says Yves. And once revealed it disappears.

Anna nods seriously. She looks at Yves. Her eyes are soft.

— It is a story that can never be told.

Yves nods. He stares into space and Anna watches him, and her eyes are full of love.

— That flat, Yves says.

— Yes.

— Probably still available.

She laughs.

— Probably very cheap Anna. We should have a look at that.

— We should.

— What are you two doing?

— I'm teaching Yves a song.

— It's very complicated Harry.

— It's very simple. I need to write it down.

— Are we disturbing people? asks Yves.

— No no you're fine. I just heard you sing a little.

— We'll keep it down.

— You're fine. What are you working on next Anna?

She is rummaging for a pen.

— Bags: A Cultural History.

— No, seriously.

— I don't know. The Two Patricks maybe.

— What's that?

— The story of Ireland's patron saint, and the theory that there were actually two of them. One sent by Pope Celestine in

431. And another one, the former slave, returning from Britain in 432. They were both known as Patrick. Or took the same name. And the same story, in time. Handsome men, strong. Not dissimilar. Leading to many miracles of bi-location et cetera. They were lovers of course.

— What about the flying cat?

— Remind me.

— The children's book about a flying cat which leads to a rash of children throwing cats out of windows.

She laughs.

— God. No.

— I liked it. Most survive. But they're angry.

— Every day when I dust my desk I shake a yellow duster out of the window. And I expect, every time, that it will be seen and interpreted as a distress signal and the police will arrive and shoot Mrs Dobson downstairs.

— The plane crashes.

— Ah yes.

— What's that one? Harry asked.

— A story book.

— Short stories.

— And in each of the short stories there is a plane crash. Sometimes the plane crashes into the story, into the characters, and that's the end of that. Sometimes

— Sometimes it's more subtle.

— Yes. Like someone's wife's plane will crash. Or there'll be a plane crash on the television.

— All except the last story.

— Which takes place on a plane.

— Which doesn't crash.

Yves and Anna smile.

— I don't get it, says Harry.

Anna and Yves look at him, and still smile, but don't explain.

Yves goes to the toilet. He hums and whistles. He sees a man from Dekker House on Hopewell Street. The man says to him

— Do you live here Stoker? You're always here. Every time I come in I see you. You seem to spend your life here.

He is being friendly. Yves smiles at him.

— No, I don't. I am rarely here. This place takes up a tiny, miniscule, insignificant part of my life. A speck. A mote. A pin-prick. It's a tiny hole in a great big wall.

The man laughs.

As he is going out, Yves says to him, still smiling.

— May your death come as a shock to you.

He goes back to talk some more to Anna, but of course she is gone.

The Flat

DOWNSTAIRS, THE GARDEN. The soil and the edge of the soil. The grass, the little grass, yellowing. The small bushes, the wood of them, the leaf, the colour. Green, cream, white, yellow, pink, purple, something rusted in the corner by a broken chair. Roses, lavender, violets, peonies. Hydrangea. Delphinium. A cat in the sun. A metal table in the mud with a fake-tile top. A watering can but plastic. A pair of boots by a door. A strip of path by the wall of the house. Two houses. The garden shared. Two houses, two back doors. Silence in the middle of June. Silence being the airplanes and traffic. The sirens. Somewhere, in a different garden, the clack of shears, of something being cut down. No voices.

Voices. On the ground floor, behind the door with the boots.

— There used to be a key for this, a big old thing. Don't know what happened to it. So now there's just these bolts.

— Ok.

— And you have to, see, there's a catch

— Ok

— On this one. You have to watch your fingers as well because when it finally slides it flies

— Oh

— See what I mean?

— Shit Laura.

— What?

— Oh, you didn't hit your finger?

— No I'm fine. And this one is easy. Et voila.

The door opens and two women and a man emerge into the light, squinting, they step down, staying on the path, forming themselves into a line, behind them the dark of the inside, the cool of it, a passageway, the house.

— It's very nice, says the man.

The cat stands up and walks to them. One of the women crouches and holds out her hand.

— This is our baby. Hello baby. How are you eh? All toasty aren't you, you lovely little baby.

— What's she called?

— We never named her. They don't really do names, do they? Not even sure she's ours at this stage. Are you baby? Whose are you? Whose baby are you? We barely see her. She's a good mouser though.

The cat brushes up against them all and walks into the dark behind them. The man turns to watch her go, and then lets his gaze run up the walls of the house. He looks particularly at the windows of the first floor. By his feet the slab step is veined and cracked like a hand. The paint of the threshold looks wet. But his eyes are upwards. On bricks the colour of wet sand, mortar the colour of dry sand, the bricks the size of letterboxes, the windows with the sky trapped in them, glinting.

He is a young man. They are young women. They are, all three of them, wearing shorts. Red, grey, khaki. The man and one of the women wear vests. The other woman wears a loose shirt. They all wear different sorts of flip-flops. They all have short hair. The man has a neatly trimmed beard. He is white. His hair is a light brown. One woman is brown skinned, with black hair. The other has red hair, dyed red hair, and is darker skinned, and she is the first to walk on the little grass.

— It's shared with next door, she says. There's a man there, Morgan, looks after it. With Alison. Between them. You green fingered?

— Not even a little, the man says, and laughs.

— Nor me. Laura does a bit.

The other woman is looking at some empty pots against the wall.

— I planted a . . . what . . . I can't remember what it was called. We got a gift, didn't we, some sort of shrub. So I planted that. I don't even know where it is now. That's the full extent of the bit I've done.

The man laughs the same laugh.

— What's the difference, asks Laura, between a shrub and a plant?

— Well a shrub is a sort of plant, the man says.

They look at him. He laughs again.

— That's all I have for you.

— Let's go in, says the woman who is not Laura. It's fucking roasting out here.

They go back into the dark. The women let the man lock the door, sliding back the bolts. He makes a show of seeing they're secure. They walk along a small passage where some garden tools and a bicycle with no front wheel are propped against the wall. The cat waits for them. They go through another door. They turn, and again the young man is the one to lock it, turning a key.

— And this goes?

— In this thing.

The woman who is not Laura is holding out a small wooden

box. He drops the key into it, she closes the lid, and places it on a shoulder-high shelf to her left. They are in a hallway now. It is bright and cool. The cat walks to the front door and waits there, as if hoping that they are going to open the front door. She chitters. She looks up the stairs.

The two women and the young man are talking about something new now. They don't come to the front door. They seem to disappear under the stairs, as if into a cupboard. The hall is silent. Take-away menus and estate-agent leaflets lie on the floor. The cat moves very slowly towards the bannisters and briefly rubs her head on the edge of the bottom step before standing still for a while, her ears upright, then back, then upright again, looking up. Her head moves and stops. Moves and stops.

Moves and stops.

A kettle has boiled while they have been in the garden, and the woman who is Laura goes to the kitchen and makes coffee for the three of them while the young man looks through the books on the shelves and makes comments about some of them.

— You're a reader then? asks the woman.

— Yeah. Well, I mean, as much as I can be, given, you know, work, all that. But yeah I love to read. It's great to see a load of books in a place though, like this. I'm looking forward to getting some shelves up. I've a few boxes . . .

— There are shelves aren't there? In the living room?

— Yeah, there are, but I think I'd like some more. I have quite a few books. And I do that thing, you know, where I buy more while I still have loads I haven't read.

She nods.

— You know the flat then?

She looks at him a little quizzically.

— My flat. You said there were shelves in

— Oh, yeah. Sorry. Yeah we used to know your . . . predecessors? Karl and Peppi. So we'd be in and out. They weren't
readers though.

She laughs.

— They had knick-knacks and pictures and odd little things
on those shelves. Not a lot of books.

Laura comes into the room with a tray of mugs and a plate of
biscuits.

— I don't know what we're doing drinking coffee, she says.
We don't have any milk I'm afraid. Or sugar. We're not used to
visitors. Will you let the cat in Nadia, I can hear her.

— Not used to visitors, Nadia repeats, smiling, in a strange
voice, an older voice. No one ever comes to see us. Poor elderly
spinster sisters. Poor cat ladies.

Her voice changes again as she opens the door.

— Hello baby. Come in then if you're coming. Come on.

They all sit a little awkwardly, Nadia and Laura on the sofa,
the young man on the armchair opposite. The window at his
back is large, almost to the floor, and the blind is down, keeping
out the sun. But the room is filled with bright light. The cat sits
formally in the doorway of the kitchen and looks at him. He
holds his coffee. Sips at it. Then leans forward and puts it on the
table. There are beads of sweat on his forehead. No one has said
anything for quite a while.

— What's your commute like? Nadia asks him.

— I walk. Or at least I used to walk from the last place, which
was just off Coldharbour Lane, opposite King's. It's a little further from here I think. But I'll probably still walk.

— Where do you work?

— Borough. Just off Borough High Street.

— Oh that's easy, said Nadia.

They spend several minutes talking about routes he might take through Burgess Park. No one touches their coffee, or the biscuits. Nadia speaks much more than Laura. The young man stops sweating, but leans forward with his elbows on his knees as if to keep his back away from the armchair. The cat has gone somewhere else.

It is Nadia who again brings up his . . . predecessors. The conversation has moved on, from going out to coming back.

— Oh Karl and Peppi used to make such a noise when they came rolling home late, she said. Which they did a lot. Or early. Or god knows.

— Peppi?

— Yeah. Peppi. He's Greek.

Laura laughs.

— He's Greek but Peppi isn't, I mean the name isn't Greek. It was some stupid nickname from when he first came to London.

— I thought it was short for something. Or a version of something that was unpronounceable in English. No?

Laura shakes her head, shrugs.

The cat brushes against the young man's leg and he jumps slightly, startled, but the women don't notice. He holds out a hand for the cat to sniff.

— They used to go out, Nadia continued, and stay out, you know, all weekend sometimes, and roll in at some completely random hour – three in the afternoon, seven at night, Sunday, Monday, whatever – looking like . . .

She laughs.

— So, the young man asks, is the entire building queer?

They both look at him, and for a moment nobody says anything, and the young man's eyes widen slightly. Then Nadia

laughs, and Laura does too, and the young man sighs exagger-
atedly and puts his hand to his heart.

— Oh my god, he says. Just for a second there. I thought . . .
god what a faux pas that would have been.

They are still laughing, and he laughs too. The cat walks out
of the room, into a small corridor and ambles into the kitchen.
It is a small kitchen, with a small window, also looking out on the
back garden, also with the blind down. She sniffs in the corners,
sniffs an empty bowl that sits in a little alcove under the sink,
sniffs a bowl full of water beside it, and rubs her back on the
corner of a cupboard. Then she jumps onto the counter top,
sniffs her way slowly to the blind and noses her way in behind it.
She surveys the garden for a moment, then awkwardly jumps and
clambers up to the open awning at the top and goes outside.

The kitchen is quiet again. The voices of the women and the
man continue, naming people in the building, speculating and
laughing. They seem much more relaxed with each other now.
Next to the kitchen is a large bathroom. Some items of clothing
hang from the rail above the bath in the dazzling light. Frosted
glass. Tiles. A mirror. Next to the bathroom is a large bedroom,
messy, dark, with a television, chairs, clothes lying around, a large
wardrobe with a door missing, a big unmade bed. The windows
are covered by dark heavy drapes. Dust in the air. Paintings.
Photographs. A fan by the bed. A full-length mirror. The voices
can barely be heard. Somewhere in the building or outside it a
cough. Another cough. The silence then. The drapes. The dark.

The silence then.

Something has happened to the conversation.

The young man is sitting on the edge of the armchair, turned
slightly to the side. He seems downcast and the air above him
quivers. It quivers for an instant then stops. The women sit

leaning into each other, Nadia with her arm around Laura, who looks into space, her expression one of sorrow. Here is sorrow.

— Really. It's fine. It's just . . . Well, it's lovely that you've moved in.

This is Nadia. She is forcing a smile while her hand strokes Laura's arm.

— And great that the building is staying queer. Pretty much, right? It's just we miss them quite a lot. Karl. Peppi. They were really great. Weren't they?

She squeezes Laura, leans her head towards her a little, kissing her hair. Laura says nothing and does not move.

— Where have they moved to? he asks.

Nadia makes a face, as if he has said something clumsy, something inappropriate. Laura briefly shuts her eyes, then disentangles herself from their embrace and stands up. She sighs, forces a smile, glances at the young man and says a damaged *Sorry*, takes her coffee cup and hurries out of the room.

— Oh, said Nadia. Don't worry about it.

— I'm . . . I don't understand, says the man. And seems about to say more.

— Really, said Nadia. It's fine. I think we assumed that Alison would have told you. But it's fine. I mean, it's not something, well, Alison does what she wants I suppose.

She stands up. She keeps on talking. He hesitates, and then stands up as well.

— She's been quite good with us really. I mean, I've had landlords that were far worse. I mean, immeasurably worse. She's not great with getting stuff fixed, but she gets to it eventually. She's put the rent up on us just the once. She's a little eccentric, and

She moves towards the door. He follows her.

— she can be a bit random, scatty, not completely on it. But it's a price we're willing to pay for having a landlord who is vaguely human, you know,

She opens the door. He walks slowly past her, stands in the doorway and turns. He is clearly confused.

— and not wanting a cut of our entire fucking lives. I mean. She doesn't take the piss. You might have to wait a while before she has someone come to look at . . . you know, a dodgy tap or whatever, but she's all right. For a landlord. Doesn't actually give a shit. But isn't obnoxious about it. At some point she'll probably kick us all out and sell the place for seventy billion quid and that'll be the end of that. But anyway.

She gives him a weak hug.

— Look I'm really sorry if I've . . .

— No, really, please, don't worry about it. Let us know if you need anything. Or need a hand with moving stuff at the weekend. We'll be here. And come down and say hello any time, ok?

— Of course. Really good to meet you.

— Let's all be friends, she says, and shuts the door.

The flat is not the same shape as theirs. He stands in a small hallway. He puts his keys on a shelf over a radiator. Everything white. Except a small round wooden table in a corner, on which stands an empty plant pot. The floor a blond wood laminate. He stays where he finds himself, staring at nothing, his lips slightly parted, an expression on his face. Some sort of expression. There is a door to his left, into a large bedroom. A double wardrobe takes up one whole wall. One of its four doors is a mirror. Opposite it is a large window looking down into the garden. There is what appears to be a blackout blind but it is not down and the room is bright and warm. The window is open. A fly buzzes against the inside of the glass, trapped by the central vertical strut. Divider. What that thing is called. That part of the window. The wardrobe is closed. On the bed are piles of clothes and books, several pairs of shoes, an open suitcase. Towels neatly folded in a pile on the floor. A stack of magazines. More books. Boxes filled with things that people bring with them.

The young man is still standing with his back to the door of the flat. The expression has gone.

The walls in the bedroom, white. The floor the same as the hallway. There is a small bathroom too, directly opposite where the young man stands. He sighs and takes off his vest and steps out of his flip-flops. He walks to the right, into a large living room and kitchen, wiping his torso with the vest which he then drops onto a dark sofa. The window is open here as well, and the blind up. He squints, blows out a breath of air, walks across the room, leans over a desk that is covered in books and papers and pulls the blind down. At the other end of the room there is a kitchen alcove and he goes there and sits on a stool at the counter which divides it from the living room and opens a laptop. There is a carpet in the living room, dark blue, laminate in the kitchen, the same as the hallway and bedroom. There are boxes on the floor. In the kitchen all the cupboards are open. He types into Google.

Karl Peppy

He reads the results but does not click on any of them.

Karl and Peppy

Same.

Carl and Peppy

Same.

Carl and Peppi

Same

87 Denman Road

A Shock

Same

Karl Peppi Peckham Camberwell death

He clicks the first result. It is a story about a couple falling to their deaths from the tenth floor of a nearby block of flats. He goes back. The second result is about a teenage boy, stabbed. He looks at *Images* for *Karl Peppi Peckham Camberwell death*. The boy. Buildings. Police. In the kitchen there is a humming fridge. There are jars on a counter top. There is a spoon on the floor. There are more books.

He pulls a phone out of his pocket and puts it on the counter and slowly types a message. He stops several times and stares into space. Sighs. Rubs his hand over his chest.

Hi Alison. Really love the flat thanks for taking the table away. Had a slightly weird conversation with the girls downstairs. Don't know if I said something wrong but they seem upset when i asked about the previous tenants. They said they they thought you told me? But I don't know about what. Am slightly concerned. Can you let me know what that's about? Thanks! David.

He sends it. He gets up and goes to the bathroom.

While he is gone, while David is gone, the phone buzzes against the counter top, slides a little. Nothing else happens.

The light is much dimmer. So it is morning. It is cooler in the flat. The bed has nothing on it now. All those things are on the floor. The bed has been slept in. There is a glass of water on the small side table. There are cables. A tablet. A box of tissues. A book lies face down. Somewhere outside there is hammering that starts and stops. Starts. Stops.

In the kitchen area David is making coffee. There are two mugs. A woman is sitting on the sofa in the living room, watching him. He has put croissants on a plate. Milk in a small jug, sugar in a matching bowl. On a tray. The kettle is boiling and he is speaking loudly.

— I mean sometimes I have to go in on a Saturday, but not . . . not often. If there's a new campaign . . . there's always some last-minute panic. Printers. Delivery. Website disasters.

— Campaign?

The kettle clicks off.

— Yeah, product launch or . . . there can be a few during the year. Different things. Oh I've made this pretty strong, I hope that's all right.

He is filling a cafetière and speaking at a normal volume now.

— Strong is good.

He carries it over and sets it on the low table in front of her. Coffee table.

— So, yeah, we sometimes have a bit of a panic on. Not just now though. Everything is bobbing along.

He brings the tray with everything else on it.

— Oh, this is very nice David, thank you. I should drop in regular.

He laughs.

— You'd be welcome.

He sits beside her.

— What sort of products then?

He is wearing a red T-shirt. The same shorts and flip-flops. She is older. White. Perhaps in her fifties. She has shoulder-length fair hair. She wears a black blouse. White trousers. There is a little pile of mobile phone, wallet, keys, a couple of envelopes, and a notebook and pen on the table in front of her. A bag lies on the floor at her feet. His face flickers something and resettles.

— Could be anything. Let's see. We did a new range of sushi

for Sainsbury's last month. Before that there was a coffee maker, a yoghurt thing that
— Lots of food.
— Yeah. New supermarket lines mostly. Can be pretty dull really if

Outside, the garden is in shade but the heat is coming. The cat is sitting on the boundary wall on the right, looking into the garden next door. Behind her, in front of the other house which shares the big garden, a man is standing on the grass with his hands behind his back, walking very slowly, looking at the plants. Occasionally he leans forward or stoops down to see something, or to reach out a hand and touch a flower or a leaf. He seems content. He turns and looks back towards the house. The other house, his house. The one next door. Then he swings slowly back around, his eyes running over the windows where David sits talking, and down, past the cat on the wall, to look again at the flowers. All these flowers. Look at all these flowers. He is like a bee. Moving from flower to flower. But all he does is smile, and look, and sometimes one hand will touch a stem. Happy.
— Yes, well, they disappeared.
— They disappeared?

David is smiling at her. He scratches his shoulder, shifts slightly forward on the sofa.
— Yes love. Vanished.

She smiles too. He laughs, looks at her quizzically.
— I mean that's the truth of it. We don't know where they went to. Nobody seems to know where they went to. Nobody really knows anything at all. It doesn't affect you though, I mean, in case you are worried about that. The flat is yours, contract's done, all the rest of it. If they show up. Well they won't. But if

they were to, they don't live here anymore. Locks have been
changed actually. Your door and the front door.

— But what do you mean they disappeared?

The woman folds her arms. Sighs.

— Well, it was February. Quite late on I think. I mean, we
didn't notice for ages. That was part of the problem, trying to
work out when exactly they'd last been seen. Anyway. Laura and
Nadia couldn't get in touch with them. So they asked me. I come
knocking. Texting. Phoning. Nothing. I knock again. A Wednesday night it was, and at this stage Laura and Nadia haven't seen
them for a week or more. So I am a little concerned. And I really
am an idiot, shouldn't have done this, but I let myself in. Of
course it's only when I'm standing in the hallway that I think, you
know, well, what if it's the worst? Not sure I'd be ready for that
at all. So I turned on my heel

She laughs.

— and I went and got Archie from opposite. You meet Archie
yet?

— No not yet.

— Anyway he thinks I'm barmy but he hasn't seen them
either, so we come in together, you should have seen us, clutching on to each other like such babies, and we look around and of
course the place is empty. And it's a bit of a mess, but no more
than you'd expect with those boys. So I just assumed they'd gone
on holiday and not told anyone. Next thing I know the police are
here.

— Shit.

— Well, just because Laura and Nadia had been on to them.
And I have to tell you David, this is a big deal for those two. For
Laura and Nadia. But honest to god I don't think anyone else
really thinks it's any great mystery at all. I mean, the police

couldn't find them. But they weren't really interested because they couldn't find anything that, you know, suggested a crime. And there were no passports or phones here. The laptop was gone. No sign of anything bad happening at all. Just messy. Clothes lying around. State of the bathroom. But there was no food left in the cupboards. Or no . . . you know, nothing that would go off. Oh some mouldy bread I think. But it looked like they'd cleared out, though they did leave of lot of stuff – TV, pictures,

She looks around the room.

— couple of terrible paintings they had, vases and lamps. All in storage now.

She looks at him again.

— And David, I've told Laura and Nadia this but I don't think they want to hear it, I don't think they've quite realised, but Karl and Peppi owed me five month's rent.

— Oh.

— Yes. And when the police heard that, well they just left it really. They said they'd stay in touch but of course I haven't heard anything more.

She laughs again.

— Doing a runner is not the sort of crime they're interested in. Though they did tell me to report it formally, for the small-claims court, if I wanted to go that way. But there's no point is there. So I'm annoyed, you know. Laura and Nadia though. Genuine upset.

— What about families? Or work?

— Oh the girls looked into all that. Peppi is Greek. No one had any contact details for his family. Karl is from Cumbria or Cornwall or something. And he left home, or more likely was kicked out of home, when he was sixteen, seventeen, something like that. The girls did some Facebooking and emailing but nothing came of it.

David shakes his head. He is leaning back in the sofa now. They are both leaning back, turned towards each other. They take sips of coffee but the croissants haven't been touched. The hammering outside stopped a long time ago. Probably when the kettle was boiling. The happy man has gone in. The cat is two gardens away. She is perched on the roof of a shed, watching another cat who does not know she is there. It is like this.

— And work?

She laughs, this time putting her coffee mug down and pulling her hair back from her face.

— Don't know where Peppi was working. I had details on the paperwork. But it was out of date of course. Restaurant in Waterloo. Laura and Nadia knew the name of another place he'd been but that drew a blank as well. Karl had been out of work. I knew this because he was in bar management and I know a couple of people who knew him, or knew of him, and he had been in a place in Vauxhall and he'd been fired, the middle of last year. And I heard about that when it happened. And that's when the rent stopped. Or shortly after. Probably hadn't worked since then. Or at least, nothing regular. He worked the bar at a couple of clubs on busy weekends. Didn't tell me anything of course, why would he? The excuses were always daft. A friend who needed surgery in Portugal or Spain or god knows. Then something about another friend stealing money. Then Peppi saying he hadn't been paid. Then they gave me some money the month before. January. Because of course I had started to talk about eviction. They gave me one month's worth, so I backed off. But they knew they were on borrowed time here David. This isn't a hotel.

David sighs. He scratches his shoulder. He picks up one of

the croissants and takes a bite and flakes of pastry cascade down his T-shirt. He puts it back on the plate. He pours each of them some more coffee.

— Nice boys. Liked them. But a bit chaotic. So I think it's all fairly obvious really.

— Yeah, he says. What was he fired for? Karl?

She smiles at him.

— I wondered that too, but it's nothing. He had a row with the owner, one of the owners. I know this guy. Awful bully. I'd heard at the time that it had been about pay. Not getting paid. And it was. Karl got stroppy about it. Refused to work a shift until it was sorted, and that's enough for this guy.

He looks down at his T-shirt and starts picking up flakes of pastry and putting them in his mouth.

— Stupid thing for them to do really. I mean. I need to get my rent. I'm not a charity. But I could have worked something out with them. Some landlords would have had them out on their ear as soon as they found out about the job. But I didn't do that David. I gave them time to sort it out. Could even have helped, but they never asked. Which is sad. And what do they do now? I don't know. I don't know how they start again. Bank accounts. References. Jobs. Any of that. I've no idea. I've a claim in against them of course. Had to. Credit records are ruined. But that's not my fault. And Laura and Nadia heartbroken.

She pressed a button on her phone to see the time.

— And, I don't want to say this really David, but I think sometimes that they would rather that Karl and Peppi were dead in a ditch somewhere than have to face up to the fact that they weren't nearly as close to them as they thought.

David looked at her.

— Well, she said. That's harsh isn't it? It is. But they've obsessed about it quite a bit more than is healthy I think.

He brushes the smallest crumbs away.

— That's a shame, he says.

He talks on the phone, telling someone that he has dead men in his flat and that's why it's cheap. He is laughing. He is laughing about that idea. He says their names, and he asks the person he is talking to whether they have heard those names, and then he asks about something else.

In the shower he carefully examines the tiles at head height. He washes his hair. The bathroom is private.

He puts books on the shelves in the living room, and spends a long time rearranging them. He tries to make the desk sit flush to the windowsill but it is slightly too big, and there is a gap of a few centimetres. He peels an orange and leaves the segments on the counter top and puts one in his mouth whenever he passes by while he unpacks the boxes in the hallway and in the bedroom and puts things where he wants them to be.

Finally the only unpacked boxes left are in the bedroom. The blind is down in the living room. It is very hot. All the blinds are down. He sends some messages on his phone. He laughs at a reply he gets, and spends a few minutes texting back and forth with someone. Then he goes to the bedroom and takes off his clothes and lies on the bed and masturbates, looking all the time at the phone in his hand. Then he has another shower and puts on clean clothes.

He reads. He just sits in the living room reading a book.

Downstairs in the garden the cat is chasing flies, a butterfly. She looks at the flat where Nadia and Laura live.

*

Someone comes to the flat. A man about the same age as David. They kiss and hug like friends, and David shows him around and they talk about the flat and about Karl and Peppi and about Alison. David tells him all about it, and about Laura and Nadia downstairs.

— They sound a little intense, says his friend.

— They are a little intense.

— Maybe they killed them. Buried them in the garden.

They both laugh at this idea as if it is funny.

Later David changes again and they leave.

He doesn't come back until almost five the next morning. He is alone. His eyes are red. Yellow. He takes off his clothes and sleeps on top of the bed, sweating a little. He twitches in his sleep. In his sleep he covers himself with the duvet. He sleeps until early afternoon. When he wakes he spends a long time on his phone.

His kitchen is empty. He drinks two glasses of water. With the second glass he swallows a large blue grey pill that he takes from a foil in a box in a cupboard. Then he sniffs at his body and puts on his shorts and tee shirt from the day before, and a pair of sandals, and leaves. He closes the door of the flat. Then there is a pause before he turns the key in the second lock. All the windows are closed. The flat is warm, the air still, and nothing seems to move.

David watches some shows on his laptop. Reads. He has bought food and put it in the fridge. Vegetables – broccoli, green beans, red and yellow peppers, mushrooms, an avocado, an aubergine, some chillis. Also cheese, a bottle of white wine. Two tubs of yoghurt. A small lemon cake. Orange juice. He has bought rice and pasta. Tinned tomatoes, tinned beans, olive oil, spices, eggs, a bag of bagels, and a bar of chocolate which he has left on a shelf in one of the cupboards. It has begun to soften but he hasn't noticed. He has eaten a meal of mushrooms and onions and broccoli and rice. He has a glass of wine now.

He makes a phone call to his mother. He tells her about the flat. About how nice it is. He describes the rooms. He says that the flat has five rooms, and names them. *Hallway. Bedroom. Bathroom. Living room. Kitchen.* This is not true. He describes the garden. He tells her about his downstairs neighbours. He talks about how hot it is in London. He asks her questions about a sister, and about an aunt. They talk for almost twenty minutes and he ends the call by telling his mother that he loves her. He finishes his wine and gets himself a glass of water and puts another show on his laptop and holds his phone in his hand, and his attention moves between the show and his phone, and every few minutes he takes a sip of the water. The blinds are open now in the living room and the sun is going down. He yawns. He puts the phone aside and turns off the show and watches some pornography on his laptop for a couple of minutes before standing up to close the blinds. He looks out over the garden, and over the walls to the grid of gardens beyond. The dark is coming up out of the ground. The sky is a deep blue. He snaps the blinds shut and watches the pornography and masturbates. When he ejaculates he pinches some of his semen in his fingers and puts it in his mouth, his eyes still on the screen. After a while he goes for a shower. He puts on fresh boxer shorts and goes to bed. He reads his book for a short while and then turns off his bedside lamp.

The flat is very quiet. He turns over and settles and his breathing slows and he falls asleep. His phone is charging by his bed. In the living room his laptop is charging. The chocolate in the cupboard has partially melted. A mouse behind the plaster in the wall pauses and scratches for a while, then moves to a tiny hole that leads to the flat downstairs where Nadia and Laura live with their nameless cat who is a good mouser.

The flat has five room names. But only four rooms. It is a strange mistake to make.

An alarm. A melody which begins softly and becomes louder. David groans and then opens his eyes, and he looks startled. He stares at the window, and then at the door. He sits up, picks up his phone, and the alarm stops. He curses. Lies down again. After five minutes the same alarm starts again. David sits upright, turns it off. Looks at the door. He throws back the duvet and gets up. He goes to the bathroom.

In the kitchen there are unwashed dishes. His laptop is fully charged. The chocolate is hard again but misshapen. There is the loud sound of the shower from the bathroom, and in the kitchen the hum of the fridge and in the distance, drilling starts.

David comes out of the bathroom in a towel. He puts his boxer shorts in a laundry basket in the bedroom. He stands in front of the mirror in the wardrobe door and takes the towel off and looks at himself as he dries his hair and his back and his legs. He dresses in boxer shorts, a blue shirt, grey trousers, socks, black shoes. He goes back to the bathroom. He curses, then he comes back to the bedroom and combs his hair in front of the mirror there. He goes back to the bathroom. He comes back again with a bottle of hair gel. He squeezes a small drop in the palm of his left hand and throws the bottle on the bed and with the fingers of his right hand he pinches the hair gel from his palm and puts it into his hair, looking at himself carefully in the mirror. In the little hallway there is nothing. In the living room and kitchen there is just the morning air and the sound of drilling which starts and stops, starts and stops. David walks through the flat to the fridge. His shoes are loud on the linoleum. He pours himself an orange juice. He swallows another blue grey pill. He looks around.

— Oranges, he says.

He cuts a bagel in two and holds the halves and looks around.

— Oh for fuck's sake. Toaster.

He smiles. He opens the grill and looks in. He sighs. He puts the halves of the bagel on a plate. He looks in the fridge. He sighs again. He puts the plate with the bagel on it in the fridge and closes it. He looks at his phone. He walks across the room and unplugs the laptop and puts it in a bag that has been sitting on the chair in front of the desk. He puts some papers that have been sitting on the desk in there as well. The desk is slightly too big to sit flush against the windowsill. He stares into the bag for a moment. Then he pulls the blind up. He takes the bag and leaves the room. He immediately comes back, sighing again, and lowers the blind, muttering unintelligibly. He goes out to the little hallway. He rummages in his bag, pulls out some headphones and puts them around his neck and plugs them into his phone. Then he opens the door of the flat and goes out and closes the door behind him. There is a small pause and then he locks the second lock.

He is at home and cooking when there is a knock at the door. He pulls on a T-shirt. It is Nadia. He asks her in and apologises for the state of the flat but the flat is tidier than it has been since he arrived. All the boxes are gone. Everything is put away. A new vase sits on the small table that was in the hall but which is now beside the bookshelves. The vase is empty. Nadia tells David that he should pick some flowers from the garden. She tells him the flat is tidier than she's ever seen it before. Only his desk is untidy, but she doesn't say this.

— I just wanted to invite you to dinner really. Oh, not tonight, Friday night? If you fancy it.

David doesn't say anything. He is frowning, looking at the vase.

— Not to worry if you can't. A couple of other friends are coming over.

— That would be great. I'm just hesitating because I have half an arrangement for Friday night. But it's not, you know

— Oh that's cool.

— It's not confirmed. Half date sort of thing. Mightn't happen.

— Oh well you can't miss that. First date?

David glances at the window.

— Yes. Well. Yes.

— Ok, well maybe another time.

— I mean, I'm not sure it'll happen. Can I confirm one way or the other with you tomorrow?

— Sure. You want my number?

They stand at the kitchen counter and Nadia tells David her number and he puts it into his phone while she looks at his books.

— What are you making? she asks him.

— Uh. Some pasta. Just with broccoli. Beans. Pesto.

— Are you vegetarian?

— Yes. Sorry.

— No, no, so am I. Laura will eat seafood sometimes but that's it. So it'll be something veggie on Friday. Burritos or something.

— That'd be great. I've texted you, so you have mine.

— Oh, it's downstairs. Anyway, I'll leave you to it.

In the hallway she apologises to David for the previous time, when he was in their flat. He smiles and tells her that there is nothing to apologise for, and says that Alison told him what had happened. She says that it's still a bit weird, especially for Laura, the idea that their friends have vanished. He says he understands. She says goodbye and he closes the door. David turns and looks annoyed. He pulls off his T-shirt and throws it towards the bedroom door as he walks back into the kitchen.

How many rooms are in the flat? There are five. There is the hallway. The bedroom. The bathroom. The living room. The kitchen. That is five. But the living room and the kitchen are combined. They are one room. So there are four rooms in the flat.

No. There are five.

The fifth room is hidden.

It is dark. There is music playing softly somewhere. The door to the living room and kitchen is closed. The small light over the sink in the bathroom is on, and the door is open. The light in the hallway is on.

There is suddenly the loud noise of the buzzer. There is a laugh from the bedroom, and David appears. He picks up the intercom and says hello. There is a muffled voice and David says 'first floor' in response and then opens the door of the flat and waits. He puts his hand on his hair. Looks down, flicks something from his chest. A man appears.

— David?

— Yeah. Come in, come in.

A Shock

— Hi. I'm Ravi.

— Nice to meet you. You found it ok.

— Sure, easy.

They are smiling at each other. David closes the door and they kiss. The man is wearing jeans and a black T-shirt. David is wearing a white T-shirt and navy shorts. They go to the bedroom, which is neat and tidy. David's laptop is on the bedside table. Ravi tells David that he has a nice flat. David thanks him. They undress while talking about sexual things. When they are naked Ravi kneels in front of David and takes his cock into his mouth. He caresses David's chest and stomach and back. David puts his hand on Ravi's head and moans quietly. There is music playing on the laptop but it is a small, restricted sound, tinny and flat. Ravi sucks David's cock for a while, and then David pulls Ravi to his feet and they kiss deeply and he runs his hands over Ravi's body. They get onto the bed and kiss more before David kneels on the bed and lowers his head to Ravi's cock and puts it in his mouth. In the hallway there is a fly. In the living room there are two. In the bedroom there is a large moth behind the blind, which is closed. The moth is trying to get out but can't. Ravi and David have sex for about half an hour. Eventually David comes inside Ravi, and Ravi comes at the same time, on his own stomach. David pinches some of Ravi's semen in his fingers and puts it in his mouth and groans and Ravi laughs. They shower separately. David lies on the bed naked and looks at things on his laptop while Ravi showers. When Ravi comes back in he starts getting dressed. David offers Ravi a glass of wine but he declines. David puts on his shorts, and they kiss in the hallway again and Ravi thanks David and leaves. They don't say anything about meeting again. After Ravi is gone David sits in the living room

183

and calls someone and tells them about Ravi. He says that Ravi is sexy, but not very friendly. He tells his friend that he is still horny and he laughs.

A friend of David's arrives. It is evening. He looks the same age as David. He has darker skin and a shaved head. He has tattoos. David has no tattoos. He is a little taller than David. He is wearing jeans and a black vest, sandals. He has sunglasses but he has taken them off and they sit on top of his bag which is on the kitchen counter. David points things out to him.

— Storage is great. There's loads of cupboards. I'm not even using half of them.

— It's lovely. Much nicer than the last place.

— Isn't it?

— New toaster.

— Haven't even used it. Threw out mouldy bagels this morning. Been getting a smoothie on the walk to work.

— Health.

— Health.

— Chocolate though.

His friend is holding the bar of chocolate that was in the cupboard.

— I forgot about that.

— It's gone weird. It's melted and

— Been there since I moved in.

— gone all flat and hardened again.

— Bin it.

The friend looks around. The bin is under the counter. He throws the chocolate in.

— What were the names of the guys?

— What guys?

— The ones who lived here.

— Karl and Eppi. Or Peppi. Peppi I think.

— It's a bit weird.

— Nah not really. They did a runner. I mean I suppose doing a runner is a bit weird. But it's not weird like the *Marie Celeste* sort of weird.

— The what?

David laughs.

— It was a ship. Found floating somewhere with no one on it. Cups of tea on the table still warm. Food on the plates. No one aboard.

— When was this?

— Oh eighteen something. I can't remember.

His friend is smiling.

— It's a novel?

— No, no. It happened. You've never heard of the *Marie Celeste*?

They cook a meal together. David does most of the cooking but his friend chops mushrooms and garlic and opens wine. David doesn't eat very much. They talk a lot about sex but they are not sexual with each other. David tells his friend about Ravi. David says that he's been on the apps more than usual but that he's been too busy to hook up. He says that anyway he prefers to go to other guys' places. David tells him that Ravi has been the only guy he's had over since he moved in.

This is not true.

David is standing on a chair. It is his desk chair from the living room. It is placed in front of the mirror in the bedroom. He is barefoot, wearing only shorts. He is putting a coat into the top part of the wardrobe. The coat is folded. He rises on his toes and stretches to put it in towards the back of wardrobe. Then he steps off the chair and takes a small pile of jumpers from the bed and steps up onto the chair again and puts the jumpers in as well. He steps down and goes out of the room. By the bedside on the window side of the bed is the small table that used to be in the hallway and which David then moved to the living room, the table which had a vase on it when Nadia called. David has moved it to the bedroom and it sits in the corner by the window, and on it now sits a large silver electric fan which isn't on. In the hallway there are four empty boxes. A rat runs through the garden, at the foot of the wall. The cat leaps away from its path and turns and waits, and tentatively goes back to find it but it's gone now, through a tangle of shrubs in the corner and a gap between bricks into the next garden and over towards a house with a boarded-up basement. In the kitchen there is the new toaster. The vase now sits on one of the bookshelves in the living room.

David comes back into the bedroom with a bag. It bulges with what looks like scarves, hats perhaps. Through the plastic of the bag it is possible to see the outline of a hand. It is a glove. He stands on the chair and puts the bag into the top of the wardrobe. He farts, and laughs. Then he steps down and half runs out of the room.

The fan came in a box and the toaster came in a box, and each of these boxes had come in other bigger boxes. David looks at all these boxes in the hallway and sighs. He folds his arms and walks slowly into the living room and over to his desk. He takes a sip from a mug that sits there and he looks out the window and sees the cat sitting off to the left staring into the bushes. It is early morning. He leans over his desk and looks at something on his laptop. He hums. He coughs a couple of times. The desk does not sit flush with the windowsill. He stands up straight and looks outside again, at the cat who is still in the same place, at the gardens with their matted green and yellow trees and hedges, bushes, plants, and he looks at the windows of the houses on all sides. He finishes whatever he is drinking. Coffee probably. Yes, there is a small cafetière on the kitchen counter. David hums and sways a little. He swings his hips, sings a line of a song. Then he turns and walks to the kitchen and puts the cafetière and the mug in the sink.

He flattens the fan box and the toaster box and leaves them by the door of the flat. Then he flattens the bigger boxes and takes them into the bedroom. He moves the chair to another part of the wardrobe and stands on it and opens another door to the top part of the wardrobe. He looks in at two suitcases and several flattened boxes. There is no room. He steps down, moves the chair back to where it was, picks up the new boxes, steps up on the chair, and sticks his arm into the wardrobe and lifts the pile of jumpers and the coat and lifts the boxes to slide them underneath. Then he stops. He doesn't move for a few seconds. He lowers his right arm holding the new boxes, and then he slowly pulls his left arm out of the wardrobe, letting the jumpers and the coat down again. In his left hand there is a folder. It is A4 sized, a pale green.

David steps down off the chair. He puts the boxes down on the bed and sits on the chair and opens the folder. It is full.

— Oh my god, he says.

He leafs through some of the contents.

— Oh my fucking god, he says.

And then he laughs, loudly, and for quite some time.

David goes out of the flat. He stops before he has closed the door, making a sound with his teeth. He leaves the door open and goes back in to the flat, into the bedroom. There is silence and he is gone. There is nothing here. The landing is bare and the stair is slightly to the right of the door to the flat. In front of it, slightly to the right. On the same landing there is another door to a different flat. The stair going up is on the left. The banister is a dark wood. There is a worn thin carpet that covers the stairs and the landing and it is of no particular colour. David comes back out of the flat, wearing a T-shirt now, and flip-flops. He closes the door. He holds his keys in his hand. He doesn't lock the second lock.

He starts down the stairs, then he stops. He has gone down three steps. Now he is standing still and staring into space. He takes another step. He makes a sound again with his teeth, or perhaps with his lips or his tongue, a clicking sort of sound. He starts to turn around. Then stops. Turns back again. Then he sits down on the stairs.

The carpet is a sort of bluish grey. David's legs are smooth. The hairs are light and fair.

At the bottom of the stairs there are leaflets and menus and free magazines lying around on the floor. There are two umbrellas leaning against the wall in the corner. There is a box beside them. There is a bicycle. There is the noise of a siren and the planes keep coming. David is just sitting there. He is looking at nothing. Near the top of the stairs. There is a doormat that is the colour of sand.

David stands up and walks slowly down the rest of the stairs. He pinches his nostrils. Then he coughs, clearing his throat. At the bottom of the stairs he turns and walks towards the door that leads to the garden and to the downstairs flat. He moves slowly. He stops at the door to the flat. He strokes his beard and his neck and knocks at the door and then takes a step back.

— David.

— Hello.

— Come in, come in.

— Sorry to bother you.

— No bother.

He pauses in the doorway, but then he goes in. He doesn't close the door behind him. He folds his arms.

— You want a coffee?

— No thanks.

It is Laura. She is wearing a dressing gown. She goes and sits in the armchair. She looks curiously at David.

— Close the door. Come in. Something wrong?

David looks at the door as if he had forgotten about it, and takes a step to it and closes it slowly.

— No, nothing wrong. I just have a bit of a weird question to ask.

— Ok.

— Do you have a picture of Karl and Peppi that I could have?

Laura frowns.

— I have loads yeah. Why?

— Well that's the thing. I can't really say. I mean. By which I mean that there isn't really a reason. I just, it's just that I am in what used to be their place, you know? And I know that you miss them a lot. So there's sort of an energy. No, not energy, I hate that sort of talk, that language. But the fact of them is, it looms large. In the flat. And just generally, you know. And I don't know what they look like. I don't have a picture of them in my head. There's this faceless fact. Of them. And I'd like to put faces to them. Does that make sense? Any sense?

Laura looks at him for a moment without saying anything. Then she looks down and up again.

— It makes a lot of sense actually.

She stands up, smiling.

— It's sort of beautiful, Laura says.

She walks over to David and puts her arms around him. He seems surprised. He hesitates and then embraces her lightly in return.

— They are lovely people, says Laura. I'm so glad you want to be friends with them as well.

David's face, invisible to Laura as she holds on to him, makes an exaggerated expression of surprise or horror, comic horror, wide-eyed, his tongue sticking out slightly. She lets go of him eventually and goes to get her phone, telling David that she is not as worried now as she had been. That having him in the flat has somehow calmed her down quite a lot. She expects that she will hear from them eventually, though maybe not for some time, but that it is pretty clear that they'd needed to do what they'd done, and that it is pointless trying to second guess them or to worry. David tells her this is good. A good thing.

On her phone she shows him various pictures of the two men. Sometimes one or the other alone, and with either Laura or Nadia or both. But mostly the two men, together. Some of the photos have been taken in the garden, some in Laura and Nadia's flat. Some in the upstairs flat. Together they pick the best photos, the nicest photos, and Laura sends them all from her phone to David's phone. They chat for a while about things. About the flat. About his work.

The cat is outside. On the path outside, listening.

Her work. She asks him what he's working on at the moment, and he tells her some things about that, some brand names. He seems impatient. He talks quite fast, and repeats himself. He turns down a second offer of coffee and stands up and tells Laura that he has to go. She walks after him to the door and he turns in the open doorway and she kisses him on the cheek and smiles at him and he nods and smiles back at her and goes. In the hall he runs his hands over his face. He jogs back up the stairs and goes back into the flat. In. He locks the second lock from the inside. He walks into the bedroom and stands there. The contents of the folder are spilled across the bed. They are photographs. Photographic prints, paper prints, some polaroids. All of them show Karl and Peppi having sex.

He checks the phone against the photos. He lays them out on the bed. Karl, he says. Peppi, he says. A photo of one man, lying on his back – Karl, he says. The other man, his face covered in cum, laughing, Peppi. He lays them out on the bed. He takes off his clothes and starts to masturbate. He goes through the photos. There are hundreds of them. He stops on photos showing three men together. He looks at the room
— Jesus.
He lays out a series of photos in which three men can be seen on the bed. One fucking another while sucking the cock of a standing man, who is crouching so that the man who is being fucked can eat his ass. In the mirror there is a reflection of a fourth man, naked, with an erection, holding the phone that is taking the photos. David groans. He looks like he is about to come but he doesn't. He looks at more photographs. He continues to masturbate. He spits on his hand. He walks around the room looking at it from different angles. He moans loudly. Saying *fuck* sometimes, or *Jesus, oh my god*. He starts to feel his arse. He is rummaging in the bedside drawer.
This is private.
In the hallway there are two ants. They are leaving. In the kitchen the toaster looks like it still has not been used. There are

dirty dishes in the sink. The bin is full and there are flies. Two flies. Three. The blinds are open but the window is closed. David stays in his room with the photographs, moaning, for a long time. When he comes out he is covered in sweat. He walks naked into the kitchen and drinks two large glasses of water. His cock is still hard but it softens as he drinks. He burps and laughs. Then he runs his hand over the sweat on his chest. He curses and goes to the bathroom and after a couple of minutes there is the sound of the shower. All the photos are on the bed. A dildo lies on the floor. There two different bottles of lubricant on the bed. The pillows are piled up. There is a smear of lube on the wardrobe door mirror. There is all this.

When he comes out of the shower he dries himself in the bedroom, looking at the photos, stroking his cock a little. Then he puts all the photos back in the folder. He puts on boxer shorts. He takes the dildo to the bathroom and when he comes back he dries it on the towel he's thrown on the bed. Then he puts it in the bedside drawer. He puts the bottles of lubricant in there too. He hasn't noticed the smear on the mirror. He pulls up the blind and opens the window. He sees the body of the large moth lying on the windowsill and makes a face. He looks around. His gaze rests a moment on the tissues by the bed. But then he walks out of the bedroom to the kitchen. He takes a sheet of kitchen paper. Then he has another drink of water. Then he looks around for something. He goes back into the bedroom, the kitchen paper balled up in his hand. He looks around. He lifts and shakes the duvet and his phone falls to the floor. He curses and picks it up. He walks back to the kitchen and starts looking at his phone. He looks and scrolls and touches it with his finger. He sits on a stool by the counter. After a few minutes doing this he gets up and goes to his desk and opens his laptop. He looks around. Then he goes back to the bedroom. He picks up the chair from in front of the wardrobe. Then he puts it down again. He picks up the folder with the photographs and opens the main part of the wardrobe and puts it on a shelf under some T-shirts. Then he picks up the balled piece of kitchen towel and looks at it, frowning. He carries it to the kitchen and puts it in the bin. He sees the flies. He makes a face. He takes the top off the bin and pulls the black bag out and ties it. He takes it to the door of the flat. He looks around. He puts the bag down. Then he goes into the bedroom and looks around. He picks up his keys which are under the T-shirt he was wearing earlier. He puts the T-shirt in the laundry basket and then glances over to the window. There is the sound of children shouting. He goes out to the hallway and picks up the rubbish bag and opens the door of the flat. He leaves it open and he takes the bag out and then stops at the top of the stairs and puts the bag down and turns around and comes back inside and goes into the bedroom. He opens the laundry basket and takes out the T-shirt that he had just put in and puts it on. Then he picks up his shorts from the floor and puts them on, and finds his flip-flops and puts them on as well and then he looks around. He walks around. Then he pats his pocket and takes the keys out and goes back to the hallway and out of the flat and he takes the rubbish bag downstairs and goes out of the building and after a minute he comes back into the building and he jogs up the stairs and goes into the flat and closes the door and locks the second lock and then he goes into the bedroom and takes off the flip-flops and the T-shirt and the shorts and the boxer shorts and he glances at the window and then walks over to it. There is the sound of children shouting. He looks out. He can't see them. They are in a garden that is not visible except for its tree and its hedges, impossible to pick out against all the other trees, all the other hedges. He glances down and sees the body of the large moth lying on the windowsill and makes a face. He looks around. His gaze rests a moment on the tissues by the bed. But then he walks out of the bedroom to the kitchen. He takes a sheet of kitchen paper. Then he has another drink of water. Then he looks around for something. He goes back into the bedroom, the kitchen paper balled up in his hand. He looks around.

This goes on for hours.

He sleeps late. He wakes up suddenly and looks at his phone and his voice makes a shrill noise and then he says *What!* loudly. He sits up in bed and stares at his phone. He touches the screen. After several minutes he makes a phone call.

— Alex. Yeah hi. I'm late. Yeah I know. Something came up, family. Yes I know. A family thing. No nothing, nothing bad, nothing, not an emergency, but I had to spend the whole morning on the phone trying to get it sorted and. Yes I know. I apologise. No, no one is dead. I'll explain when I see you. I'm on my way now. Yes. Ok. Ok. I know. Did it go ok? I'm really sorry about this. Ok. See you soon.

He gets dressed and leaves very quickly. He doesn't lock the second lock.

There is the sound of a key. In the second lock. Rattling. Then there is a pause. Then a key is put into the first lock and the door opens and it is David standing there, looking puzzled. He glances around and then comes in. He closes the door behind him and locks the second lock. He looks confused and unhappy. He puts his bag down in the living room. He pulls up the blind and opens the window. He gets himself a drink of water. He sits down on the sofa. He spends a few minutes just staring into space. He takes off his shoes and pulls his knees up to his chest and sits with his arms around his legs, his face hidden. Then he sits cross legged. He moves his legs, swings his body one way and then the other, uncomfortable. Then he stands up frowning, and curses, and takes off his trousers and his socks and sits back on the sofa cross-legged. He folds his arms and looks down at the floor. He doesn't do anything for a few minutes.

The flies that were around the bin are not there any more. There is no black bag in the bin, but there is one on the counter top. One fly is dead on the kitchen floor. There are no more dirty dishes in the sink. There are clean dishes on the draining board. A second fly is buzzing against the glass of the open window. It needs to fly over the barrier of the window frame to get out of the window but it doesn't, it keeps on buzzing against the glass. In the bedroom the dead moth is still on the windowsill.

David makes a phone call.

— Hi Rob. Yeah. No, no. I'm just in. Had a shitty day. Jesus. No, no I'm ok. More or less.

He has a long, one-sided conversation with Rob. He tells him about sleeping late, about missing an event that he was supposed to be organising. He tells Rob that the event was important. That it was supposed to be followed by a meeting at which David was supposed to make a presentation, and he'd missed that as well. As he tells Rob the details of these things he sighs often and looks around the room. He tells him about all the people who were there. He tells him about his boss Alex and how Alex had told him that he had completely let the entire organisation down, that it had been a sort of betrayal, and that David thinks this language is ridiculous, and that there is no way that he, David, is *that* important to this campaign that they are launching, that Alex is being a prick, that there are others who have been more central, especially Marcia who had after all assembled . . . and here David trails off and curses and then tells Rob that he has forgotten to take his pill, and he stands up and goes to the kitchen while still talking, and he pours a second glass of water – the first is still on the coffee table in the living room – and he opens one of the cupboards and puts Rob on speaker phone and puts the phone down by the sink and he takes one of the small letter-sized boxes out of the cupboard and takes a foil of pills from the box and pops one of the pills out of the foil and swallows it with the water, and Rob asks him is he ok though, and David says that he is fine, that he's just pissed off, that Alex is being unprofessional and vindictive, and that if he can't deal with a member of staff having a personal emergency, you know, a family crisis, if he can't deal with that with courtesy and calm, without, you know, fucking exploding, then maybe he shouldn't, David says, maybe Alex shouldn't be running a team like theirs, and Rob asks him what family crisis, and David, who has left the phone on speaker by the sink and is looking in all the cupboards one by one, tells Rob that no, there wasn't actually a family crisis, but as far as Alex is concerned there is, or there was, a family crisis he means, so maybe, David says, maybe he, meaning David, should talk to someone in HR because this is, what this amounted to is bullying actually, and Rob tells him to calm down, to maybe have an early night and see what he thinks about it in the morning, and that he should, David that is, David should relax, that he sounds extremely stressed, and he asks whether he wants Rob to come over, and David laughs at this saying no he is absolutely fine, a little stressed maybe but Alex is being a prick, and Rob tells him again that he needs to calm down, and David tells him he is calm, but he lowers his voice which has become quite loud, and he stops looking in the cupboards and stands looking towards the window with his hand in his boxer shorts, and Rob says that he has to go, he has to have his dinner, and that he'll call David tomorrow, and David says ok and Rob cuts the call and David just stands there looking towards the window but his eyes are unfocused, and he takes his hand out of his boxer shorts and turns around and then takes off his T-shirt and his boxer shorts and leaves them on the floor and picks up his phone and touches the screen and there is a ringing tone and David touches the phone and the speaker goes off and he holds the phone to his ear and he stands in the kitchen gently playing with his cock and he says hello and then he has more or less the same conversation again with some other person.

He gets dressed. His shorts. His shoes. A T-shirt. He puts his phone in his pocket and looks at the door of the flat. He walks into the living room, the kitchen, the living room, the kitchen, the hallway, the bedroom. He looks at the bedroom and then he begins to tidy up. He sniffs at a towel and puts it in the laundry basket. He closes the door of the wardrobe. He stares at the mirror. Not at his own reflection but at the mirror, and then he goes to the laundry basket and takes the towel out again and goes to the mirror and wipes it clean. He sighs, mutters, sighs. He goes to the bathroom for a few minutes. He has a drink of water. He stares at the books on his shelves. He takes some from the floor and puts them back on the shelves. He goes into the kitchen and starts looking in the cupboards and touching his phone screen and saying things out loud in a voice that is both more cheerful and more harsh than his voice before.

— Bread. Chocolate. Snacks. Like crisps, nuts. Nuts. Crisps. Hummus. Bagels. Crisp sandwich. So sandwich bread. And bagels. Miso soup. Milk. Jesus, milk? Ok.

He opens the fridge.

— Milk. Yoghurt. Hummus. Orange. Orange juice. Some dessert things. Cakes.

He closes the fridge and the cupboards. The last cupboard door he closes swings a little on its hinges and knocks, makes a knocking sound, and David, who has turned away from it jumps, startled, and turns around and stares at it, at the cupboard door.

— Jesus.

He opens it and then flips it closed and it makes the same knocking sound, three raps very much like someone knocking on a door. David moves away from it, shaking his head. He puts his phone in his pocket and walks through the hallway and opens the door of the flat and goes out and closes the door behind him, and then the pause, and then he locks the second lock.

The cupboard door has always been like that. When Karl and Peppi lived in the flat whoever was in the kitchen would deliberately cause the sound to happen and the other one, sitting usually in the living room would say

— Come in.

There is a man, older than David, in the hallway. He is leaning his back against the closed door of the flat. David is naked and on his knees sucking the man's cock. The man pulls off a T-shirt. He gives David instructions. David stands up, turns around, bends over, and the man slides down the doorway. The light is on in the bedroom. The living room and kitchen are dark. David is moaning loudly. He is pulling at his buttocks. He loses his balance slightly and laughs, and the man slaps his arse and stands up and tells David to suck his cock again. This is private. On the little shelf over the radiator there is a bottle of poppers, lube. In the bedroom David's laptop is on the bedside table, playing pornography full screen, silently. It is night. It is very warm. The bed is made, the duvet neat. They are making a lot of noise. The cat can hear them. In the garden she is standing still, on the path by the house, her ears up. After a while the noise stops.

— That was great. Want to hang out for a while?

— Nah, I have to get back. Another time.

— Maybe we can get as far as the bedroom.

— Nah this is good. Sexy fucker.

He leaves without showering or even washing. David closes the door after him and smiles and then laughs, and takes a shower. Afterwards he sits on his bed naked, looking at his phone.

There is a knock at the door. Another knock. A long silence. Another knock, louder. Then Laura's voice

— David are you there?

Silence.

— David?

David comes back with a bag of shopping. He is pale and his skin is wet with sweat, and there are stains of sweat on his T-shirt at the collar and under the arms and at his shoulder blades.

— Jesus, he says, in the hallway, where he stands for a moment as if collecting himself, before putting down the bag and turning the key in the second lock and leaving it to hang there.

— What a fucking nightmare.

He goes into the bedroom and takes off his clothes. He looks around and then opens the laundry basket and takes out the towel and dries his skin. He wraps the towel around his waist and takes the bag from the hallway into the kitchen and puts things into the cupboards and the fridge. Then he makes himself a sandwich with crisps. He pours a glass of milk. He takes a bite of the sandwich and chews it slowly and then sips the milk. He goes and walks around the living room. He picks up a book and opens it and reads, and walks around the middle of the room. He doesn't finish the sandwich.

David is awake when the alarm goes off on his phone. He looks at it as if shocked. He picks it up and touches the screen and it goes quiet. He drops it on the bed.

— Fuck, he says.

He looks at his laptop. He goes back to what he was doing.

Later, he types a long email on his laptop while lying naked on his stomach on the bed. He reads it aloud. Then changes some things and reads a couple of sentences aloud. His voice is deeper. He works on it for almost an hour, tapping at his keyboard, reading, then tapping some more. Eventually he reads it all out and then sends it. It is to Alex. It is about bullying. His arm is bleeding.

It is the middle of the night. David is sitting naked on his bed. He is cross-legged, his back against the headboard. He has his laptop open beside him, and two closed books and the folder of photographs of Karl and Peppi, also closed. He is holding his phone in one hand and a third book in the other hand, and he is reading. He reads for a moment, then looks at his phone, scrolls with his thumb. Then he goes back to reading. After a minute or two he looks at his phone. He does this for a while. It is the middle of the night. The lights are still on in the living room and kitchen. The hallway and the bathroom are dark. In the bedroom the bedside light is on, and the fan is on, and there is also a small towel, a hand towel, on the bed. David puts the book down. He looks at the phone, touches the screen. He clears his throat. He uses his fingers to touch a message into his phone.

Hey Ravi. Want to come over?

He clicks his tongue, clears his throat again. He puts down the phone but keeps looking at it. He feels for the towel and picks it up and wipes his face and his chest. He puts it down and picks up the phone. He looks at his arm. He puts a finger to his arm just below the elbow and presses, and then rubs the skin with his fingers and scratches it briefly with his nails. He looks at the phone. He touches the screen and then holds the phone to his ear. He stares at nothing. He looks at the phone, then puts it back to his ear. In the silence of the flat it is possible to hear the ringing tone inside David's phone, and then the interruption and the generic voice of the voicemail service. David touches the screen to end the call and drops the phone on the bed and picks up the book again.

— Suit yourself.

It is the afternoon. David is in the living room. He is naked and he is lying on the floor on his back and he has his phone in his hand and he's touching the screen and scratching his arm. He makes a phone call.

— Rob? Yeah. How are you? Yeah I know. What time do you finish? Ok. Could you come over? Here. To the flat. Yeah. Well, I don't know. No I didn't go in. No, no it's fine. I just think that this thing with Alex has probably blown up out of all proportion you know? And I'm . . . what? I'd rather not. Can you not come here? Why not? I don't know what you mean.

He closes his eyes for a moment.

— No, just come here for fuck's sake. I'm not going out.

That is the end of the phone call.

David leaves the flat. He has a towel with him, a book, headphones. Then he appears in the garden. He is wearing shorts and a short-sleeved shirt that is open. The cat comes over to him and the grass is dry and a yellow kind of colour. The cat brushes against his legs and David squats and strokes her head and she purrs. He smiles at her. He looks around. He is wearing sunglasses. He shakes out the towel and the cat trots away and watches him. He lays the towel on the grass. Then he takes off his shirt and his sandals and he sits on the towel. He looks around. He looks at the windows of Laura and Nadia's flat. He looks at the cat. He lies back. He puts his headphones on, presses the screen of his phone and puts the phone down and picks up the book and holds it above his face. He stays like that for a while. Then he turns onto his stomach and props himself up on his elbows and puts the book on the grass and reads it like that. He seems very calm. His legs sometime bend at the knee and every so often he touches a heel to his buttocks. He brushes at his shoulder. He shoos away a fly. The cat sits near him.

After a while Nadia appears. They talk for a while, laughing about things. Everything is fine. Nadia goes inside and comes back with two glasses of wine and sits on the grass and David puts aside his book and sits up, and they chat to each other happily, taking turns stroking the cat.

It is a nice day.

David opens the door of the flat and walks down the stairs and goes to the door of Nadia and Laura's flat and knocks. He has left the door of the flat upstairs open and he is naked. He is sweating. He knocks a second time. He waits. There is no one there. He knocks a third time. He turns and walks back to the stairs and goes slowly up. He pauses halfway and looks around.

He stares. Then he starts to cry, and goes back up to the flat and goes inside and closes the door. He stops crying and has another glass of water.

Later he is shivering. He gets dressed. It is still hot.

— It's a nice flat. I mean for one person. I mean in London. What are you paying?

— A lot.

— I thought. I thought you said it was a deal.

This is the friend with the tattoos. He is sitting on the sofa with David. They are slightly slumped against each other. They each have a glass of wine.

— Well it's not . . . it's not a *deal*. But I want to live on my own. You know. I can't stand. It's pretty great for a one-person place. It's pretty good. Like you say.

David looks towards the window. His friend follows his gaze. There isn't anything there.

— And I don't know how two people would live here to be honest.

— A couple.

— Sure but even a couple is going to need space. There's basically one room to . . . hang out in.

— Bedroom.

— I couldn't do it.

— Everyone else does. But yeah. Maybe they drove each other crazy. Maybe each of them ran off. In different directions.

David is quiet for a moment.

— I really love it here, he says then. I'm really happy here.

— That's great David.

He pats David's thigh.

— You deserve a bit of that, you know?

— I mean I feel really good here. It just has this atmosphere. It's quiet. And I love that. I can read. It's relaxed, but I feel energised as well, when I'm here. Full of ideas. I really look forward to coming home from work, you know. Because of the flat, not because of work. I hate leaving in the morning. Do you know what I mean?

— Well, no. I hate my place. But that's other people isn't it? If they fucking washed up

— I couldn't stand that.

— I mean they're all right. I even really like Marsha and

— This place is just really good for me. You know? I feel more alive here. It's doesn't feel like a one-bedroomed flat. It feels like a headquarters.

The man with the tattoos laughs.

— Headquarters?

— It's my headquarters.

— What are you planning?

— Life.

— Oh Jesus.

— Headquarters of love.

— Headquarters of getting boned.

They laugh about this and make more comments related to sex. David tells his friend again how happy he is in the flat. He talks about it a lot, describing the flat as something other than a flat, as a home. He says there is a special kind of energy to it. He doesn't ask his friend anything. He never says his name. His friend seems to become tired, and bored, and he leaves. When he's gone David puts on headphones and listens to music on his phone and dances for a while in the living room. Then he goes to bed and reads.

*

He goes to answer the intercom but it buzzed more than twenty minutes ago. He holds it to his ear and makes a noise. Then he makes the same noise. He looks bad. He walks around the flat. He stops when he sees his phone, which is in the kitchen. He looks at his phone. He says something. He makes a noise. It sounds like he is trying to say something but it is as if his lips or his tongue are swollen or not working, though there is no evidence of this, there is just a yellowness to the skin of his face, and he shivers in short spasms and there is blood on his left hand, on the fingers, the nails. He is wearing tracksuit bottoms, a jumper, and he has a towel wrapped around his shoulders. He is barefoot. He stands there. He looks at his phone. He stands in the kitchen looking at his phone. He stays there, in the same place, standing there, for nearly an hour.

He cannot speak.

There is a knock at the door. It's Alison. Behind her on the stairs are Laura and Nadia. David looks startled.

— Hello.

— David, says Alison. She sounds relieved. Behind her, Laura turns and walks back down the stairs. Nadia laughs.

— What's going on?

— Well we couldn't reach you.

David hasn't asked them in. He's is wearing a shirt and jeans and is barefoot. His hair is neat, his hands are clean. He looks very handsome.

— How do you mean?

— There was no answer at the door.

— I'm just back from work. What's happened?

— Well, nothing apparently.

— Oh it's our fault, says Nadia. Were you away for a while?

— Yeah I was at my mum's for the weekend.

— The girls heard some noises.

— No, that's the thing, we didn't hear anything really. Or we imagined things. Laura was worried that . . . I'm really sorry.

Alison looks embarrassed. She rolls her eyes for David. Nadia, behind her, can't see.

— Ok, says David. Well I'm fine thanks very much. I go to work, you know. And I sometimes spend the night at a friend's, or go away for a few days, and that can happen any time, and I'm not, I'm not really happy that my movements are being monitored or whatever. It's sort of creepy to be honest. It really is.

Alison nods and turns.

— Completely understand that. Apologies. I won't be knocking on your door again unless you ask me to.

— I'm really sorry, Nadia says again.

They go downstairs. David doesn't say anything else. He watches them. His face is handsome. He looks so young. His eyes are beautiful. He closes the door.

He sits at his desk. He is reading a book. He is wearing just shorts. It is morning. There is a mug of coffee and he sips from it and looks out of the window and sees the cat. The cat is there. And he looks towards the happy man who is in the garden again, going from flower to flower. There are butterflies over the roses, the violets, the delphiniums. David looks at everything but does not seem to take it in, to really see it. He is smiling. He looks back at his book. He reads for a moment and then looks up and smiles again. Then he looks once more at the book and he reads aloud. Then he closes the book.

*

There is nothing for a while. What is a while. No one comes. No one calls. David is not in the bedroom. Or the bathroom. The hallway is empty. So is the living room, and the kitchen. He is not in these rooms.

He is in the other room, the fifth room.

The only ones who know this are you, and I.

The Pigeon

HE WOKE AND lay still. He had again kicked off the duvet in his sleep, and there was a chill in the air, this hour, and his body was cold, his legs goosebumped and his shoulders dull and slightly trembling, and he in fascination like a wounded creature – this was his thought – he lay still for a while, dying, an arrow in his back, fallen on snow, some sort of deer or big cat dreaming as it died of being a human boy, a human man, a useless dream. Then he stretched out his arm and pulled the duvet back over his skin. He felt himself begin to disappear in the warmth, to dissolve on the tongue of it, and he fell a long way down asleep, as slow and safe as a child. In his sleep he was part of something.

Ronnie called at just after seven with the van, Pigeon racing to get out the door before Ronnie started on the horn, annoying people.

— Why can you not wake?
— I am awake. I did . . .
— You look like you still asleep.
— Ronnie I've been up for a half hour. I've had a shower. I'm wide awake. I'm early. Shut up.
— You not early.

— I'm not late.

Ronnie stopped at the end of the road and Pigeon got them coffees from the corner shop and that cheered Ronnie up.

— That place is better than the coffee places. Coffee places have better sandwiches than the sandwich places. Chinese places have the best chips. Nothing as it seems.

They spent the best part of an hour getting over to Hammersmith. The radio going. Pigeon dozing. Ronnie smoking, sighing at the traffic, muttering back at the people on the radio. He liked the news shows, the talk shows. *Scandal* he would say. *Scandal* and *Idiot* and *Lies. Lies. Lies.*

He had a reputation for moodiness, Ronnie did. He was known for his sulks. In The Arms once when Pigeon had been there someone had called him Ronnie the Walk Out, and he'd walked out.

— They give up so easy, these people, these suffering people. They doubt and they relent. You must not relent Pigeon. You hear me?

Pigeon didn't know what he was talking about.

— I hear you Ronnie.

They were working on a bathroom in the house of a lady who left them a pile of cheese sandwiches on the kitchen table every day, and plates and cups and saucers laid out, and sometimes a note telling them about a cake in the fridge or ice cream in the freezer. Every morning when they arrived Ronnie would spend twenty minutes having a shit in the downstairs toilet while Pigeon put the kettle on and set up Ronnie's workbench in the back garden and brought in whatever they needed from the van. Then he made a pot of tea and a start on the sandwiches and looked out at the garden where the woman had a bird bath and an old iron bench and a table and chairs, all crowded together on a tiny little patch of yellow grass and hard earth. Ronnie was trying to persuade her to let them cover it – decking or marble effect porcelain tiles. When Ronnie was done they'd sit together eating the sandwiches and drinking the tea while Ronnie read the news on his phone, telling Pigeon what was happening in the city and the country and the world, in that order. There was, Ronnie insisted, no good reason for thinking that mankind was anything other than scum.

— A reputation is a gathered thing. You cannot throw it off easy.

Pigeon asked Ronnie when there'd last been snow because he couldn't remember. He thought maybe it was years ago. But Ronnie insisted that there'd been snow last winter. Late snow. He said he remembered because he'd slid all the way down Camberwell Grove in the van, his nephew Gary screaming like a girl in the passenger seat, Ronnie pumping the brakes and just praying that whatever he ended up hitting it wasn't a Jaguar *or a Telsa or a Rolls fucking Royce.*

— Tesla, Pigeon corrected him

— I know I know. I misspeak out of defiance.

— Yeah?

— Not rich people going to save the planet Pigeon. Dead people will save the planet.

— How?

— By dying.

Ronnie was a pessimist. The van hadn't hit anything in the end, it had just come to a sideways halt outside the pub, and he and Gary hadn't stopped laughing for an hour. Pigeon had heard the story before. But he thought it had been two years ago. At least. But Ronnie insisted.

— Took us half day to get to Elephant and then we give up.

Went for a fry. Left the van off Walworth Road and went home on the bus. Great day. Lovely day. Late February. This year.

— Ok. I don't remember that.

— You sleep in till June.

He had been late once for Ronnie. But that had been enough. Ronnie hated it more than any other thing. He'd blown the horn until people were shouting out windows at him, Pigeon having to come out in his socks, his boots in his hand, his face not even splashed, his mouth like a compost box. And Ronnie just stared at him, a slow shake of the head and his eyes narrowed with contempt as if Pigeon was contemptible, was nothing, was just more human scum. It had been five minutes. But Ronnie had hung it on Pigeon like a name tag. *You must be awake Pigeon. You must be awake in the world or you are not in the world at all. Lazy youth no prosper.*

His dream had faded. Only snow and trees remained, and the memory of being cold. He ate the last of the sandwiches and thought of cold places. The north. Scandinavia. Russia. He could just walk, and it would get colder. Take a boat up into the ice. Deckhand. Trawler man. Something like that. Dirty at first, the ice, then clear clean white. He'd never been further north than Leeds.

He tidied things away and Ronnie went upstairs to the bathroom and organised what they were doing. Lady wanted the whole thing the other way around. She wanted a pedestal bath. She wanted a bidet. She wanted a toilet like the captain's chair on Star Trek with all the buttons. She wanted the door in a different place. So they had stripped out what was there and Pigeon had carted it all out to the skip, and now they were playing Twister with the pipes and Ronnie would shout STOP STOP every half hour or so and look at his diagrams. Pigeon had long since given up trying to have an opinion about what Ronnie had been doing for *twenty damn years* before Pigeon *was drama in your mother house.* Pigeon was twenty-three and his parents' second child. So. But he just stayed quiet now and Ronnie would kneel on the floor and redraw his diagrams while Pigeon swept up around him, and they would undo about fifteen minutes out of every thirty, rolling the time back like stripping a wire. Pigeon hated this work. Or maybe he didn't mind it. He didn't pay attention to either the work or what he thought of it. He went off in his head, and he had lots of time for that, and that was good, and he had stopped worrying about it because the last thing Ronnie wanted from him was thinking.

It was hot. He thought his dream was simply that. It was memorable because of that. He thought of the swimming pool in Camberwell and how he liked it, in theory, while in practice it was always full of kids and in the water you had to keep moving or you'd just see plasters or clumps of hair floating past. He thought of being on his back on the grass in Burgess Park, shirt off, music on, couple of beers. Boring. Useless. He wanted to be away. Swimming in a sea, like he had in Ibiza. But somewhere else. Sober. Dawn. His skin in the low sun. Off the coast of Senegal. Palestine. Sri Lanka. Or walking through some low hills in, what, in the northern parts of India, Kashmir, or sailing in the blue Sea of . . . Marmara. Turkey. He wanted to be wandering through the fog of Patagonia though, really, down in the cold south, naked in the glow of the earthworm, unloved on his own terms in a place he could not imagine.

There. In his mind the world was a tumble of words that he loved.

He'd never been further south than Ibiza. Never been further west than . . . Dublin. East . . . Amsterdam? Probably Ibiza again. A small narrow patch of the world. Twenty-three. Useless.

He was in a room, a big bare room, waiting while Ronnie tried to figure out how to carry a rich woman's waste away from her. A bathroom bigger than his family living room. Bigger than the bathroom Rajit's family had. Bigger than the bathroom of the expensive Marylebone Hotel where he'd once spent a night with an Italian. That place. This was a bathroom with nothing in it, where he could crouch and half-close his eyes and look out over the dust and the bare wood like he was looking out over the plains of Patagonia, where a giant slow-moving monster called Ronnie scratched strange lines in the desert sand.

— Aaaaah. I know where it wrong. Take that board back up.

Ants came out of him in this other dream, close to a nightmare. Saturday morning, so he lay on top of his duvet for a long half hour thinking it through. A forest. On a slope. Him walking downhill, the sun on his left warming him, and he's happy but he's being careful where he steps because he's barefoot. He puts his hands on tree trunks as he passes. There are patches of grass, bushes, little clearings full of sunlight. And then he feels a tickling on his chest and scratches it. It's morning. A big forest morning and he's walking downhill and there is a lake at the bottom, he knows. More tickling on his chest and he looks down and it's an ant walking on him, and he stares at it and picks it off as if he doesn't want to hurt it. A small ant. Half-sized. He doesn't know why it's half-sized. He doesn't know how he knows that. And then there's another. On his bare chest. He's naked. He sleeps naked and he pushes his duvet off so in his dreams he's always naked and outdoors. And if he's cold he's cold. And if the sun is up and on him then it's the weekend and he's somewhere warm. And now there are ants, all over him. And he's not taking care now, he's brushing them off, knocking them off, slapping at them, specks of their blood on his palms. And he feels them in his arse. And his cock. And he looks down at his cock and lifts it up to look at the opening and the ants are climbing out of there and he goes to shout or scream and they're in his mouth and he wakes up, slap, he slaps his stomach once, and then he just freezes, because he knows immediately that it was a dream and there are no ants. But he gives himself a once over, just to be sure. He gives himself a once over twice. And then gets up to pee and he looks in his mouth in the mirror and it's just dry, and he needed to pee so that was what that was. A dry mouth and a full bladder and his body finding a way to get him up and sort it out. At eight on a Saturday morning.

He went back to bed and thought about it. His body. Not just body. But the thing that is his, as if he is something else. He never got as far as the lake. Even when he fell back asleep the forest was gone and the ants were gone and he was instead in an impossible weightless place without border where he rolled his naked body amongst other naked bodies and the whispers that he heard were as prayers, wordless but solemn, a murmur of touches, mouths on his, hands on him, until a clear low voice like Ronnie's said close to his ear *you want to come now don't ya?* and he woke up and rolled on his back and came, and then dozed with a wet belly like a man who'd been shot.

Eventually his belly dried out and rumbled and sent him to find food.

His brother had told him to read books. As in, the specific books. *Read this. Did you read that? Read this one.* He just told him to read them. Didn't say oh this is really good I think you'd like this. Never asked him what he thought of any of them. Just *read this. Give it back when you're finished.* Started when he was about twelve. He still did it sometimes, and they'd laugh. But now they talked about them too, lightly. Came back from Manchester every few weeks for a couple of days. *What did you get out of that? What do you think of that?* It was mostly history, politics, both of which Pigeon liked, but he couldn't follow his brother very far into theory, and that's where his brother lived. He was all French guys, 1950s guys, Italian guys.

Pigeon has the looks. Daniel has the brains, his mother said. Her own children. One of you ugly, one of you dumb. Effectively. Both of them furious. She was right though, except that it was Daniel who had a girlfriend. Proper girlfriend, together for years. She was a union organiser, and it was all politics for them, all the time. They'd joined the Labour Party when Corbyn had been elected. And after he got his PhD maybe Daniel would teach, or maybe he'd be a politician. Pigeon laughed in his face about it. But truthfully, he would love it. He would. Seeing his brother on the television, giving people shit. He wasn't ugly.

Pigeon did have the looks though. Tall, good skin, big clear eyes, natural muscles, a smiling face that people just loved. And he wasn't dumb.

When his father died he'd been dressed up in a suit, eight years old, and they'd made him bring flowers up on the stage. Not the stage. The altar. And when he had, the crowd had lost it. Not the crowd. The congregation. Such a cute kid. Little angel. They'd all of them, every single one, burst into tears. Quite a thing to turn around and have a hundred people bawling at you. He'd stood stock still, terrified, until Daniel came up and got him, which just made everyone cry more. Whole building filling with tears. Pigeon floating to the rafters and swimming there, looking down at his sunken dad in his sunken boat.

*

A SHOCK

His mother said he'd been raised by pigeons. They'd lived on the top floor of a block in Peckham that was gone now and that Pigeon had no memory of, and there were pigeon coops on the roof of this place, and his mother said that he'd spent all day talking with the pigeons who came down to the windowsill to talk to him. She said he had all the knowledge of pigeon London in him. All their schemes and shortcuts. Their plans and dramas. All their getting under people's feet. He'd liked the idea that he had a special knowledge, but he could not retrieve it.

And the story was all wrong. The sound he'd made as a baby was not the sound that pigeons make. Pigeons and doves make a deep trilling sort of noise, like the purring of a cat, but louder. The sound he'd made had instead been a literal *coo, coo*. He knew this because he still made it. If anything, it was more like the sound of a cuckoo. From what he could tell from YouTube anyway. It had taken him ages to figure this out, but he had, while he was still very young. He may have liked the pigeons at the window when he was a baby. He may have talked to them, but he didn't make their sound. The sound he made was much more likely, he'd realised, to have come from his mother as she leaned over him, held him, rocked him to sleep, fed him. *Coo coo.*

So he was called Pigeon for no good reason at all.

At some point in the process of working this out he had sat in the playground at school and waited for a couple of pigeons to come over to him, and he had tried to talk to them.

Coo?

They came closer, and he thought that maybe . . . but they pecked around his feet and looked at him expectantly, hustling for bread, for lunch-box crumbs.

Coo coo coo?

And of course some other boy had spotted him, heard him,

and everyone had had a good laugh. The weird Pigeon, talking to the pigeons. The name stuck harder. But it was a mistake. It was a stupid mistake.

If it weren't for his mother, for Daniel, he would leave. Just disappear out of London, out of England. What were these things? He would rather vanish.

How did she not know that pigeons made a different sound? Could she not hear them? How had no one corrected her? All those aunts and uncles cooing at him. Laughing when he cooed back. What sort of nonsense was that?

Pigeons coo. But that word doesn't match the sound. It is not, he decided, *onomatopoeic*. Pigeon looked this word up when he was maybe eleven or twelve, and to his astonishment, to his rage, the word *coo* was listed in the definition as an example of onomatopoeia. Dictionary was wrong. Just wrong. He wanted his brother to do something about it.

Daniel laughed at him. Pigeons do coo, Daniel said. They make all sorts of noises, and *of course* coo was onomatopoeic. It was, he said, exactly like *moo*. Was *moo* onomatopoeic? Pigeon didn't know. Yes it was, said Daniel. Cows don't make the actual sound that we make when we say *moo*. They don't have the lips. But *moo* is our approximation of that sound. Given our lips. It was the same, he said, with *coo*. Pigeons coo. They don't make the sound of the word *coo*, but they coo.

Approximation.

But, Pigeon had said. But but but. It's a crap approximation. It's nothing like the sound that pigeons make. It's not the trilling in the throat, the warbling, the floppy watery sound of it. Daniel didn't care. *Take it up with history* he said. Which was something he said a lot.

But maybe Pigeon had got it all backwards.

There was another sound that he heard sometimes in the evening, or in the morning, and it was much more like the sound of the word *coo*. He'd thought it was owls. For years he'd assumed that there were owls hidden everywhere. In the trees where he walked to school, in the parks where he hung around in the evenings. In the gardens of the houses coming up the hill. In the big trees that stood beside their block, on the roof, in the eaves. But he'd never seen them because they kept themselves hidden. They were night birds. They were in their nests, they couldn't be seen. At some point in his teens he'd told someone that he liked the sounds of the owls in the evenings. A girl. They'd been walking through a park. *Owls?* she asked. *What owls?* And he'd waited and picked out the sound the next time he heard it and said *there, that sound.* And she had liked him quite a lot he thought, but even still she laughed. Not a mean laugh. She'd laughed and shouldered him gently, playfully, and told him

— That's pigeons you daft git. There's no owls in London.

He laughed, shouldered her in return.

— I know, he said, I know. I just like to imagine that they're owls.

And she'd thought that was cute or whatever, and they'd kissed by the playground for a while. But when he got home he spent the whole evening on the web trying to find out what the hell was going on with birds.

So, maybe. Maybe they do coo. But they didn't coo like him. And he didn't coo like them. He was not what people said he was, and the sounds he made were his own.

And he kept on making them. For a while as a teenager he'd tried to stop. Tried to train himself out of them. But they just came. Little *coos*. Quiet little *coos*. Sometimes not so quiet. People usually thought he was saying *cool*. But he was saying *coo*. Sometimes he was more confident with it. *Coo*.

People liked it. They'd smile at him.

But most of the time it just came out of him. His lips didn't even move. The noise just came. *Coo*. When he thought of something, worked something out. When he saw something that he liked or didn't like. When he read something and understood it or didn't understand it. When he got home and Daniel was there. When he woke up and it was the weekend. When he got paid. Not loud. But people heard it. People heard it and he didn't know what they thought, but he had stopped worrying about it.

He couldn't vanish. Vanishing was what other people experienced when you went somewhere else. When you left no word. You created a vanishing that only other people knew. But you were wherever you were, un-vanished.

Vanishing is not a gift you can give yourself. Unless in falling asleep. Unless in waking up.

He had seen Ronnie's cock. This had been an error. It wasn't his fault. Ronnie had taken a piss in the back garden of a house in Deptford where they were putting in a shed. Pigeon had swung around at the sound of running water, looking for the source, half afraid that he'd hit a pipe, and there was Ronnie's cock. Just an ordinary cock. Nothing wrong with it. Nothing exceptional about it. Just a cock. But Pigeon had cooed. *Coo*. And he'd swung away again and cursed himself silently and felt the blood rush around him in confusion.

Ronnie didn't say anything, but the whole rest of the day he was in a mood. As if, Pigeon thought, he'd taken the coo as an insult. Some men get very weird about it, they get defensive, they all think they should be bigger or whatever. And Pigeon didn't care, he really did not care, but he wondered if Ronnie had thought that he'd been making fun of him. Because he hadn't. It had been a coo of surprise. But how do you walk that back? That sort of misunderstanding? Wait until the drive home and tell him he had a nice cock?

— Lovely penis, Ronnie, by the way.

— Thank you Pigeon.

That was not a thing that could happen. It should. It should be a thing that could happen, he thought. He didn't want anyone to feel bad about their body. Amount of grief guys had about that stuff. That was just . . . that should be the thing that couldn't happen.

And in all this chatting with himself was hidden – badly – the terrible notion that maybe Ronnie had taken it as something worse than an insult, something more like a sigh, something with desire in it. It was only days afterwards, quiet, that Pigeon allowed himself to think fully that maybe that's what Ronnie had thought. Pigeon didn't fancy Ronnie. Not even vaguely, not ever. He couldn't even conceive of him as a sexual being at all. He was like a child or a relative or a Labrador. His legs just walked, his chest just breathed, his head just sat on top of him. The fact that he had a cock at all had never previously been something that Pigeon had considered.

He found all of this embarrassing and distracting. He made himself stop thinking about it.

His mind was a fog sometimes. You put him somewhere, he would stay there. He could not think. He was not stupid but it was like he was not fully there. It was like he was wrapped in a duvet in his mind.

He dozed a little sometimes after lunch. As the day got on. He slowed down. He was aware. Ronnie also was aware. A couple of times he'd clapped his hands loud beside Pigeon, or shouted his name, made him jump. Usually it was when he was waiting for Ronnie to get to the end of some complex reconsideration of the plan, poring over his pieces of paper. And he wouldn't have music playing, Ronnie wouldn't. Said either it was shit music and that would soften their brains, or it was good music, and that would distract, and either way they would not do a good job and would not prosper.

— You have a girl?

— What?

— A girl. Girlfriend.

— Not at the moment.

— Ever?

This was new.

— Ever? What you mean ever? You know I've had girlfriends. You met some of them.

— I did?

— Yes.

— Ok ok.

— You met Lorna.

— I don't remember.

— From Lewisham. You met her in The Arms. You told me she was too pretty for me.

Ronnie grinned.

— Oh I remember. She was pretty. What happened?

Pigeon hadn't wanted to go away with her the previous August, to Spain. Her and her sister and her sister's friend and all of their boyfriends. So she'd dumped him.

— She was too pretty for me.

Ronnie laughed.

— She leave?

— Yeah.

— You chase her?

— Nah.

— That's good. Don't make a bad situation stupid. She leave for someone better looking? Someone more money?

— More money.

Ronnie laughed some more.

— Well you need to prosper. Prosper into pussy.

Ronnie thought this was hilarious. He rocked back and forth and wiped his eyes.

Pigeon nodded, smiled. Lorna's sister's boyfriend had once sucked him off in the bathroom at a party somewhere in Elephant and then threatened to kill him if he mentioned it to anyone. *I swear bruv. I fucking swear.* Tears in his eyes. Pigeon had told him to *chill. Relax.* Gave him a hug. So the guy calmed down and a couple of weeks later he wanted some more and Pigeon knew this was not an ideal situation and he didn't want to spend too much time with this lot any more. There was a little frenzy under their friendships.

Was that complicated? Unusual? He didn't know. So many people doing things on the quiet, taking what they thought were chances, but they were only chances because they thought they were. No one talking. He just didn't think it was much of a deal. He didn't know how weird he was, if at all. Sometimes he thought he was going to hell via his mother's broken heart. Sometimes he would have a glimpse into someone else's something and think . . . nah, everyone is at least as weird as me. I'm fine.

— Time.

— Ok.

— You pack up. I write the note.

Every day Ronnie wrote her a note to say what they'd done. It always seemed to take exactly as long to write as it took Pigeon to carry everything out to the van.

Daniel was surprised when Pigeon told him he was going to do some work for Ronnie.

— Shame.

— Why?

— You like Ronnie.

— Yeah.

— Yeah I'm just saying. Like, you're friends?

— Yeah.

— And now he's your boss. So. Changes. What happened his cousin? Or whatever. Gary.

— They fell out. He's not my boss.

— He's paying. He fixed the rate. Yeah?

— Yeah.

— He's your boss.

— Yeah. But he respects me. He's not, you know. He's not an asshole about it.

— No, I'm not saying that, as such. But. Do you know how much he charges people for the whole job, whatever it is?

Pigeon sighed with a *sheesh*. He didn't know what he was doing defending Ronnie. Guy was an asshole.

— No.

Daniel laughed.

— Yeah. He's the boss. I like Ronnie. But he's . . . I bet he's a prick of a boss.

Pigeon looked at his brother. Just an expression.

— He has that cranky thing. Fun in the pub when it's politics or something. But, yeah. I can see that he'd fall out with Gary. I like Gary. Haven't seen him since ever. I like Ronnie too. But no. Don't take any shit. What's he paying you?

— You want me to work or not? You always telling me to snap out of it, do something, take initiative. So I went to Ronnie and I persuaded him and now he's paying me and I have a job.

— I know.

— Now it's not good enough for you.

— I'm not saying that.

— You are though.

They went through it.

Daniel had liked it best when Pigeon was doing call-centre work out in Croydon and going to the library and thinking about university. He liked it because he could nag him about joining a union, about organising. He could talk about courses that Pigeon might be interested in, do well in. Business studies or something. But Pigeon hated going to Croydon. Hated talking to the other people there. Call-centre chairs and library chairs had the same sweated grime to them, the same stink, they sat in the same dead air, and all he heard on the phone was just garbage people, and he wasn't going to the library at all, he was just saying he was to his mother to account for various hours in which he was doing other things, and he wasn't thinking about university he was thinking about Patagonia and Kashmir and the mountains of Chile and Colombia. All those peaks. There is a world.

Daniel apologised. Said he was proud, that he loved him, and that Pigeon was right to be annoyed. They hugged, and that was that.

*

The lady worked in TV, they thought. There were letters lying around the kitchen from the BBC. There was a folder usually on the kitchen counter with the logo on the front. In the hallway there was a framed picture of her all dressed up with Graham Norton. He had his arm around her shoulder and they were both smiling at the camera. And there was another picture of her with Laura Kuenssberg and the lady was talking and wearing a lanyard and carrying a notebook and Kuenssberg was listening to her, arms crossed, as if it was important, as if they were working. And there were pictures of her with other people too, people they didn't recognise. Ronnie thought one of them might be Stephen Fry, but he wasn't confident.

— Another of those kind. They everywhere.

In the downstairs toilet there was a digital radio on the windowsill. In the living room they could see a huge television, and lots of boxes and bookshelves filled with DVDs, as well as some books. It was all a nice cosy clutter of things. She lived on her own. There was no sign of a man, no sign of kids. She'd found Ronnie through another job he'd done in Battersea for a friend of hers. Another bathroom. Not with Pigeon though, he'd done it on his own. Tiles. He liked doing the tiles himself. He liked precision. He liked doing the finishing touches. Pigeon had never been around for the end of any job.

He dreamed he had his own volcano. Even in his sleep he thought this was stupid. But there it was. A huge mountain that seemed to be outside his mother's house. Or maybe his mother's house was instead now to be found on the slopes on a large smouldering mountain where the air was fresh and you could see the cities down by the coast where people killed each other. It was his. In the sense that it did his bidding. He destroyed an entire version of London with a glance. He swept away an approaching boat with a pyroclastic flow. He flattened the homes of the people he didn't like, and Ronnie as well. Ronnie running from a collapsing fiery approximation of his block on Champion Hill. Naked for some reason. At which Pigeon woke. Woke up and wondered what that was about. Did he not like Ronnie? Ronnie was a boss. That was that. A prick of a boss.

Ronnie had disappeared. Pigeon called his name, loudly. House was quiet, bright, the sun a little lower. He'd left his phone somewhere. He had fallen asleep on the bathroom floor. Waiting for Ronnie to figure out what they'd done wrong this time. Looking at the dust, lying down at first to follow what Ronnie was doing with the pipes for the bidet, and then just staying there, sinking his head onto his arm when Ronnie left the room. For what? To pee downstairs probably. If it was to get something he'd have sent Pigeon. So he closed his eyes, just for a second. There'd been a wide desert and a mirage of a complicated temple in the distance and he'd walked toward it with the sun on his face knowing it was a mirage but it was beautiful anyway, and then he recognised it as the copper of the bathroom piping and he was awake again and Ronnie was gone. He lay there a minute or two. He lay there expecting Ronnie to come back, thinking that he'd dropped off for a few seconds. Maybe he dropped off again. But at some stage the fact that he'd been there a while became a possibility. He might have fallen asleep. His shoulder and his hip hurt from the floorboards. Might have. Fucks sake.

He got up and his bones all snapped but the place was quiet. He got up and went to the stairs and listened and the place was quiet and he called Ronnie's name loudly and the place was quiet. Downstairs the kitchen was tidied up, their mugs and plates put away. The back door closed and locked. Ronnie's workbench gone from the garden – all his stuff gone. Pigeon walked to the front door and it was locked. He stood there looking at it like it had said something to him. Tried it again. The bottom lock was locked. The bottom lock which the lady had been so particular about. *You have two front-door keys. The Yale lock but also this bottom one. You don't leave the door open ever ok? In and out while you're here, the Yale is fine. When you leave you lock the bottom one as well ok?* He tried it again. He bent over and looked through the keyhole. He crouched and opened the letter flap. Couldn't see much, the skip with boards up the side, a length of cracked plastic pipe against the sky, but he was pretty sure that he was able to see where the van had been parked and it wasn't parked there any more.

Fucking hell.

He went back to the kitchen. The note was on the counter by the kettle.

Radiator done and working. Bidet piping done. Bidet and toilet arrive Monday. Tomorrow is sink and bidet to finish. R.

Then he couldn't find his phone.

There was a dismantled bed in the corner but no mattress, a box of Christmas decorations, parts of at least two bicycles, a mirror, two kitchen chairs, an armchair piled high with board games, CDs, books, porn magazines, a kettle, a lampshade, video cassettes, documents, photographs. Clothes. It was hot. Lots of clothes. In black bags, in boxes, and on a rack down at the end. It was gloomy but he could see fine. Light came through the eaves. By the water tanks there was an old torch but it was dead. He was sweating. But it was not . . . he was not . . . he was ok.

What are you doing?

A Shock

He looked at his hand in the gloom. He was properly locked in.

He'd assumed Ronnie had taken his phone. The phone was gone. It would have been either on the new ledge they'd stuck over the new radiator in the new bathroom, or it would be in the kitchen, and it was in neither place, and in no place in between. In the kitchen there was no sign of the back-door key. It hung usually in a cupboard but it wasn't there. Pigeon was pretty sure that he wouldn't have been able to get out over the walls at the back anyway. No side passages in these terraces. Just a tangle of tiny gardens hemmed in. And him clambering around out there was going to get the cops down in less than no time. A neighbourhood like this. They'd probably shoot him.

All of the ground-floor windows were locked. No sign of keys. He didn't know if that was Ronnie or just the way they always were. Probably the way they always were. He could squeeze through a front one upstairs and drop to the street. He didn't want to do that. It was too high. And he would be seen. They would gather and drag him to a cliff edge or a police station and he would hang there until they let him go.

He looked at the mirror, not into it. It showed him the lines of the roof beams at a broken angle. He thought for a moment that it was sweating, but it was just mottled, old.

He was sweating. He could smell it.

He'd assumed that Ronnie would drive around for a while and then come back and get him, all *no prosper*ing bullshit from ear to ear all the way home, and Pigeon just raging in the passenger seat. He'd have a proper go at Ronnie, he fucking would . . . but he knew he couldn't keep it up. He didn't have the fury. Nothing but a sleepy child. Maybe he needed a little lock in, needed his nose rubbed in it. *Stay in your dreams. Stay in your* *scratchy dreams.* In a stranger's house. Used up for nothing much and left behind with the cut-offs and the shavings, with his hands between his thighs and his dribbling mouth and his lazy, empty head. *Little lesson for you Pigeon.* What did Ronnie hate in him? Softness. *You not much more than a boy and you still asleep.* Not laziness. Ronnie was lazy as. He hated the softness. The quietness. The hint of something. *You must be awake Pigeon. You must be awake in the world or you are not in the world at all.* Such a crock of stupid bullshit.

After a while he'd decided that Ronnie wasn't coming back. Why would he? *You must not relent.* Ronnie the sulk. Ronnie the Walk Out. Furious Ronnie. All humankind is scum.

His hand in the gloom was a ghost. He could smell it.

Oh man. What was he doing? He had rolled into a slow panic that had taken him room to room looking for a way out and then for a hiding place because here he was, in a house that wasn't his with no way of relenting, stuck, waiting to face a woman he had said three words to, *hello, goodbye, thanks,* ever, in total, and he was supposed to explain that he had fallen asleep and been abandoned.

Something in him had decided to hide. In the attic.

Oh man.

He shifted things off the armchair thinking he'd sit on it. But there was too much. Why has she a pile of porn magazines in her attic? For fuck's sake. Instead he got a heap of musty old coats and jumpers and put them in the front corner. Over the front door, roughly. Somewhere about there. Laid them out and sat down. Put his back against the plain board that divided her attic from next door. It was hot. He should use the toilet. He had no idea what time it was. But there was a radio down there . . .

He lowered himself down through the hatch and swung his

leg for the bannister and put his weight there and let his arms fall toward the wall over the front-bedroom door and hopped down. It was noisy. No way he could do that when there was someone in the house. Downstairs he looked at the radio and it was 17:22. They'd never stayed later than four. He pissed and tried to shit. He had no idea what time she came back. So he would just . . .

He couldn't shit. He didn't know even why he was trying, he'd had one earlier, he never had a shit around now. He went to the kitchen and found a plastic jug, quite big, and he filled it two thirds with water. He looked in cupboards for some sort of snack food that wouldn't be missed. He was thinking energy bars or something, but there was nothing but crisps and they were noisy, and oranges, smelly, and he left it. He wasn't hungry.

What was he doing?

For a second he thought it was Friday. That he would need to stay hidden until Monday. But it wasn't. It was Thursday. He went back and looked at the radio. It was Thursday.

He could just wait for her in the kitchen and she would be a little baffled maybe but she would just let him out and that would be that. He had his Oyster card. He had some money. He'd get home, eventually. Then he'd go over to Ronnie's. Knock on the door. *Phone, please.* Take the phone. Then maybe he'd punch Ronnie. Or maybe he'd not say another word. Just look at him like he was human scum and walk away and never say another word to him as long as he lived. Go back to the call centre or do Deliveroo for the summer and then go up to Manchester and do something near his brother. Study. Snap out of it. Get out of London. Which is only a fraction of the world. You know? A tiny dense little fraction. It is not the full extent of things. There is fresh air. There is a cold drink of water.

He looked at the front door. The thought of it opening made him sick.

She might not even recognise him.

He took his jug back up and took his time climbing with it but he made it without spilling any and he lowered the square of wood back into the hatch and let his eyes adjust and then he felt suddenly emotional, as if he was going to cry.

This was something.

He knew he wasn't dreaming but he knew that he had learned how to do this by dreaming. How to be beside things. Out of them. How to find a solitary space. How to hide in the roof. How to stay where he was until the coast was clear.

He set the jug down carefully and went and got some more clothes to sit on and he sat on them. He took off his shoes.

He was doing this.

He got up. Ridiculous.

What if she comes through the door just as he's dangling through the hatch. So what? Maybe he had to check the water tank. What's he doing with a jug? So maybe he had to test the water. Take some water. Put some back. Who the fuck cares, she's not going to care, he's just the plumber's boy still in her house she won't give a shit she'll just let him out and away. She won't even look at him.

Even if she doesn't recognise him. Just. *I'm Ronnie's . . . I work with Ronnie. We met. Hello. Goodbye. Thanks.*

He sat down.

It would serve Ronnie right if he was discovered camping out in the attic. *What are you doing locking people into my house? You're fired.* Then all that public trouble. All that talk.

He was doing the right thing. He was comfortable enough.

He could be quiet. He could think things through. Sleep a light little sleep. Make it to the morning and she'd be gone and Ronnie would arrive and that would be it.

He was in the eaves. Pigeon in the eaves. Near the eaves. He thought that if he could make himself as small as possible that he could perhaps make himself smaller still. That something would take over and he would be transformed, down, and down again, into something tiny like a bird. He could strut. Stick his head through the holes and coo at the street.

He was falling asleep. He snapped out of it suddenly and shifted. His back was sore against the divider. He wondered if he should lie down. But he shouldn't sleep. Why did he always need to sleep? He was worried about snoring. Someone had told him once. He didn't much believe them. But he was full of involuntary noises. The coo and the fart and the burp. Why not the snore? She wouldn't hear him. Even if she did. Those noises don't register. Who is in their house, in their bed, and they hear a noise and they think *oh my god there is someone farting in the attic?* He laughed, stopped. Smiled while his belly jiggled. He couldn't laugh, he couldn't fart, he couldn't snore. Ok!

Sometimes a car went by, voices, footsteps. He could hear it all clearly. But nothing from inside. He became bored. He thought about the porn magazines, and immediately stopped thinking about them. Don't make a bad situation stupid. A couple of times he thought he heard her and he stopped breathing. But it wasn't her.

Maybe he should go and wait. Get up, go through the hatch. Even put all the clothes back the other end of the attic before he went. Bring the jug down. Wait in the kitchen for her. *Hi there, yeah, I know, I know, misunderstanding with Ronnie, he thought I was making my own way home. He locked up. Thinking I'd already gone. I know I know. No, I don't have a phone. I don't believe in them. I like to read books. I'm pretty faggy to tell you the truth I don't even carry a knife. I know, I know, what sort of youth. A non-prospering youth, that's what. Ok, you have a great evening, take care now, all the best, god bless.*

He stayed where he was.

After a while he lay down.

When he woke it was to the sound of the front door slamming.

His brain reassembled the world in an instant.

So he was doing this.

He stayed very still. Footsteps to the kitchen. Reading the note. Quiet for a while. Then her running up the stairs. A click. Another click. Light switches. She was looking at the bathroom.

— Fuck's sake, she said, quite loudly.

They had not done much that day.

She was right under the hatch. He imagined her looking at it. No, she was in the bathroom. He could hear her on the boards. She cleared her throat. She was talking to herself but he couldn't hear what she was saying. Then she seemed further away. Her bedroom. Just for a second. A little silence. Then she coughed again somewhere much closer and his body tensed. Feet. Her footsteps. She went downstairs. He breathed and wiped his head, and his hand glistened in the dark. It was dark. A foggy grey light showed him next to nothing of himself.

So here it was. Here he was. For the duration.

He needed to shift his position but he waited. The downstairs toilet flushed. He could hear the radio. It seemed to move around. She took it to the kitchen. He heard pots and pans. He lifted himself and scuttled out from the divider, lay down on his back. Tried to get comfortable. This was it. He was here. This was where he was.

Perhaps he never leaves.

He was pressed between the flat of the floor and whatever he put on himself. He was face down. Then he was on his back without moving. In the dark he was crushed without moving. On his back, his brother's body lying on him, legs and hips and belly to legs and hips and belly, laughing at him, making as if to spit in his face, in his mouth, and rolling off then, Pigeon pushing him off, acting like he was pushing him off, but it was his brother who rolled, who left it, who said sorry later on. One time. He thought of the man from France, and now he's face down, that big man with the cold belly who had lain on his back in the heat so that he could barely breathe, checking all the time, looking at him, and every inch of him covered by every inch of him, knees in the back on his knees, cock in the crack of his arse, cold belly in his back, shoulders on his shoulders, pressing him like a ball of blue tack. He put other men on his back. So that he could not move. Faceless men. Pale bodies in the attic. He did not want to know their faces. Just men. And so his brain flashed their faces at him and the cop was strongest and he just smiled at that claptrap, that nonsense. This is what the mind does, what the cock do. This nonsense. Tries to scare you, shame you, give you what you don't need as if it's something that you secretly want, when it's not. When it's not.

He thought of Mr Guptha's thighs and his big neck, his bunched up cords, the bulge in his crotch you could see sometimes when he walked down the aisles – one way looking at faces and the other way looking over shoulders – and you could feel him getting closer like a sound wave, like a pool wave, hitting you, flattening you, and he would go past and Pigeon would crouch in his desk like he was on top of him. On his back. He was rock hard, he realised. Not then, now. He realised it when it suddenly hurt and he had to lift his hips and get his hand down there and straighten himself out. Hard and fucking wet. Jesus. He imagined his cock poking through the ceiling, through the lady's ceiling, pointing at her out of her ceiling like a light fitting. He imagined her standing on her bed to see what it was, and licking it, putting it in her mouth. All those men on his back. All that woman sucking his cock. He fell asleep like that, seeping out a pool of hot wet mess into his M&S briefs and his canvas work trousers that he knew were sexy. He fell asleep and dreamed of dying at the bottom of the sea, part of the world at last, part of its mulch and its mess, its waste matter, its sag and decomposition, living forever in the soil of the future, living forever like a slice of what happened, a single thin slice of time, cut out and put down.

In his sleep he did not snore. But the coos came before dawn. And when she woke it took a while to make them out, but they reached her and she lay there and listened. Then she got up to go to the gym and shower. She dressed. She made some sandwiches for the plumbers. For the polite older man, and the sullen younger one. Not the brightest people she had ever met, not the fastest workers. But you get what you pay for.

She went outside and locked the front door and heard the coos again, above her head. She looked up, puzzled. A pigeon looked back at her from the eaves.

The Meeting

THERE WAS TALK in The Arms. Ronnie had been in, defiant. Harry asked him straight out had he really locked that young lad into a house and left him there? Ronnie leaned sideways against the bar and looked at no one in particular and said that no, it wasn't true. It had been a misunderstanding, and that Daniel Salisu was a liar and a troublemaker and that socialism was too cowardly to ever hold sway in the United Kingdom where it took hard work and early rising to prosper, and Pigeon Salisu had never risen early in his life, he was incapable of waking, he was lost in a dream of idleness, and he had left his phone in the van and how was Ronnie expected to know that?

— Pigeon name, pigeon life.

Harry laughed, shook his head. Stan scowled at Ronnie and Ronnie scowled back. But he left after one drink, muttering.

Later, when the others arrived, Stan went to the bar for his second pint before starting.

— Anna isn't going, said Harry, but Stan didn't know what he was talking about.

— Anna who?

— You don't know Anna? She comes in sometimes.

— I don't think so.

— Well, she's not going, but Yan probably is.

— Yan?

— Yes, Yan.

— Who is Yan?

Harry laughed, shook his head.

— You know him. His name is a bit . . . variable. Yan. Always here. Except tonight. Yves, Yan, Yanko? Priestly sort of oddball. You hate him.

— Stoker.

— Right. He's going. He's harmless you know.

And Harry went through to the back bar.

— Going to what? Stan asked no one. He sipped his beer. The place was quiet. He checked his phone for Maria, gathered his thoughts, was about to turn away when Harry came back through, talking.

— You having a meeting?

— Yeah.

— Want the backroom? I can turn the music down.

— Nah you're all right. It's fine in here. Just a few of us.

— Here, Stan.

Stan put down his beer. Leaned on the bar.

— What's the name of the older guy? I can never get it.

— Prentice?

— Prentice. That's it. Bit of a muppet.

— What happened?

Stan looked towards the table where Prentice was chatting with Sal and Fatma. Andrew had arrived as well. Sanjay was outside smoking.

— Ah nothing. He's just an awkward sort. You know Ronnie?

— Not really. I know Daniel Salisu though. He's a good guy.

— So are you going?

— To what?

— To the fucking party.

— What fucking party?

— Jesus Stan. I told you not five minutes ago.

— No you didn't. You started telling me who was going and who wasn't going but you never told me to what.

— The party. Those two, that couple, always in here, not always. Gay couple. Northern, one of them. They're having a party. They were in last night and told me a bunch of people to invite. Including you and yours.

— Oh that's nice of them.

— Nice lads. Probably Tory.

— And drinking in here?

— I serve everyone.

— Not a very Tory sort of establishment Harry.

Harry gave him the details and Stan picked up his pint and went back to the beginning of the meeting.

An email from Sanjay, announcing a full meeting for the Thursday, had gone out late, on the Tuesday afternoon – just two days' notice – and there had been a string of back and forths about that, on email, in WhatsApp, on Slack, and in The Arms on the Tuesday night when Prentice and Hilda had bumped into Sanjay, and then Flo, and all of them complaining – *well we won't get anything done if people don't come to the meetings*; and *what sort of notice is two days have you not heard of childcare, shifts*; and then, *it's just a matter of making arrangements*; and, *lots of people aren't going to be able to make this one*; then, *there's always someone who can't make a meeting, you have to question people's motivations really*; and, *well actually you don't we're all coming with different motivations and different abilities and resources and this is something that has to be respected.*

239

Prentice went up to the bar and spoke for a while with Harry, trying to persuade him that as a Jew he would be very welcome to join their local group and Harry explained, a little baffled, that he wasn't a Jew. Which in turn baffled Prentice.

— Hilda told me you were Jewish.

— No I'm from Nottingham.

— Well, I mean, there are Jews in Nottingham, I'm sure.

Harry laughed.

— I'm sure there are. But I'm, well I don't know what I am, Church of England I suppose, I've never really thought about it.

— Church of England also very welcome, said Prentice.

— Why does people's religion matter though? Harry asked him.

— It doesn't, it doesn't, it doesn't at all. I just thought you were Jewish. That would matter. You know. Well, it wouldn't matter, but given the, given the situation. It would be good to have more Jews really, locally, involved, to head off, well, to demonstrate that we are not anti-Semitic. I mean, we're really not. You're in the party though?

— Barely.

— Well, would you join us?

— I don't think so mate.

Prentice went back to the others and entered into furious consultation with Hilda. He told her that he'd never been more embarrassed.

— You can't be embarrassed without being assed, Hilda said.

— What?

— You can't say *embarrassed* without saying *assed*. It's part of the word you see. So don't be assed and you won't be embarrassed.

— I'm embarrassed I married you.

A Shock

Hilda laughed wildly at this which seemed to reassure Flo and Sanjay and Janice – who had just turned up as well – huddled together at a slight distance trying to eavesdrop.

About ten minutes later on WhatsApp Stan told everyone that a meeting with two days' notice was *not practical* and that it had been scheduled *without a full meeting of, or consultation with, the steering committee and it was therefore cancelled.* He then called a meeting of the steering committee for the next night, the Wednesday.

Sanjay went outside to call him. The others watched through the window as Sanjay paced and smoked and argued, and then was mostly silent, nodding, and, towards the end, smiling, as he wandered towards the edge of their field of vision, and then wandered out of it, and didn't return.

— Bit of pantomime, that, said Prentice.

— Where's he gone?

— He's hung up on him. That's what's happened there.

— Stan hung up on him?

— How do you know?

— Well I don't Janice, it's conjecture.

— He's left half his pint.

— Stan's embarrassed him.

— He's embarrassed himself.

— They're as bad as each other.

Janice and Flo left together and walked down towards Peckham on the main road, complaining, mostly about Stan. Neither of them was on the steering committee, but Flo pointed out that they could be if they wanted to be, given that there wasn't currently a gender balance and that there was at least one open position for a woman which either of them could probably just take, and then have it confirmed by acclamation at the next full meeting. Flo tried to persuade Janice to put herself forward, and Janice tried to persuade Flo, and by the time they got as far as the fire station they had decided that they would bring it up at the next meeting and decide closer to the time which one of them should take it because it was becoming a joke now, this constant bickering between Stan and Sanjay. They thought it was a stupid male thing, a pissing competition. Dickering, said Janice.

— Not bickering. Dickering.

And they laughed.

Janice lived in the Pelican Estate. Flo walked on towards her place off Peckham Hill Street, but she stopped into the Spoons for a last couple because it was only just gone eleven and she wasn't tired, and the next day was just a matter of getting the kids out, and her shift at Boots didn't start until one because it was Thursday. She quite liked Sanjay. He had persuaded her to get involved, which took some doing, so he must have something going for him. In Spoons she did her sums and bought a pint of the second cheapest lager and sat on a high stool at a high table and tried to work out what was happening on the muted television. There was a game that sometimes got going in The Arms, when people would pretend that they'd just got a news alert on their phone and they would call out what it was, what they wished it was.

— Prime Minister dead.

— Vatican on fire.

— The President has fallen down the steps of Air Force One and is lying mangled at the bottom, bleeding out, and no one's coming to help him.

— Beyoncé buys flat in Peckham.

— Queen seeks divorce.

— There's a fucking meteorite. Size of Camberwell. About to hit Camberwell.

Always got the loudest cheers, those ones.

Flo sat there with a grin on her face staring at nothing and was startled, flustered, nearly knocked over her glass, when Sally Morris tapped her on the shoulder and asked could she join her. Sally was peculiar, but Flo thought it was nothing very much, just the grind of things, a little punch drunk from living, something Flo sometimes reeled from too, so much time pushing back against the bullshit that when suddenly and briefly there was nothing pushing you you fell over and looked like a tit. Sally was single now, far better for it, but wasting her evenings in the Spoons was not smart she told Flo.

— I need to get a hobby, she said. Do you have a hobby?

— Trying to improve the lot of the working classes, said Flo, and they both had a good laugh, and Flo stayed much longer than she'd intended.

Around the corner two kids crashed a stolen moped into the side of a parked Zipvan and one of the kids shattered his kneecap and the other ran off, leaving the stolen moped blocking the road and his friend trying not to scream and trying to stand up, eventually giving up on both and lying by the kerb making a racket while passers-by called an ambulance and the cops came first and turned the boy over like they were flipping a burger and put a knee between his shoulder blades and cuffed him. He had nothing in his pockets but a smashed-up phone and a balled-up fiver and a house key.

Prentice was still in The Arms talking a little to Harry. Prentice wasn't really following, but Harry seemed to be telling him about how the pub worked. Prentice hadn't asked him that. He'd asked why they'd started serving food earlier in the year and then stopped after about a month. But Harry was talking about his tenancy and his contractual obligations to the owners, who were, he said, effectively a property company who made him serve a range of shit beers and blamed him when no one drank them.

— Is it the mice?

— What?

— Did you stop serving food because of the mice?

— Fuck off mate. Kitchen is pristine. Kitchen is pristine. Get the odd mouse during the autumn but they come in the front door like all our customers. Really mate, who told you that?

— No one. I was guessing.

— The food guy didn't work out. Don't start telling people I have mice. I don't. Might start doing some Thai stuff during the winter. I've been talking to these guys. They roll up with all the gear. Little van. Very efficient. Lovely stuff too. You like Thai?

— No.

— You're missing out. Nothing better than a Pad Thai. Peanut and the chicken and the big noodle. You're missing out mate. Yes sir what can I get you?

Prentice blinked hard and tried to rename the tiny dizzy spells he'd been having lately as something else. Maybe an eye thing. Maybe he needed new glasses. Or they were too tight, these ones. But he'd had them for years and the dizziness had come on in just the last few weeks. Couple of months maybe. He'd sat down in the caff one afternoon the previous week and thought he was having a stroke. His arms went funny, everything blurred. A real shock that. He'd spoken out loud to hear if he was slurring and Hilda had stared at him but thought he was just being daft. *One two three testing one two three.* Or she'd decided to think that. It had stopped anyway. Or it had passed through him

244

like a wave of particles from space, which, he knew, was a constant phenomenon. That had been the worst by far. But the regular ones, like just now as Harry moved off to serve someone else, they were like squeezes. Like everything was being given a little squeeze, a little squeeze of the head, a passing angel, he thought, checking for freshness. Not sore. Just everything went odd for a second. He knew death was in the vicinity. The angel of death. He sipped his stout. He would die, thought Prentice, suddenly, and that was a blessing surely. The next time Hilda nagged him about seeing his grandchildren at the weekend he'd moan but he'd relent. He hated the journey – all those buses – and they would hardly notice him, but you have to do your final rounds, your final hugs and kisses so that nothing was left acrimonious and what happened next might be better. Hilda would be fine.

Harry rang the bell soon after and Prentice chuckled at the notion of last orders. He'd had enough. He surprised Harry a little by shaking his hand before he left. On the way home he whistled and thought about Hilda. She'd be fine.

Harry locked up and did the tills and swept the floor and cleaned the toilets and laid out some traps and went to bed with his book. He read for a half an hour about the forest and the light, and then put in his earplugs and fell asleep. He dreamed. Downstairs a mouse called Troubadour Anx improved the scurry tunnel under the north wall. She worked for several hours, taking short breaks to feed on human food which though abundant these days she found disgusting. After improving the lateral volume of the tunnel she checked the three gaps, one outward to the lane, two inward to the main room. Then she crossed the room in the open, quickly, and cut through a gap where the bar counter met the east wall. Obscured by a crate of empty bottles was the entrance to the system of ramps both Troubadour Anx and her brother Altar Phen had designed and constructed over the last several weeks. It led upwards through the cavities of the wall to the ceiling above, where a vast empty space stretched in all directions, held between the ceiling of the main bar below, and the floor of the almost empty human room above. Some support struts remained. Some essential beams. But they had cleared it of its rubbish. This would be where the meeting would be held.

The next night. The Wednesday. Stan took his second pint back to the table, and they got started. Though all that amounted to for ten minutes was Sanjay and Stan arguing about whether, *firstly*, Stan had any business giving the other members of the steering committee a public ticking off over the scheduling of the next general meeting, or, *for that matter*, whether it was his place to summon a meeting of the steering committee just like that – Sanjay snapped his fingers – as if he was some sort of *autarchist arsehole*. To which Stan replied, good humouredly he thought, that he was more of an *anarcho-syndicalist arsehole*. But Sanjay was genuinely angry, and Stan let him have his say, knowing as he did that he, Stan, was in the right, and that Sanjay's attempt to hold a quick meeting to ram through a set of proposals that would serve only to further distance them from the party was out of fucking order.

Harry half watched them, and half read the paper. He could hear the odd word. A mocking laugh from the Asian guy. Then he saw Prescott or Preston or whatever the old crank was called clear his throat and start into a speech. A couple of the others exchanged tired glances, and Harry grinned at the back page of the *Standard*.

— Good golfing John?

John sat with his back to him staring at the big screen.

— The Italian is making a mess of it.

— Is he?

— Double bogey, the Italian.

— Double bogey, said Harry.

— Double bogey, said John. He's not a finisher. Every time. Just falls apart at the end.

— Don't we all John. Don't we all.

— Aye.

He served a woman in the back bar and shifted some crates looking for crisps. Found only droppings on the empty shelves. He went into the kitchen for the spray bleach and crouched and sprayed and scrubbed for a good ten minutes before anyone asked him for anything. The woman again, wanting another vodka.

— Quiet tonight, she said.

— Bit more lively in the front bar.

— I like the jukebox though.

He gave her a few fifties in her change. She was playing the Motown favourites. Dancing in a small way in front of the machine. Smiling. There was a couple in the corner, deep in conversation, making their half pints last almost an hour now. In the front bar there was John, the anarchist plotters, the two guys from the phone shop who always had a pint after they closed, and a man at one of the high tables in the corner picking his nose and reading a book – one of the silent, sullen regulars who contributed nothing to anything. He'd been the one looking for crisps. Harry had a blind spot when it came to crisps. Never ate them, never remembered to order them. And didn't much like having them around. Mice don't drink, but they like crisps.

He went into what he still called the kitchen, though he had tried *office* a couple of time, to blank looks. There was a phone, and a battered laptop for the cameras and for doing their online, and there was lost property, a cupboard with keys, a safe, all of that. But there was also a grill and a sink and a fridge. He wanted rid of the grill. He'd cleaned it and thrown a towel over it – as you would a corpse – and Ahunna had said she'd a friend who could use it. But that had been a while ago. He'd ask her again. He was looking at the roster when he heard a familiar creak and the traffic pulsed louder. But it stayed louder, and he went out.

It was him of course. Yves, Yan, Stoker. He was standing in the open door with his back to the room, looking out at the sky where the sunset glowed a deep unhealthy red over the rooftops, streaked with trails of smoky cloud, bruised orange and purple. His hands were on his hips. Stan was staring at him grimly, ignoring his little meeting. The nose-picking man was looking at him too, with a smile. And Harry smiled as well, glad that at last there would be someone to talk to, even if the talk went in a circle that had nothing in the middle.

His friend seemed to lift his shoulders and lower them again in a great sigh. He took his hands off his hips and his foot from the door, letting it swing shut, and he turned to the room.

— The city, he announced with a look a great joy, is on fire.

In the little envelope of his bed Harry read his book. He had expected it to end badly for the woman in the forest, and it was ending badly, and it pained him and he did not want to finish, and he put it down.

In the quiet seeping glow of the street he considered the ceiling and his own wellbeing. He would be all right, he thought. Another year maybe, of this. And then a different year, of something else. Though it would not be a disaster if all the years continued the same. It might suit him just fine. His thoughts spun slower and fell warm around him. He slept. He dreamed that something woke him. There was a noise. He lay there for a moment, then checked his ears. He'd forgotten to put the plugs in. He turned to his bedside table and saw a light beneath the door. He'd forgotten to put the light out. He sighed and moaned and got up. Pushed his feet into his slippers. Picked up his keys out of habit. Turned to go out and saw the light beneath the door vanish.

Harry stood very still. For a moment. There were switches for the light at the bottom of the stairs, and at the top, right outside his bedroom. He looked for his phone. It was there. On the table. Beside a glass of water. He listened but could hear nothing in front of him. There was only the odd car at his back, and a very delicate hum like that of a fridge or a distant crowd.

His feet were itchy.

Have a think, Harry.

At the bottom of the stairs there was a door, which he knew he had locked, and bolted, which led to a small hallway. Street door on the left, also locked and bolted, and a door to the back bar on the right, locked and bolted. And everything was alarmed. They'd tried before, but they'd always set it off before they got anywhere. And what sort of burglar turns on a light? Maybe the electrics were playing up.

He tutted and sighed and stepped to the door and opened it. Something moved and something brushed his leg, and he very quickly reached out for the light switch and flicked it on. Something on the stairs. No. Nothing on the stairs. Nothing anywhere. Dry mouth. Blotchy lino and a bare light. He walked down the steps. There was a smell. A smell and a hum. At the bottom he flicked the light switch on and off a few times and the dark came and went. He opened the panel on the alarm controls and all the indicators were as they should be. He turned off the internal. He'd just have a look. The smell was like the cellar, and the hum was a chittering thing, and a sort of heat, he thought, as well – the heat you get when the place is full.

He really should have known.

He opened the door and the shadows seemed to shimmer and part to admit him. He saw mice on the bar counter. He saw more on the floor. He kicked out and walked ahead and turned then into the front bar where the light from the street struggled through the windows and the floor was newly covered by a carpet that could not settle, that squeaked and smelled and roiled, that rippled, and he suddenly did not want to take a step, so he stopped, and there was nothing he could see that was not moving, even the windows were crossed and over written, and Harry felt something hit his shoulder, and saw a mouse bounce off his chest, and then another, and another, and his head was now being pelted and his shoulders smacked, and he held an arm over his face and looked up, and saw that they were legion and untold, impossible, endless, and were coming through the ceiling like a sweat, and falling from the lights, and a patch of plaster floated down, bringing with it a tumbling cargo of more, small and excited mice, hundreds of them, thousands, more than it was possible to see. They came through the walls. They came through the floor. They scrabbled at his feet and then this ankles. They seemed to want something, and to speak in tiny voices that he could not hear, and plead with him in ways he could not make out, and they seemed to present to him petitions and requests, and they seemed to him to know a different aspect of the world and showed it, not unkindly, like a death turned inside out. When he thought of moving he found that they were up to his thighs and he could not move, and they kept on falling, and rising, and laughing, and they scampered over his face and they looked into his eyes and whispered to him and told him that he would be all right, really, he would be fine, and they kept on coming, and they kept on coming, and he wondered, as his eyes were squirmingly covered and then went dark, if the whole world was ending this way, drowned in mice, or if it was just The Arms, or just him, whether it was only his life that was ending this way, or whether it was everyone's, and he wondered then, and the mice wondered with him, fascinated and incomprehensibly alive, what the difference was.

The Song

HE IS SHORT and wiry and looks from the back like a boy. But when he turns, his face is deeply lined and his eyes a sunset pink and he is probably the oldest person there. He wears a dark suit jacket that shines at the elbows and is too big for him, and greasy jeans that are an inch too short for his old black formal shoes and his sky-blue socks. Under the jacket he is wearing a white shirt that beams out from his torso and his wrists, and he has a thin flowery scent of fabric softener about him, which must be the shirt. His hands are veined and liver spotted and in the right one he holds a tumbler with a small measure of whiskey. In one jacket pocket there is a half bottle of Jameson's and in the other a small battered bottle of mineral water. He looks like he's just had his hair cut, severely. He smiles. He smiles widely at everyone.

— Well it's actually my own isn't that terrible? he is saying to a woman half his age in a floral summer dress. It's my own special magic glass. Ah it's not magic, I just like it so I brought it with me. Are you sure you don't want a small Jameson's?

— No, no, thank you.

— I could get you a glass

— No I don't drink. Thanks.

— Oh say no more, fair play. I am a demon for the Jameson's.

For whisky in general actually, I'm not that fussy. I'm not very fussy at all really.

His smile is wide and he laughs and rocks back and forth a little from the waist, and his left hand touches the woman briefly on the arm.

They are in the middle of the front room of a mid-terrace house. You know the house. Or you know what it is like, reflected. You have been nearby. You have been very close.

Around them people stand in little groups, and sit on the sofa and the chairs. Through an arch, in what is a sort of dining room, there are more people standing around with drinks, and a table has been pushed back near a wall and behind it a young man in glasses crouches over turntables. The music is not very loud. People are able to hear each other. How many people? More than twenty. It's early. Maybe thirty people, in both rooms, in the kitchen, in the hallway. There are some in the back garden. From far above they look so small. From a hundred metres up. It is still hot. It's always hot.

— Your dress is absolutely gorgeous. I do love summer clothes. It's so lovely to see all the lovely dresses during the summer isn't it? And all the handsome men in their shorts. It's always so lovely to see, in the parks and all of that. And all the little children in their little sun hats, oh I love that, all the little babies with their cute little hats, they're such a joy.

He looks around at other people and then back at the woman.

— Do you have any? Children I mean, not hats.

And he laughs again, and rocks back and forth again, and touches the woman's arm again. She laughs too, but she isn't quite laughing at the same thing that he is. She looks at him with a mild sort of bafflement, amused, as if he is something not quite there, as if he is an illusion, a trick, someone playing a joke on

her. Her name is Katherine, and she is there with her partner
Fran, who is in the kitchen, or that is where Katherine assumes
they've gone, it's where they said they were going, and then this
man started talking to her. She wants to ask him what age he is,
because she is curious. But she isn't going to ask him that, it's not
something you ask anyone, it doesn't matter, age doesn't matter
at all, and this man is very nice, very chatty, probably gay she
thinks, a bit queer maybe, and oddly dressed. Though it occurs
to her that if he was in his twenties he wouldn't be very oddly
dressed at all, he'd be dressed like a lot of the hipster guys are
dressed at this party, or in the same spirit anyway. Except for the
shoes. His shoes are shined and flat and pointed and she has
glanced at them a couple of times and they make her uneasy, she
doesn't know why. His socks look like clean socks that are kept
in a dirty drawer. He has asked her about children. She isn't
going to answer that. You don't ask people that. She would have
to come up with a question of her own. A swerve.

— What's your name?

— Michael, he says, but he thought about it for a flash, his
eyes darted, and she doesn't believe him.

— I'm Katherine.

— Oh a lovely name, that's a gorgeous name, but I'll tell you,
I'll forget it. I'm not good with names at all. Faces are my forte.
I am an encyclopedia of faces. I've never forgotten a single one.
And I am like the archaeologists with their reconstructions. I
might meet a boy and twenty years later I'll meet the man and
I'll know it immediately, oh I met you I'll tell him, I met you in
1994 in a pub in Greenwich, you were with your mother, lovely
Caribbean woman lived in the flats on Lewisham Road near the
big Tesco. Is she still with us? That sort of thing. I don't know
was the big Tesco there in 1994? I don't know. Faces, as I say,

that's my forte. I'm not great on names or supermarkets. But your name is lovely. What is it again?

— Katherine.

— Lovely name. I'll do my best. Your face is inedible. Indelible. But we'll have to see Katherine, won't we, we'll have to see as they say. And hello there who's this.

It is Fran, and Michael, if that is his name (it isn't, obviously) looks Fran over with a great smile as Katherine does the introductions, and Fran smiles and shakes the man's hand and the man holds it for longer than is comfortable for Fran, and they do not enjoy the sensation at all.

— Aren't you looking all lovely as well, oh the two of you so nice, with the lovely summer frock and then this shirt, what would you call that? Mint green I'd call it I think, will that do it? Mint green, and those tiny flowers, so lovely the pair of you. I look like an undertaker next to the both of you. Don't I? Bring out your dead! Bring out your dead! Oh stop. Two girls as lovely as the pair of you. Am I right with that? Is it two girls? I'm sorry to be blundering around like I don't know what. I'm a terrible old-fashioned thing, I just don't know how to ask. Everyone should be whatever they want to be is the way I think about it, but sometimes I put my foot in it and get in terrible trouble so I think it's best to just ask straight out and hope that asking isn't in itself disrespectful. Is it?

— I'm non-binary, says Fran.

— Well, there you are, says the man, and lets go of Fran's hand. I know a woman, she lives around here somewhere I think. Maybe around here. Lovely woman, she must be getting on a bit now, but I knew her when she was young and she had a girlfriend, and I knew her too. Can't for the life of me remember their names now of course, it's not my forte. But lovely good-looking funny women, a real delight the pair of them, great company, devoted to each other, together a good old while, they had a house around here. And then sure didn't the other one then transition to a man? In her, oh I don't know, in her thirties I suppose she was, and she ducked out of sight for a while, because in those days it was, well it's not easy now I know, but the whole thing then was terribly cruel, people would be terribly, awfully cruel. And she re-emerged, but she was a man. Ah listen to me, mangling it all up again. He was a man. So this woman, around here, had fallen in love with a woman, and then the woman became a man. Extraordinary really. It was extraordinary.

— Did they stay together? asks Katherine.

— Oh god yes, they did, absolutely. Love you see. Love is love. I don't need to tell you that. Absolutely devoted to each other. I don't know of course what changed in the bedroom so to speak, if anything, I mean I didn't, well you wouldn't ask would you? They stayed together. And of course people talked and there were some nasty things that happened. The bigots. Even around here, in those days, it was all anarchists and squatters and punks but there are always the bigots, there always are. The horrible people. But they stayed put, they did, they stayed put and they had each other and that was all they wanted, and people eventually left them alone really. Fran would you like a drop of Jameson's?

He is pouring some for himself, skilfully balancing the tumbler in the crook of his elbow. Fran shakes their head.

— We . . . I'm just going to go say hello to a couple of people in the kitchen.

— Oh I'll come with you. Lovely to meet you Michael.

— And you dear. See you later now. You promised me a dance now and I'll hold you to it.

— No I didn't, laughs Katherine.

They squeeze their way past people to the kitchen, Fran leading Katherine by the hand. When they are out of sight Fran
looks back and smiles.

— What the fuck?

— I know. I know.

They go out to the garden and Fran laughs and they stand
together rerunning the conversation for a few moments and
looking around shyly and being shyly looked at. They do not
know anyone. Some people are sitting on chairs under the
kitchen window, listening to a man who might be Spanish or
Greek – Mediterranean anyway – as he stands and talks, and one
of them watches Fran and Katherine and smiles and seems to like
seeing them, though it is clear that he does not know them – no
recognition has passed between them – and he looks at them
surreptitiously.

This is David.

You know David.

From the flat.

He has come out for once. His hair is neat, he is pale, he is
thin. He is sitting there, looking surreptitiously at Katherine and
Fran, as if there is something about them that cheers him. He
smiles.

He's looking ok.

He sips his beer and looks at his phone. The Mediterranean
man is still talking, telling them about the course that he is teaching and how his students are fantastically curious and sceptical
and are not at all what he had expected in London, not what he
had expected at all. He says that he had expected a *bunch of rich
uptight white kids* and what he had found instead was *a fantastic,
just a fantastic, really fantastic room full of people from all over the
world* – this impresses him so much, that there are people from

China, from India, from Nigeria and Sudan, people from Colombia and Argentina, and Italy and even one from Spain, as well of course as people from the UK – and they are already very sophisticated in their thinking, and it has delighted him, he is generalising he says, but generally speaking he loves them, he really thinks they are fantastic.

David looks across again at the couple whose names he cannot know. They are peeking over the fence into the garden next door. Perhaps he feels a simple affection for them. For their queerness, for what he might view perhaps as their innocence. Perhaps he is thinking like that. They are younger than him, and perhaps he is noticing that as well, and liking it. Though his eyes flit somewhat, self-consciously almost, as if he feels that he should not be feeling, or thinking, whatever it is that he is feeling, or thinking. It is impossible to know.

The man is still talking, though no one has asked him anything. He's wearing an FC St. Pauli T-shirt.

— And this by the way is one of the already great misunderstood ideas of capitalism, or of contemporary capitalism, late stage as they say, though I am pessimistic about that, and anyway, these ideas of selfish behaviour, the perpetual self-interest of individuals, this is not established by evidence, and that of course is now widely accepted, and the Left is largely triumphant about this, because it seems to say something about human nature, that we do not act always out of self-interest, while of course this claim for human nature simply mirrors the fallacy of the Right who made as well a claim about human nature when the evidence was different, or was not understood, but anyway, in any case, the interesting thing, and from the point of view of those of us on the Left, those of us who are on the Left, the bad thing, is that this idea of self-interest is established in relation to groups, the evidence is clear, it is really incontrovertible, and it is that while we are unpredictable as individuals we are predictable as groups, depressingly predictable, and we will act in a group in ways that we would not act as individuals, and of course this can be harnessed in all sorts of ways, by the Left in terms of forming movements and organising and so forth, which are ways in which acting as a group seems to us positive and beneficial, and there of course are ways in which the Right can also harness a group, and these are broadly similar methods, with different characteristics of course, but the point is the harness, the harnessing, that it can be done, that we, when we are grouped together by perceived shared interests or actual, of course, shared interests, or by class, which amounts essentially to the same thing, or by nationality, which certainly doesn't, or by race or by gender or by age and so on and so on.

David does not seem to be following. He looks at his phone. His expression has changed and he looks a little annoyed, or impatient. He sips his beer. There are two people sitting next to him, and the talking man stands in front of them, as if standing in front of his fantastic students.

Christ.

David stands up.

— Excuse me.

And he walks around the talking man, who turns slightly to let him pass but who does not stop talking, and walks towards Katherine and Fran, but he seems to have forgotten about them, he doesn't even look at them, he walks past, looking annoyed, as if he has remembered something that he has forgotten to do. He walks towards the door into the kitchen but then stops and turns around and goes the other way, towards the end of the garden, which is not far, just two or three paces, but there is no one there, and he stands and looks away from the house, looking at the sky, and then down at the grass under his feet, such as it is, and he seems ill at ease. He seems anxious. Perhaps he stood up too quickly. He has started to sweat.

There is a light in the ground that looks like a buried piece of the sun, or a tenth of a foggy moon, yellow as with the light of a streetlight. Something just below the surface of the thin grass. But it is an illusion. We do not bury lights. And if we do we put them out. Don't we? It's just a little yellowing of the thin grass. Just that.

Everyone ignores him. But when he turns he looks as if people are bothering him, he looks annoyed at everyone, and he walks to the kitchen door and goes in.

It is more crowded than it was. David turns his shoulders sideways, his hips. He moves sideways.

— Excuse me. Excuse me.

People talk and the music seems louder. They talk so much.

Well I'm not saying that exactly

There is no case

Fuck's sake

She was on her eighth fucking vodka at this point

No one has the time Ravi, you know?

David looks sharply to his right. But it is a different Ravi. David looks even more annoyed.

Is there? In the house? Is there?

Weird

Watch out

It has to be Sanders. No

Prefer the Stormbird

No one eats that stuff do they

Careful please

Guy is a creep
Well he was fucking her brother, that's why
And if

He pushes past a young man wearing a low-cut T-shirt, so low that the tops of his shoulder blades are visible, and David moves a little slower, and stares at the man's skin, and at his fair hair, and he pushes past him very closely, taller than him, moving the front of his body across the back of the other man's body, much closer than he probably needs to, almost stroking him, a balled hand resting very gently on his shoulder.

— Sorry. Ooops. Excuse me.

He passes through and looks back. The man looks at him. You know this one as well. They stare at each other for only a second. David smiles, but the other man doesn't.

Regardless
I don't think it's very good
Bounce
Love this
Balkan overdrive
Is there really?
Oh fucking councillors my god
A real ache
Persimmons
June halla
Moss was
I don't want to dance
Fucks sake

David comes to the kitchen door where you can see through to the living room door and he looks in, and in the crowd a man who is dancing catches his eye and gestures at David, smiling, beckoning him over. And the woman he is dancing with turns and looks and shouts out David's name, and also beckons him over. David smiles back. He holds up a finger and motions with his head towards the front of the house, and he mouths something which is impossible to read, but his whole body language seems to say *Yes, yes of course, just hang on a minute, I just have to go over here, and then I'll be back to you . . . in one minute*, and he pushes past a clump of people standing in the corridor by the stairs and he makes his way to the front door and has to ask people to move so that he can open it, and he opens it, and there are people outside as well, so it is hard to know why it was closed at all.

— Oh hi. We thought we were locked out.

David looks behind him, the way he's come. As if briefly looking for someone.

— Are you leaving?

— Yeah. I have to go home unfortunately.

— Already?

— What?

— You're leaving already?

— I'll be back in a bit, he says.

— Oh ok.

— I have to go home.

— Ok, says Maria. Take care.

She knows him, she's sure. But she cannot recall how. Maybe he is one of Stan's. She watches him hurry through the gate and turn to the left, running his hand over his hair, and she watches him for a moment as he walks away, pulling a phone from his pocket, glancing at it, holding it in his hand. She looks into the house, wondering, because he seems a little upset, or annoyed, wondering if something has happened, if he's maybe had an argument with someone.

The house is more crowded now. More people have arrived.

Are still arriving. All these men. Stan is somewhere but she can't see him. People are dancing in the living room. It's pretty loud. One of the women who had been outside pushes past her shouting *WOO WOO*, sticking her arms in the air, moving straight to the centre of things. Easy. She watches her for a moment, trying to be envious of that sort of energy. But she isn't, she really isn't.

Maria. This is Maria.

You know exactly where this is going.

A young guy stumbles on the stairs, makes a noise, a half shriek, slides down a step before catching himself. Embarrassed, he smiles at Maria and she smiles back.

— You ok?

— I find stairs very complicated.

She laughs, and he goes towards the kitchen.

Everything is hip-hop and London jazz, a low smell of weed, distinct bodies, a bee buzz of conversation, slaps of laughter. It's ok. She sips her warm beer. There are two more bottles in her shoulder bag. She is wearing jeans and she should have worn shorts, something else. She edges into the kitchen. All these men. The guy from the stairs is in conversation with someone, and he smiles at her again as she squeezes past. She says hello to Flo, who has forgotten her name. She sees the man from The Arms that Stan doesn't like. She wonders whether Gary will be here. She hopes so. She misses Gary. She recognises more faces than she knows names. Some people smile or nod at her and she smiles or nods back, but she finds herself wondering when she was last at a party. Maybe one of these days, she thinks, a party will be good.

She goes towards the garden. She is half thinking that there will be weed there, and she might be offered a little smoke, and that would do her some good. She'll see how it goes. She might drink her beers and wait for Stan to find her and then go home.

She hopes he'll stay. If he wants to leave with her maybe she'll stay. But she can't do that. She would like to walk for a while, on her own. She is tired of the bike.

A man leaning against the sink has raised his voice. He is pointing at someone. She has to go between them.

— Excuse me.

— Not fucking on – sorry – not fucking on mate, I'm not having it.

Oh god. There is some muttering to her left. From where he is pointing. Someone else is moving past her in the opposite direction, and the general noise of voices has suddenly dropped.

— Hold on, hold on.

— Not having it.

She makes it to the door, where people are coming to stand and listen. She squeezes through. She is too apologetic. Is she? Why is she ducking her shoulders, her head, as if it has started raining? She is incurious. Is she? She doesn't want to be in the kitchen watching two men shouting at each other. She doesn't want that. And that's what they seem to be getting into.

Everyone is looking at her as she walks outside but they aren't really, they're looking at the kitchen, at what is going on in the kitchen. No sign of Stan. Where is he? Upstairs maybe. In a bedroom with someone. She laughs, almost out loud. She walks to the end of the garden. It isn't far. Thin yellow grass, bright as if painted, a fence that she can't see over, butterflies, the sky brighter now than the ground. There's a border of bushes, including a nice rose in the corner. A pile of stones, a couple of chairs. Behind her, raised voices. She wants to be in a different life. The words of the argument include *offensive*, *arsehole*, *homophobe*, *curtains*. She thinks she heard *curtains*. People used to say *curtains for you. It's curtains for you.* She wonders about that for a while and thinks that it must come from the theatre. Theatre curtains. *Show's over, mate. You're going home in an ambulance.*

She finishes her beer. She doesn't want to sit down. Through the kitchen window she can see the guy, the strange older guy who is sometimes in The Arms, the chalky man in the shiny suit. Stan hates him. She can't remember his name. He is staring open-mouthed at the . . . belligerents. An expression on his face like a child's. Belligerent. Bellum. He is looking at her. He is looking straight at her. She turns to face next door. Southern bellum. She puts her empty beer bottle down into the soil of the border, pressing it in a little so that it won't fall over, and she takes another from her bag. Does that look bad? Carrying beers around, hidden in her bag, at a party? They're not hidden. That's just where they are. Where is Stan? Bellicose. She is bellicose. She burps. What sort of mood is this? A bit giddy. She might dance later. They should dance in the garden, the house is too hot.

— Well that was a terrible business.

He is at her shoulder and what can she do? His mouth is closed now. But he still looks a little shocked.

— What happened?

He takes a deep breath. Theatrical.

— As I understand it, and I'm not at all sure that I got every detail, well, I'm not sure how it started but the man with the beard said something to the man without the beard, something about his boyfriend, and I believe that it wasn't very nice, and so the man he's said this to, the younger one, he's shouting at the man with the beard who was just laughing at him, and it seems that this man, the man with the beard had made a doggetry comment about this younger man's boyfriend, a doggetry comment about his boyfriend, which this man took very badly, and he was shouting at him, and seemed very angry, and the other man got very sheepish then as the younger man said what he said, and then someone else got involved to say that the man with the beard has had a recent bereavement, and this didn't help at all because the other man was terribly offended that someone's death might be offered as an excuse for what he described as

Someone else comes over and stands next to them. The guy from the stairs. He is wearing a low-cut T-shirt. He is handsome, Maria thinks, in a grubby, careless sort of way, as if being handsome annoys him a little.

— ageism I think it was, and, hello there

— He said something about his boyfriend.

— What did he say do you know, I missed that bit.

— Well, says the guy, they were chatting, and the man with the glasses pointed out his boyfriend to the other guy, the guy with the beard, and the guy with the beard looked at him and said *disgusting* or *that's disgusting*, or something.

— What?

— Yeah. *Disgusting.* And then he clarified, as if this would be ok, by saying that the *age gap* was disgusting, that he was talking about the age gap.

— Oh my god.

— How young is his boyfriend?

— He's not the younger one he's the older one. He's maybe fifty or so, and the guy in the glasses is maybe early thirties, something like that.

— That's it?

— Oh my goodness.

— I know. I know right? I'm Tom by the way, sorry for just barging into your conversation

— Hello Tommy very nice to meet you, and I'm, I'm, I'm Michael. And this is, well I actually don't know, I did the same thing you did I just walked over and started talking. It's amazing isn't it, how something like that will get people talking to each other isn't it? Strangers I mean. I mean an accident or a death or a fight I suppose, it's always the same, always gets people talking who otherwise

— I'm Maria.

— Hi.

He gives her a conspiratorial sort of smile, she thinks. She wonders if he has come to her rescue. Do men do that? Do they think twice? Do people like Tommy keep an eye on people like Michael? What is wrong with Michael anyway? He seems fine. Startled and worried like a child, and talkative, so talkative.

You know Tommy. You know Tommy, and Maria, and the man they're talking to. You know where they are. You know what's going to happen.

— Did you hear then Tommy about the bereavement?

Tommy laughs.

— Yes, I did. I did. And that seemed to make the guy in the glasses even angrier.

— *How dare you, he said*, said Michael.

— That's right.

— *How dare you use grief as an excuse for your shitty behaviour.*

— Something like that.

— Oh there'll be a mood now won't there?

— I think they left. I mean the guy who said it. I think his friend took him. They were heading for the front door anyway. Seems calm now.

— That's a terrible thing to say about something like that sure love is love is what I say, that's the way I look at it anyway, and you can never really know what brings people together, who are we to judge, and a thing like that, well, *disgusting* is a terrible word to use about people don't you think?

He drinks from a little glass.

— Do you know either of them? Tommy asks her.

— No, no I don't.

— I don't really know the younger one but I know his boyfriend. He's lovely. Very sweet. I mean it's not even a big gap. You know? I know of bigger gaps. Such a stupid thing to say.

Two talkative men. She likes them both. Michael has produced a bottle of whiskey from his pocket and is pouring himself some. So she is like him. They are like each other. Why does Stan hate him?

— Will you have some Maria? Some whiskey? No? Tommy? Will you? Go on. I don't have a glass though. Take a swig from the bottle ah go on sure why not a big swig of, it'll put hairs on your chest, won't it isn't that what they say? There you go, oh not too much now, don't take it all, ah I'm only joking.

They all laugh.

David is at home by now. Gary is asleep, in a friend's place in Whitechapel, his camera beside him. He's fine, he's just tired. Harry is fine too. He's working in The Arms. It's busy. Ahunna is on as well. She still hasn't taken the grill. They might come to the party after closing – Harry will call someone, find out if it's worth it. Ronnie is at home watching TV. Anna is out. She's having dinner with a friend in a restaurant in Brixton. They are telling each other stories. Pigeon is on a date, sort of. They're having a drink, also in Brixton, and they might go dancing afterwards. Pigeon doesn't really like her though. She's not laughing at his jokes. Stan is in a corner of the front room, sitting on the sofa, sweating, trying to have a conversation with Sanjay. They're not arguing, they're actually getting on fine. Stan thinks that maybe it's a breakthrough. He's too hot though. He might head for the garden in a bit. That's everyone. Almost everyone.

— I bring my own because there's never usually whiskey at a party. And I only really like the whiskey really. Wine hurts my jaw. Do you get that? I am allergic to something in wine that gives me lockjaw. No, I'm serious.

— Lockjaw?

— A pain anyway.

Tommy laughs.

— And beer just makes me. Well it's an older man thing, I won't bore you with it.

— Pee, says Tommy.

— Well, yes, says Michael. But every five minutes my god, a bladder the size of an eggcup. But I shouldn't be talking like this it's very vulgar.

Maria thinks that Michael is laughing only at what is happening, at the jokes he is making, at the little scene the three of them are creating in the garden with their drinks and their voices and their unfamiliarity with each other. Things that she and Tommy are also laughing at. But she thinks too that she and Tommy, with the glances they exchange, are also laughing at Michael. At the ridiculousness of Michael, at his clothes and his voice and his whiskey pocket, and his innocence – his apparent innocence – and his mischief, his apparent mischief. And furthermore she thinks, as she looks at Tommy, at something around his eyes, she thinks that she is laughing at Tommy too, at his youth, at his fascination with Michael, at his attractiveness and his sexiness, his apparent sexiness, his apparent body. And she is slightly wrong about all of this. Maria is slightly wrong about everything that is happening, and is wrong too about the laughter, and its varied sources and causes and effects.

Slightly.

— The mood will be ruined now we should do something about it, have they turned off the music, oh, have they?

— No I don't think so.

— No, there it is again, it went down a bit there for a second I thought. Oh! I know! Do you know what?

He grips Tommy's arm, but looks at Maria.

— Do you sing?

Maria shakes her head.

— Sing? No. Not really.

— Let's sing some songs. You. Do you sing. I bet you do look at you face of a choirboy of course you do voice of an angel, you do don't you?

— I really don't, says Tommy.

— Most people can carry a tune. They just don't have any confidence about it. It used to be at parties when I was your age there would always be songs. We need songs. It'll get rid of the mood. Lift the mood. That's all it takes. It's a great thing, music, singing together, singing songs. We need songs. I'm right amn't I right?

— I'm not sure it's that sort of party really, says Tommy.

— Oh look at those butterflies aren't they just the most beautiful thing?

Maria turns and sees two, three, white butterflies on the wing, scattering themselves against the flowers and the fence. Above them the bricks and the roof tops. About them the city-less sky, all a deep royal blue, crossed by dots.

— You only see white ones these days, mostly, says Michael. It used to be a famous place for butterflies, Camberwell. Crowds of them, all colours, everywhere you went. But now you get the white ones mostly.

— They fly like they're in a panic.

Michael stares at Tommy for a moment, and then laughs. He thinks this is very funny.

— I like that. That's very good. Butterfly panic. I like that.

The rest is simple.

He forgets for a few minutes, Michael does, but then he remembers and he puts down his glass on the grass and in his pockets he finds pieces of paper, a pen. He has already forgotten Maria's name, but he writes it down when she tells him, even though she insists, laughing, but also slightly worried, that she does not sing, she will not sing.

— Oh I know I know, here, I'll make a note of that.

He takes Tommy's name as well, and then he goes to others in the garden, and Tommy and Maria listen in as he tries to persuade them that what the party needs now is songs, and that if they want they can give him their name and he will get it all organised and then call them when it's their turn.

— He's brave.

— I hope people aren't rude to him.

— Well I hope that he doesn't end up with only our names. Do you mind if I?

He has produced a small joint.

— Not at all.

— Like some?

— I'd love some.

They smoke together and watch Michael and they smile, and the butterflies panic around them and the darkness covers the ground but the sky is a bright beautiful blue. They talk about nothing, relaxed now, and Tommy tells her some secrets, and she tells him some in return, and they are becoming friends suddenly, and she was not expecting this. Michael has gone inside the house. They watch the butterflies. They try to have them land on their outstretched hands, but that doesn't happen. Then Tommy has to go to the bathroom.

— I'll be back, but just in case, give me your number. I don't want to lose you.

And they swap numbers. And he goes.

— Be careful on those stairs, she calls after him.

He laughs without looking back.

She is wondering what she should do. She takes the last beer from her bag and opens it. She moves towards the kitchen. She is fine now. Everything is fine. And then the music stops.

She squeezes into the kitchen. There are voices coming from the living room, and she worries for a moment that it is another argument. But then she hears Michael's voice, and laughter. And she is immediately worried that he is about to make a fool of himself. That he will be mocked and ridiculed. She hears the laughter. She goes and stands amongst people. She leans back on the kitchen counter. She can't make out the words.

— Is it the same guy? someone beside her asks.

— Same guy. He's doing the singing thing.

— Oh god. Did people say yes?

— I don't know. Maybe. I think he's going to start it off though.

This is Katherine. Katherine and Fran. Maria listens to them. She says nothing.

— Oh god, says Katherine again.

And then Michael begins. He whistles first, and people laugh, and someone starts to whistle as well, but they are quickly shushed. Then Michael sings, to the same melody as the whistle.

And he sings in French. And his voice is clear, and strong. It is loud. It seems to shimmer. It fills the spaces around them like a bright cool air, but serious. Serious. He has a beautiful voice. Beautiful.

— Wow, says Katherine. He can sing.

— I know this, says Fran.

— What is it?

— Old French thing. Old war song.

— What's it about?

And Fran begins to quietly translate some of the words for Katherine. They lean against each other, beside Maria. She is moved by the strength of Michael's voice. So moved. She thinks she knows the song as well, but she cannot place it. A verse, and then some whistling, and then a verse. There is silence in the house. Silence everywhere.

J'ai changé cent fois de nom
J'ai perdu femme et enfants
Mais j'ai tant d'amis
Et j'ai la France entière

As Michael sings, Maria leans closer to Fran so that she can hear the words in English. Katherine is staring at the floor. Fran is smiling, Maria closes her eyes. Michael sings, whistles, sings. His voice is a perfect thing.

Le vent souffle sur les tombes
La liberté reviendra
On nous oubliera
Nous rentrerons dans l'ombre

And he whistles.

— The wind on the graves, says Fran. Freedom will come again. We will be forgotten. We will go into the shadows.

And the song is over.

Maria is not surprised to discover that she is crying. Just a few tears. Through her closed eyes. And no one sees. No one knows. No one but you.

There is applause. Generous, genuine applause. She can hear Stan, she thinks, shouting, *well done, well done*. She cannot tell if he is sincere or not. She doesn't know what he thinks.

She opens her eyes, wipes her cheeks and laughs a little. Silly. Fran and Katherine have moved away, towards the door. The crowd are trying to get Michael to sing some more. It seems sincere. Maybe even Stan. Maybe people are ok, are good sometimes. Then there is silence, and she can hear his talking voice, Michael's voice, but not what he says. Then there is laughter, and then silence again as they listen to him speak. He is addressing his crowd. She smiles.

The kitchen is almost empty. She sighs, puts down her empty bottle, looks around. All the things she wants to know, and all the things she wants to say, are perhaps impossible. She looks at the wall opposite, over the table, where something seems to glint. She takes a step towards it, unable to understand what she is looking at. Hips to the table edge, she leans over, raises her hand as if to touch it. Perhaps it is a stain. Or an insect. Or someone has thrown a grape, and it has stuck. Her hand stops. It is an eye. There is an eye in the wall, glistening, peculiar, completely alive. It is looking at her, and it seems impossible to understand, but Maria is not frightened, she does not scream. There is no shock.

Perhaps it should have started this way.

Perhaps it does.

Acknowledgements

The line 'Take off your life like trousers' is from *The Wall* by Anne Sexton, from her collection *The Awful Rowing Towards God* (1975).

The words 'sheep boy, idiot son of Donkey Kong' are from *Safesurfer* by Julian Cope, from *Peggy Suicide* (1991).

The song sung at the party is *La Complainte du Partisan*, written by Anna Marly and Emmanuel d'Astier de la Vigerie in 1943.

I am grateful to Barbara Epler, Philip Gwyn Jones, Laurence Lalayaux, for their support, their encouragement, and for the work they undertook to see this book published.

I am grateful to the Arts Council of Ireland for financial assistance in the form of a bursary.

I am grateful to Taha Hassan for everything.

I will always be grateful to the memory of my friend David Miller.